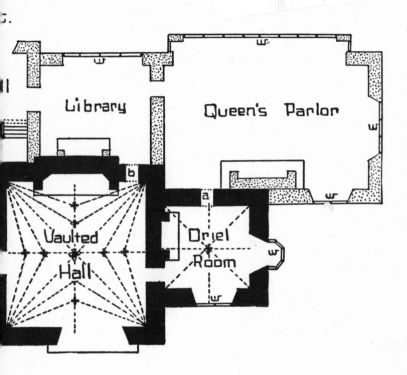

Library

Queen's Parlor

Vaulted Hall

Oriel Room

■ Original Priory Walls —15ᵗʰ Century.
▧ Anthony's temporary repairs—1559
▦ Anthony's new wing— 1565
▨ Peregrine's wing—1669.
a. Anthony's door, Richard's sliding panel
b. Door cut by Anthony
c. Door cut by Peregrine
d. Anthony's window, Peregrine's door

# QUEEN'S FOLLY

## Other Books by Elswyth Thane

FICTION

RIDERS OF THE WIND

ECHO ANSWERS

HIS ELIZABETH

CLOTH OF GOLD

BOUND TO HAPPEN

QUEEN'S FOLLY

BIOGRAPHICAL

THE TUDOR WENCH

YOUNG MR. DISRAELI

PLAYS

THE TUDOR WENCH

YOUNG MR. DISRAELI

"A Little House
'way down in Worcestershire"

# QUEEN'S FOLLY

## *A Romance*

## BY ELSWYTH THANE

*No dwellers—what profiteth house for to stand?*
*What goodness, unoccupied, bringeth the land?*
*No husbandry used, how soon shall we starve?*
*Housekeeping neglected, what comfort to serve?*

TUSSER, 1557

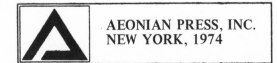

AEONIAN PRESS, INC.
NEW YORK, 1974

TO MOTHER

Who made the drawings

# CONTENTS

# ILLUSTRATIONS

*The Old Priory Door is drawn by Olive Wren.*
*The other four illustrations are by Edith Thane.*

*1553 – 1588*

*During the historical research on* **The Tudor Wench** *a man walked out of contemporary records on to the page. He carried a secret message to Elizabeth which probably saved her life at the time of the Lady Jane Grey tragedy. For a few minutes he stood in Elizabeth's presence at Hatfield, when she was ill and frightened and in danger, and just nineteen. She must have thanked him. She could hardly have forgotten him. He has been waiting rather a long time for his story to be told. But he is nameless. History acknowledges him for a few hours only, and after three hundred and eighty-three years there is no way to trace him. Except that he stood there that night and watched her read his crumpled message, one can be sure of nothing. What became of him? Did he ever see her again? Perhaps it was something like this . . .*

# I

## 1553

TWO horsemen rode headlong through the storm toward London. Greenwich Palace lay behind them in the sudden darkness, the Thames flowed somewhere on their right, the road was a black morass beneath the feet of their labouring horses. Their way was lighted only by blinding lightning flashes that showed trees and bushes atoss in the wind, and the pace they kept was suicidal.

Wet to the skin, with mud in their eyes and down their
necks, they pelted on; choked with wind and rain,
crouched low in the saddle. Thunder rattled all round
them, the sharp, shattering thunder that follows instantly
where lightning strikes, and trees fell groaning beside the
road. By Providence, and the instinct of their desperate
horses, they came to the Surrey side of London Bridge
and reined in to pass the gates.

It was only just past nine o'clock on a July night, and
lights still glimmered in some of the houses on the Bridge,
but the road between was deserted. They crossed at a
sober walk, their faces shining with rain, and not a word
between them. If anyone had noticed them, a whisper
might have passed that one of them wore the Duke of
Northumberland's livery. The other was a gentleman,
young, but not sumptuously dressed, and wrapped in a
common groom's cloak as though to seem more simple
even than he was. Buttoned close inside the doublet of
each, but dampening for all that, was a letter signed by
Northumberland. Little Edward VI lay dying at Greenwich, and the Duke summoned the King's sisters to his
bedside.

Silent, enduring the storm, their horses breathing hard,
Northumberland's messengers emerged from the gates at
the far end of the Bridge and entered Candlewick Street
at a trot. The streets of London were emptied, by the
weather. At St. Paul's the horsemen separated, with a
gesture of parting only, and Northumberland's livery
turned northward toward Hunsdon, where Mary was,

4

while the other kept on through Lud Gate and Fleet Street and Temple Bar, and so along the Strand to Charing Cross and the open fields which lay either side of the hedgerows bordering the road. And as he went, his face impassive, the sound of his companion's horse swallowed up in a second in the roar of wind and rain, he made sure once again of the small soggy roll of paper between palm and glove of his left hand.

At Hyde Park Lane, which his tired horse reached at a canter, he began to bear to his right, toward Hatfield. His message—both his messages—were for Elizabeth, Anne Boleyn's daughter, the red-haired one, the Protestant heir. His mind revolved unceasingly round the dangerous situation in which he found himself, and the surprising scene in the stables at Greenwich which had landed him there.

The boy King was dying, everyone knew that. He was not yet sixteen, and he had never been a healthy child. After him there were no more male heirs to the Tudor throne; nothing but girls. Edward had two sisters— Mary, who was thirty-seven, and Elizabeth, who would be twenty in September. And he had three girl cousins, granddaughters of the old King's youngest sister—Lady Jane, Lady Catherine, and Lady Mary. Except for the Scottish line and its child Queen Mary Stuart, who was betrothed to the Dauphin and lived in France, that was all.

The Duke of Northumberland ruled England now, and its ailing King. By nagging, bullying, and endless persuasion, he had induced Edward to make a will setting aside his sisters and naming Lady Jane as his heir. And then, to cement his own power further, Northumberland married his fourth son Guildford to Lady Jane, who was barely sixteen. Thus, except for the King's disinherited sisters, Northumberland held England in his hand.

Mary, the rightful heir by her father's will, was a Catholic, and Rome was abhorrent to many Englishmen. But Elizabeth and Protestantism were one. It was only by virtue of Protestantism that Elizabeth's birth was legitimate. She was not likely to waver in her allegiance to the English Church. And Elizabeth came before Jane in the succession as devised by the old King's will. Tonight Northumberland was sending for them both to Greenwich. And once they had left the obscure security of their country establishments and come to Court, he would hold them also in his hand.

Head down against the whipping rain, the horseman drove home his spurs, while his mind circled round and came to rest again in the stables at Greenwich and on his own small place in the Duke of Northumberland's plans. He had grown up with the Duke's children, and was the same age as Guildford's brother Robert, whom he served as page, confidant and friend. He and Robert had watched with awe while the Duke's ambition soared. He knew that Robert was apprehensive, and he knew why. Robert had seen the Princess Elizabeth at Whitehall two years ago, when he was first gentleman-of-the-bedchamber to Edward; had even talked with her, in

6

the presence of the little King. Robert said she was not beautiful, but—. And there the sentence would hang, while his eyes grew absent, looking inward. Robert acknowledged a growing dread that if his father succeeded in making Jane Queen, Elizabeth—and Mary too, of course—might be killed, or sent to the Tower for the rest of their lives. And therefore tonight Robert risked his neck, and the neck of his friend who rode to Hatfield, to warn her.

If Northumberland succeeded there was high treason in that damp pellet of paper inside a sodden glove. But Robert had left him no choice, even if he had wished to hesitate. Things had been very quiet all that day at Greenwich, while the Palace shimmered under exceptional summer heat. A thunderstorm was on the way by evening, and the air was thick and stale and tinged with yellow. During the last few days it had become increasingly difficult to get a private word with Robert, as the tension of the King's illness and Northumberland's uncertainty grew, but it was customary for the two boys —neither of them was yet twenty-one—to meet in the stables to see Robert's horses fed each evening. There, in whispers and elliptic sentences, because of the large ears of grooms and guardsmen, the news of the day was exchanged. Robert was known to love his horses, and he said they pined if he did not visit them each evening. Besides, his father the Duke could not keep track of everybody all the time.

Tonight Robert had crossed the courtyard openly,

through the sultry twilight, two folded papers in his hand. On the way he collected one of the Duke's men, with a nod, from a group near the door of the guardroom. In the entrance to the stables, silhouetted against the ominous sky, with his horses whickering a welcome from their stalls, he paused and spoke to the man briefly, and handed him one of those folded papers. The man tucked it away securely inside his doublet and started toward his own horse, at the other end of the stables. Robert turned, and peered into the fragrant dusk inside.

"Anthony—are you there?"

"Here, in Zara's stall."

Robert came to him swiftly. His eyes were bright and he was breathing rather fast. Zara nuzzled at his doublet for a sweet.

"It's begun," he said, and glanced over his shoulder. The Duke's man was saddling, three or four stalls away. "They're sending for Mary and Elizabeth to the King's bedside."

"Is he worse?"

"Yes. Much worse, suddenly. Something has gone wrong. They are not ready—" He thrust the paper into the other's hands. "Take this—inside your doublet, quick." He raised his voice so that the Duke's man might hear if he wished. "A message from my father to the Princess Elizabeth. Humphrey to Hunsdon—you to Hatfield. Hell for leather." And then, lower—"Don't stand there, man! Where's the saddle?" He reached behind him and clapped a saddle on the mare's back. "Take

Zara, she's the fastest. Find her bridle—hurry!" He bent
to the girth. "Tom's hat and cloak are on the peg, there.
Take them. Find his gloves as well."

"I can ride without gloves!"

"I said take his gloves," repeated Robert impatiently,
his head bent to the girth, and then straightened with
a jerk and reached a long arm. "Here they are. Put them
on." He watched while this was done. "Now take this,"
he whispered, and passed a white pellet of paper rolled
very small, and laid a finger on his lips. Treason.

Humphrey led out his horse, mounted, and looked
back inquiringly.

"Ready!" called Robert, and Zara followed him,
saddled and bridled and still nuzzling, into the fading
light of the courtyard.

Wearing the groom's hat and cloak and gloves, with
Northumberland's letter inside his doublet and the pellet
of paper in his left palm, Anthony Brand swung into the
saddle and they were gone through the gate in a clatter
of hooves. Robert stood still and watched them go. He
was not smiling.

They rode into the teeth of the threatening storm.
Almost before they were clear of Deptford it broke, and
by the time they had reached London Bridge there was
not a dry thread between them.

Through Barnet, asleep on the edge of its haunted
heath, pounded Anthony Brand on Robert's mare Zara
—alone now, and grateful for that; past the turning for
St. Albans, where some men might have hesitated, and

up the hill to the park gates of Hatfield, where an ancient fellow with a sack over his head would have asked questions and was nearly ridden down. And so at last, under great oaks that lashed at him with dripping boughs, to a heaving halt beneath the gracious brick façade of the house which sheltered the red-haired daughter of Anne Boleyn. One light burned upstairs.

The mare was done, and swayed where she stood, with the rain streaming off the tip of her tail and washing the mud from her quivering legs. He reeled to the door, cramped and shivering, with the taste of mud on his tongue, and water gurgling in his boots at every step.

His first pull at the bell appeared to snap something somewhere and there was no answering peal within. He beat upon the solid oak with his fist and rattled the heavy iron latch. No one came. He shouted. There was no reply, and thunder mocked his puny noise. He took the hilt of his sword to the panel, and swore because they did not come to let him in out of the wet. At last the bolts shot back reluctantly, and an old man in a nightcap—was she served entirely by dotards?—showed a frightened face in lantern light at the crack.

"I come from Greenwich with a message for her Grace." He crossed the threshold in a single stride, and a pool formed instantly round his feet.

"From the King?" quavered the old man.

"From the Duke of Northumberland."

"What is it, Wickham?" A maid was coming down

the narrow stone stair in the wall, a lighted candle in her hand.

"A message from Greenwich," repeated Anthony, stepping toward her, and she drew back. "I must see her Grace at once."

"You can't—not tonight—not like that—"

"The message will not wait." He set his foot on the bottom stair.

"Go down to the kitchen and dry yourself. I will tell her Grace there is a message."

He threw off the groom's cloak and tossed it over a bench, where it clung and dribbled rivulets on the stone floor. He took off his hat, and even his hair ran water.

"Tell her Grace I must see her privately," he said. "And bring me a towel."

The maidservant stared at him in the light of her wavering candle. Standing several steps below her, he seemed in his slender height to tower. There was a smear of mud across his cheek, but she saw that his eyelashes were so long that they had pointed with the wet, like a tearful girl's. Her glance went on to his mouth, and lingered.

"Well, my dear," he said, so abruptly that she started, "must we keep her Grace waiting?"

Still she hesitated, the candle shaking in her hand.

"M-Mrs. Ashley has gone to bed—" she whimpered.

He was level with her now, and she turned obediently up the stairs. He took her elbow firmly from behind, and his gloved fingers soaked her thin sleeve.

"My message is not for the governess," he said.

So they mounted the stairs together, and she shivered in the chilly grip on her arm. At the top she broke from him and ran along the passage to where a door stood ajar, with light showing through the crack.

"Your Grace!" she cried on a high note of terror. "Your Grace, a man has come from Greenwich—"

The door closed sharply behind her in his face. He waited wearily, his hat in one gloved hand, each boot in a puddle of its own making.

But in less than a minute the door opened again, and the maid stood there.

"You may come in," she said, round-eyed.

He passed her into the room, and stood still in his tracks, staring.

Her Grace the Princess Elizabeth sat at a large oak table littered with books. She wore an old blue cloth gown with a faded look, cut square at the neck and with big lawn sleeves set in to freshen it. She had no jewels. Her cap was laid aside and the candlelight shone on her ruddy hair, brushed back from a high intelligent brow, a little loosened in its natural soft ringlets round her ears, plaited into a heavy knot behind. Her face was pale, with wide, watchful eyes and a narrow chin. She was not beautiful, but—

"You have a message for me from the Court," she said, as he was silent. Her voice was clear and sharp as a bird's pipe. Her eyes were level on him.

12

Suddenly he was conscious of his own draggled appearance, and the mud smear stiffening on his cheek.

"I—I am sorry to appear before your Grace like this," he stammered. "I meant to—I asked them for a towel—down stairs—"

"You have brought me a message," she repeated with the faintest stress, enough to rebuke him for wasting her time.

"Yes, your Grace—from the Duke." He stripped off his right glove and plunged his hand into his doublet, drew out the limp folded page of the letter. "If I might speak—privately—" he added with significance.

She held out her hand for the paper. He squelched across the room to her in his wet boots and surrendered it unwillingly, and then fell back a step, with a glance at the maid, who hovered.

For a moment, with Northumberland's letter in her hand, Elizabeth debated. A written message from the Duke—and then something else *privately.* What would that be? She had perhaps one friend at Court. She was sure that Cecil, for all his caution, was her friend. But would Cecil ever undertake to meddle with the Duke's man? She thought not. Perhaps it was some gossip of the fellow's own, picked up in the stables or—no—he was not a stable and tavern lout. Who was he, then? Whom did he serve, besides the Duke? Could she trust him? Did she dare to trust him? She spoke over her shoulder to the maid, as she broke the seal of the Duke's letter.

13

"Go and wake Mrs. Ashley, Kate. Ask her to come here. And fetch this man a towel."

The girl was gone silently, like a cat.

But by then the first words of the letter had riveted Elizabeth's attention. Edward was ill, and wanted her. Her eyes softened. Poor, lonely Edward, cheated of childhood always, with no one to love or to trust. So he wrote to her, asking her to come. . . . The fact that the letter was not in Edward's handwriting took on consequence. He was too ill to write, perhaps—or else he did not know that a letter had been sent. Rumours had reached even to Hatfield, since Lady Jane's marriage with the Duke's son—rumours that Jane would try for the throne when Edward died. And the summons was not Edward's own. She must go carefully. She must not lose track of things. . . .

In the long silence while she read, and tried to see through the paper to Northumberland, the drip from the wet clothes of his messenger could be heard, a small echo of the rain which splashed against the window-panes. A long shiver shook him as he stood. The air of the room, with the casements closed against the storm, was damp and somehow bleak. He marvelled at how bare of comforts she lived, for a king's daughter and a king's sister, and realized anew the peril she stood in always—orphaned, almost friendless, with an uncertain income—a frail girl alone against the Duke of Northumberland. Robert was right to take this chance to protect her. Robert was right. . . . His eyes rested on her profile.

Suddenly she raised her head.

"You have ridden all the way from Greenwich in this weather?" she asked.

"Yes, your Grace."

"That's hard going. You will want food, and a hot drink. Go down to the kitchen and dry yourself. Ask Kate for what you need—" Her eyes strayed back to the letter. She wanted time to think.

"Your Grace—I have—there is something more."

She measured him with a long look. She rose and faced him, her back against the table, the candlelight haloing her hair.

"More? What more?"

He glanced again about the shadowy room, and drew off his left glove. His left hand came out to her, and within its curled fingers lay the little pellet of soggy paper. She took it from him swiftly, concealing it in her own palm.

"From whom?" she demanded.

He swallowed. Robert was right, oh, yes—but why make the risk they both ran any greater than it had to be? And Robert's finger to his lips—that might mean discretion even now.

"I was not to say that, your Grace," he answered quietly.

Frowning, she unrolled the second message. Five words, in a handwriting she did not know: *The King will die tonight*. Her breath came quickly. Not Cecil, after all. But who? Whom else but Cecil could she trust?

"Who gave you this?" she insisted.

"I was not to say, your Grace," he repeated doggedly.

She turned, and held the bit of paper over a candle, watched it smoke and shrivel to her fingertips, dropped it on the floor, set her foot on the ashes. A trap? Which message was the trap? Edward was ill, and wanted her. And then—privately—Edward would die tonight. One's impulse was all to run to Edward at once. He had the right to die in a sister's arms when he asked it. But suppose one arrived too late. Suppose the succession was disputed. Where was Jane now, if she meant to claim Mary's throne? In London, surely. There were two terrible words for what was in the air: *civil war*. The Catholics would rise for Mary—the Protestants would support Jane, if it came to that. And Elizabeth's own Protestantism put her on the wrong side now, against her sister Mary, whom she was bound to uphold. But Elizabeth's right was better than Jane's. What did they want with her at Court, then? To back up Jane, or to oppose her on her own account? Ah, but Jane was no concern of hers. Not yet. Mary was the heir, and whatever happened it was her place to move first. Had Mary been summoned too? What was Mary doing and thinking, only fifteen miles away, at Hunsdon? It was Mary's business to deal with Jane. If Mary did nothing at all, it would mean that she had received no letter. One could only sit still and do nothing, as long as possible. Give Mary time to decide, and to act. Then play the same game. That was safest. In any case, it was best not to be at Court, if Edward died tonight. But she sighed. It seemed heartless to let Edward die alone among those ruffians, the Council. She would hardly have resisted a personal appeal from him, one which she could be sure was genuine. But as for this document before her now . . .

And this man, this mystery, with his humble words and obstinate mouth, and his eyes that clung to her face, and saw her hair, uncovered, without the cap, and none too tidy—this man must be solved, also. Perhaps when he was dry and had had a drink or two, he would be less like a groom out of livery—more like the sort of man whose chivalry could be appealed to, whose generosity might come to one's rescue, allowing one to read the riddle of his presence if one's very life depended on it. . . .

"Oh, go and be fed!" she snapped at him, all nerves, and then quickly, as he made a formal bow and turned on his heel, not at all like a groom—"No, no, never mind my tempers!" she begged, and held out her hand to him as he looked back, and smiled. "You have done me a great service. I'll send for you—later."

He was shaking with weariness and chill, in his wet clothes, longing for the kitchen fire. For a moment he stared at her, dazed, and at her outstretched hand. In two strides he reached her, bent and touched his lips to her slim fingers, straightened dizzily, and started backwards toward the door. There he encountered the governess in a flurry, clutching a cloak about her night-rail, and the maid Kate with a clean towel in her hands. He snatched the towel and passed it hastily over his face and hair. As he did so, the door of Elizabeth's room closed gently on his heels.

He followed Kate downstairs, still mopping at himself. At the bottom, he returned the towel to her.

"I must see to my horse," he said.

"The stable boys have gone to bed—" she began.

"I know. I always see to her myself." He was at the door, fumbling with the bolts.

"I'll lock this door behind you," said Kate, bringing her candle to his side. "You can see the kitchen lights from the stables. I'll let you in that way. Wickham will build up the fire."

The worst of the storm had passed, as he stepped out again on to the doorstep. He found the mare about where he had left her, sheltering dismally against the wall of the house, and led her quickly to the stables, which he noticed were clean and dry. Old Wickham followed him there, wrapped in a horse-blanket against the rain, and carrying a cup of hot posset.

"Kate mixed it for 'ee," said Wickham simply. "It will keep 'ee from an ague. We got no garments here to fit 'ee," he mourned, eyeing the young man's slender length. "But I'll send the girl to bed and ye can strip in front of the fire and dry out what ye wear—"

They worked together on the mare for a quarter of an hour before her rider was satisfied, and left her munching comfortably. Returning to the kitchen, he found an ample

18

supper waiting, homely country fare—bean pottage, a boiled salad, pale green cheese flavoured with herbs, a hunk of good two days old bread—and more hot drink. The staring girl was shooed away by Wickham, and Anthony's wet clothes were hung up to dry before the hearth. When he had eaten he insisted on dressing himself again, all but his boots and doublet, and stood turning himself as though on a spit in front of the blaze to finish the drying, while Wickham—who had shared the posset—rambled on about the crops, the parlous times, and the wars he had seen in his youth.

The rain had stopped and stars were out in a sky already turning hot again, when Kate tapped at the door and put her head in.

"Her Grace wants you to come upstairs now," she said.

Anthony reached for his boots and drew them on; buttoned his doublet carefully, and buckled on his sword. Then with a single movement he collected cloak, hat, and gloves, and started for the outer door.

"Tell her I have gone," he said, and as Kate cried out he added over his shoulder—"It will be true by the time you get to her!"

He ran to the stables in the starlight, his foresight having placed each piece of Zara's saddlery where he could lay his hand on it in the dark. Old Wickham was after him, futilely, begging him not to cross her Grace. He rode off at a gallop, and left the old man bleating in the courtyard. Robert might have laid their heads on the block, but there was no need to sharpen the axe.

He looked back once at the dark, graceful outline of the house against the sky, and the light in an upstairs window.

## 1558

FOR one reason or another, more men than his son
Robert desired to thwart Northumberland. Someone
warned Mary too, as she rode toward London the next
day, and she turned north instead. All England rallied
to Mary at Framlingham, proclaiming her Queen, with
an army at her back. The Duke's conspiracy collapsed
and he died on the scaffold, and so did poor Lady Jane
and Guildford. Not Robert, though he spent some anxious time in the Tower, as a member of a treasonous
family.

Robert's impulsive effort to save a helpless, gallant
creature from disaster, even though he betrayed his own
father, could not be held against him. His father had not
hesitated to stake his sons' lives on his venture, along
with his own. They had been given no choice but to
fall in with schemes which they knew to be treasonous
to the old King's will. Robert had a right to a small
side stake of his own, for a chance to live if his father
failed. Anyway, it was Mary, and not Elizabeth, whose
righteous Tudor indignation and prompt Tudor courage
destroyed Northumberland.

Within a few months Robert was free again, making
himself agreeable at Mary's Court. He saw Elizabeth

there once or twice, but briefly, for the Protestant heir was still not in favour; spoke with her again, long enough to claim that bit of paper Anthony Brand had carried in his glove, and win her instant gratitude and her cautious trust. Then Robert went to Flanders to the Spanish wars, and Anthony went with him. Sometimes they spoke of her, anxiously. She was not out of danger yet.

Mary ruled England for five dismal years of foreign entanglements and religious persecution. Mary married Philip of Spain, and died of a broken heart, and other things, when he would not stay in England with an aging, childless wife. And then it was Elizabeth's turn to be Queen.

Elizabeth at twenty-five inherited an exhausted treasury and enormous debts, a dispirited realm, debased coinage, and an ill-fed, restless populace seething with religious grievances. In November, 1558, she rode to London from Hatfield, where the news of Mary's death had reached her—young, red-haired, and smiling, with her lifelong graciousness to the mob—and her way was lined with people who sobbed aloud for joy, and recalled with maudlin sentiment the good old days of bluff King Hal. In London, along gravelled streets, through crowds which laughed and cried and shouted and sang themselves hoarse, through thunder of cannon and the ringing of churchbells, she made her progress to the Tower, on horseback, wearing a purple gown. The Lord Mayor rode before, carrying her sceptre;

and just behind her, magnificently mounted, gorgeously clad, rode Robert Dudley, Master of the Horse.

There was one among the knot of velvet-clad gentlemen clustered near the spot where she would dismount at the Tower who had not seen her for the whole of those five years. He was not Robert's shadow, he had no taste for Court life, and he had only heard from Robert's ardent lips how little she had changed—taller, perhaps, even quieter, always pale, with her curling ruddy hair and watchful eyes. They had not been easy years for Mary's Protestant sister. She had still no one to trust, save Cecil when it was safe for him, and Robert who was always out of England with Philip. Until now. Now she had the world at her feet. And that must be a very pleasant feeling, after five years of Mary.

Bareheaded like the rest he waited, a tightness in his chest, measuring her slow progress by the rising roar of her delirious people as she neared the Tower. It was a sound a man of twenty-five had never heard before in England—the full-throated, jubilant, heartfelt cheer which greets a beloved sovereign. And it was for her, after the barren life she had had. His throat closed.

Through a mist he saw the head of the procession winding toward him in the winter sunlight, with plumes on the proud horses' heads and golden trappings down to their hocks; saw the Queen on her white horse, with a bright coronet on her hair, her thin cheeks aglow with excitement and the sharp air. She laughed and kissed her hand to the crowd, and bowed, and beamed on them, drinking in their homage greedily. She had always been hungry for love.

Robert was mounted on a young horse which had never heard royal salutes before, and he was having trouble as he tried to rein in at the entrance to the Tower. Each gun that went off overhead sent the frightened beast to its hind legs. Robert, who had a seat no man could better, held in his mount with a wrist of iron and cursed softly in Flemish epithets. The Queen glanced round, and broke out into unmalicious laughter. Everything pleased her today.

It was all over in a minute. Controlling his expression, Anthony stepped forward and caught Robert's bridle expertly. Robert swung down, furious, and went to give his hand to the Queen for her dismounting. Anthony, soothing the dancing horse, still saw her eyes were upon him, and dared not believe that she knew him. But while her foot was in Robert's hand he heard her question, and caught his own name in reply. She passed on, without another glance, into that grim pile which was both palace and prison.

He was to attend Robert in London, at least till after the coronation, and he had lodgings over a bookseller in Fleet Street. It was only a few weeks later that a Court page sought him out with a sealed letter. He opened it, under the curious eyes of the page. He could only guess that the single line of exquisite handwriting was her own. The Queen, in the third person, desired to see him that afternoon at three. He sent the page away with a gold piece. His heart was pounding, and there was a weakness in his knees.

It was not till then, sitting on the edge of his bed with his giddy head in his hands, that he realized what she had come to mean to him. For years he had thought of her secretly, cherished her image in his heart. But he had somehow never dreamed of seeing her again face to face, of seeing her often, even from a distance. It was terrifying to have her ride back into his life on a white horse, secure in her own right, powerful, radiant, intolerably dear to his soul. He was stunned that she should have remembered him. Robert, yes, no doubt. But a man she had seen only once, when he was drenched to the skin and caked with mud. . . .

Three o'clock found him in her ante-room, dressed in his sober best, avoiding the questions and glances of people he knew. The same page came and led him through various passages to another room, small and bare, where he was left alone and began to wonder. It was sparsely furnished with a square oak table which had a stout brass-bound chest in the middle of it, a shabby chair each side. The window was narrow, with an outlook over rooftops. Almost a prison room. He stood staring out at a strip of dull winter sky.

The door opened softly behind him, and closed again. She stood just inside, smiling at his astonishment. Mean as her surroundings were, she was dressed like a queen today—all in white, with jewels in her hair and on her fingers. Majesty became her slender dignity. She dazzled the eye.

"We haven't long," she said, very low, and crossed to the table with a rustle of silk. "So I cannot stop to make speeches. I sent for you because I am superstitious. You saved me once. Oh, yes, Robert, too. But it was you who took the wetting! I had nothing to give you then, even if you had not disappeared. But now—"

"I have had my reward," he said, and it was her turn to be astonished.

"What do you call a reward, then?" she demanded.

"Another sight of you today," he said. "And to have you remember."

"I have little enough of that kind of thing to remember," she remarked drily. "I tell you I am superstitious. I sacrifice to my gods. There must be something that you want—a young man like you. Are you rich?"

"No," he smiled.

"Your family?"

"A married sister in Cheshire is all."

"You seek a place at Court, perhaps?"

He shook his head.

"Only while Robert needs me. I fancy that won't be long."

"Why do you say that?"

He shrugged.

"Robert has got what he wants—you have given him that. He is born to Court life. I am not."

"But you are his friend."

26

"We were playmates—boys together. But now his fortune is made."

"And yours?"

He spread his empty hands.

"But what will you do," she persisted, "if you leave Robert now? Where will you go?"

"I'd thought of asking Robert to give me the management of one of his country places," he explained haltingly. "He has several—and I could save him from being robbed right and left by dishonest stewards, I think."

"That would suit you? Looking after some place in the country?"

"Yes." He lifted a fastidious nose. "London stinks," he said.

They were both unaware that he spoke to her without her title of Majesty. It was still new to her, and his lips were unschooled in Court manners. They were both absorbed in this low-voiced interview, so soon to be over, so fraught with their own emotion.

She had known all along that he was somehow different from the rest, or he would have stepped forward long ago to claim her attention. This caught her fancy. Why? Robert had been ready enough to receive benefits. Robert had not thought of that pretty speech about another sight of her. What ailed this man that he had kept out of her way and seemed to expect nothing now that she had come into her own, and partly because of him? He faced her now, handsomer than Robert, and just as self-possessed. But his eyes were different from Robert's, and his ungilded compliments rang true. He had all but said that Robert's ways were not his ways. So he looked no higher than the stewardship of one of Robert's houses! Had he no home at all of his own, then?

"There is some girl you want to marry," she ventured, with a twinge of jealousy.

"No," he smiled.

"If I could give you whatever you wanted most," she pressed him, "what would it be?"

"If you were willing—" He stuck there.

"Tell me what it is. Tell me what you want."

"Your portrait," he blurted simply. "Painted as you stand there now—so that when I am old and sad and tired I can still warm my hands at it and feed my dim eyes on the glory of you as I see it today. That is what I want—the only thing I shall ask of you—ever!"

There was a silence in the bare little room.

"What, only that?" Her breath caught on the words, and both hands came out to him in something like gratitude. "You shall have it," she promised, and he bent his head to her fingers. "But wait—have you got a roof to put over my head?"

"No—I have nothing. But there are rooms set aside for me in my sister's house, where I keep all my things—"

"I refuse to lodge in your sister's house." She turned to the table and threw back the lid of the chest. "Look," she said, smiling. "Here is your reward, if you had not made all the wrong answers!" She lifted out stiff folded parchments with dangling seals. Beneath them the chest was full of gold pieces.

He gasped.

"But I can't take that!" he cried. "Besides, I—I'd rather have the portrait!"

"You'll have the portrait," she answered, humouring him. "But you'll have these deeds as well. I meant them for you. I *stole* them for you—from Cecil!" Her merry eyes met his dazed ones above the gold. "He's forgotten it—I'm afraid it's only a *little* house, 'way down in Worcestershire, and falling to pieces." She tapped the folded parchments. "But a few good farms go with it. I never dreamed you would want to go and live in the country, but because I had so little else to give you I thought you might sell the property for what it would fetch. Why bury yourself on one of Robert's estates? This one might pay, with cherishing." She put the deeds into his hands. "There's enough money there in the chest to mend the roof and keep you from starving for a while. I've lived near a year on less myself."

"But—it's a fortune!" he said incredulously. "I could buy cattle—I could build barns—I could—"

"You could turn into a country bumpkin," she told him shortly. "You are wiser than Robert, aren't you? Now go, I have no time to myself these days. Take the papers with you. I'll have the chest brought to your lodging tonight."

"But I—can't—"

The door behind them opened quickly and a girl's anxious face looked in.

"Your Majesty—"

"Coming. Go and tell them I am coming."

The girl's face vanished and the door swung to. They were alone again in the perilous privacy of royalty, in the bleak little room. Elizabeth laid her hand on his sleeve, and its fragile fingers clung; her face, in its delicate frame of wired lace and pearl, was lifted to his.

"Let me look at you," she said, very low. "Let me remember this. Grey eyes, and mousy hair—dark lashes, like a girl's—Lord, he blushes, too!—a mouth to set some woman worshipping all her days—you will be kind to her, Anthony Brand, and never say harsh things to make her cry—"

"There is no one," he insisted. "Oh, believe—believe—there is no one like that, for me!"

"And there is no one like you—here. I am grateful for such a man—even if he is down in Worcestershire raising sheep." A moment more their eyes held each other. Her upturned face was very near, and how was he to know that Robert would have presumed to kiss her as she stood there? Then the fingers on his sleeve relaxed and she receded from him a little, a little remembered Majesty, and smiled. "When you have bought your cattle and built your barns—and before you are too old to sit a horse—come back and tell me about the place. And if they should try to tell you that the Queen is busy or tired or cannot see you—bid them bring me this." She drew a ring swiftly

from her left hand and pressed it into his, palm to palm.
"It is a Spanish jewel from brother Philip, and it has
never seen an honest man before. No doubt it will feel
strange at first in your company—" Still smiling, she was
drifting away from him, backwards toward the door.
"—as I do."

"But I would give back the farms and the gold for just
the picture!" he cried.

"It will follow you to Worcestershire."

She was gone.

Still dazed, he found his way through devious passages
to the ante-room again and hurried through it, hoping to
be unobserved. On the stairs he met Robert, likewise in
a hurry. And Robert looked surprised to see him there.

# *1559*

*A LITTLE house, 'way down in Worcestershire, and falling to pieces.* He saw it first from a sudden turn in the lane on a chilly day of March thaw.

It stood on the western slope of the Cotswold Hills, where they dip down suddenly into Evesham Vale. It was placed low and cosily, cradled in a fold of rolling land out of the wind. A film of ice covered the water in the ruts of the lane, which was overgrown with hawthorn and coppery elder. Stale snow had lingered in the hedges on the heights behind him. But as he descended toward the valley spring came up to meet him.

The trees were greeny-grey here with bursting leaves, the blackbirds were trying out their notes, lapwings were lovemaking in the hedgerows, and a flock of starlings chuckled and chittered at him from the branches of a budded elm. The first pale primroses peeped out from the greening banks, the sweet-briar hedge was in tiny leaf, the hazel buds were red. The lambs of the pure white Cotswold sheep were noticeably older and stronger than those on the bleak upper hillsides he had crossed that morning.

The long grey front of the house faced north, shaggy with unkempt ivy, the loosened fronds drooped low over

32

the narrow trefoiled windows set in pairs, whose precious glass had been pilfered lead and all from the stone mullions of the ground floor rooms. The overgrown shrubbery and winter-weakened boughs leaned all askew in the wind. The door was broad, rising to a slightly pointed arch, deeply recessed in a bold moulding, with a single worn stone step. It was set in a high squarish block at the west end, with a tall traceried window above, and a steeply pitched roof. To the east, with a deep jog, ran a low two-storeyed wing. The chimneys were square and few.

Like so many ruined houses in England then, it had once been a priory, and at the time of the dissolution of the lesser monasteries it had been carelessly tossed with a handful of small benefices to one of Henry's flatterers. This much Anthony knew already from his papers. By its appearance this raw March day he guessed that it had never been lived in since its seizure twenty years before. For a time, no doubt, its barns were kept in repair and its crops were harvested. But now it stood forgotten, as she had said, masterless and stripped, but serene in the Gothic beauty of its grey Cotswold stone. His heart went out to it in its loneliness and austere dignity. And he knew as he beheld it that not for a dozen spruce new timbered manors in a pride of slender chimney clusters and myriad marching casements would he resign this forsaken gem with its exquisite arches, trefoils, and dripstones. It was his, now, to have and to hold, with near three hun-

dred acres of land; his, and he had never owned stick or
stone before; his, to love and to cherish. . . .

He dismounted in the lane and approached the house
reverently on foot. But before he had gone half way a
sudden spatter of raindrops overtook him so that he broke
into a run and flung himself precipitately into the shallow
shelter of the doorway, against the weatherbeaten oak
door, bound with rusty iron. His horse followed at a jog-
trot and stood unhappily in the grass-grown cobbled space
before the step.

For a moment he admired the door—his door. Like a
blind man, he ran his fingertips over the smooth curves
of the deep, undecorated moulding, traced with delight the
graceful lines of the long iron hinges and elaborate lock-
plate. Then he remembered that he had no key. No one at
the hedgerow ale-house two miles away had known of
a key. Gently he set his shoulder to the oak. Gently it
gave before him, creaking, and the great door swung
slowly inward. This was his welcome home.

He stood in a high, dim hall, facing a plain stone fireplace with a hooded canopy. Breathlessly he followed
with his eyes the thin stone ribs of the vaulting in their
flight from the slender triple piers against the walls to
the carven bosses along the central rib above his head. It
was a ceiling like the sweep of wings.

His heart had not beat so since he stood in the presence of the Queen. A moment he paused there, noting the
delicate leading of the tall traceried window in the wall
above his head, too high to be reached by vandals. His

The Old Priory Door 1559

*Drawn by Olive Wren*

spurs rang on the stone floor as he walked to the door on the right. Its hinges were loud as he pushed it open. A smaller room was there, vaulted in miniature, with a delicious oriel window facing west, a pair of trefoiled lights to the north, and a small stone fireplace. He was pleased at the cosy depth of wall which showed where the north window was let in. It would be a warm house, and dry.

He was pleased with everything, though those two rooms were all that stood whole enough to keep the weather out. When he had re-crossed the hall to a narrow passage on its left, which gave on to the east wing, he found that only the north wall, which he had seen from the front, was intact. The refectory and kitchens had been there, with the dormitory above. But the entire south wall had gone, the floor of the dormitory had caved in on the refectory, bringing part of the east wall with it, and the stone had since been carried off at will to mend the barns and pigsties of the peasantry. The remains of a fine fireplace were still there, the chimney running up the north wall between two sets of trefoiled windows. A spiral stone staircase in the thickness of the wall in the corner next the passage wound upward toward the sky. Underfoot was a shambles of slate from the roof, and rubbish. The cloisters no longer existed.

He stood among the ruins, his face aglow, and saw a new wing rising there, a great panelled room with a fine mantelpiece and a big bay window; above it a comfortable bedchamber for himself, panelled too, for wood was warmer and he loved the look of polished oak; a good modern wing, but carefully done in local stone, so as not to mar the house from the outside.

Meanwhile he would live in the little room with the oriel; it would be very adequate once it was furnished and had a fire.

His bed could go there, and his writing-table, and he could eat there too. Some sort of kitchen would have to be pieced together at once, round the old refectory fire-place, and a country wench must be found to come and cook for him. And there must be workmen; a glazier first, a clever man, to match the leading which was left and the exact pale greenish tone of the glass—the replaced windows must not show that they were new. A stone mason second, to make what he could of the damage till the new wing could be planned and begun; carpenters—joiners— gardeners—a stable boy—he would draw them all from the land roundabout, his own people, from the farms he owned, along with the house. And the roof must be seen to at once. . . .

For an hour he poked about the house and grounds without encountering a soul. Then he rode in the driz-zling dusk to the inn at Evesham and sat up half the night making lists of things to be done at Worcester, where he meant to buy his furniture and find a surveyor.

But the cold grey morning light brought sanity. He had not all the money in the world. The place must pay its way as they went. A glazier, yes, for the damaged win-dow in his own room. And the gaping wound in the east

wing would have to be stopped somehow or no woman
would work there. That was all for now. The farms must
come first, and the barns. It was time to get on with the
spring planting. He must find out how things were with
his neglected tenants, see that they had what they needed,
and straighten out his rent roll. If the harvest was good,
perhaps . . .

First of all he would establish himself modestly in the
little west room and get acquainted with his people and
tend his land through the summer. There would have to
be oxen for ploughing, and a sow, and some sheep—(there
was money in wool)—a milch cow, and hens. He could
raise his own food and his keep would cost nothing. And
he would have a good dog, for company. Perhaps next
year he could think about the new wing.

But next year was still too soon. And the year after
that he bought five acres of water meadow, and set out a
young apple orchard. And the next he built new out-
buildings at the home farm. Sometimes the locked chest
under his bed was very nearly empty, and sometimes it
was almost as good as new. Once he saw the bottom and
went cold. But that was a good year for oats, and the tide
turned slowly from then on, so that money always came
in a little faster than it went out.

He was no miser to count farthings. Whatever the
place demanded of him he gave freely. But by shrewd
management and endless toil, and careful buying in of
good stock and skilful selling off of surplus mouths to
feed, and calculated slaughter—by the hard-won good

will of his tenantry, who at first could not believe their eyes and ears, and who began incredulously to prosper—the place was finally paying its way and a bit more.

He was no vainglorious country gentleman, either, but lived in his boots and shirt, laying hold of any tool, never ashamed to learn, willing to laugh at his own blunders, tireless, good-humoured, but watchful of laggards. Weakling colts and early lambs were brought to the kitchen fire and tended with his own hands. He was out at dawn after a plain porridge breakfast, a sheep-dog at his heels, and he did his accounts by candlelight. The old ones nodded their heads together at the hedgerow ale-house—"The best dung for the land is its master's foot walking over it," they quoted with approval.

Whatever faults the monks had had, they took a genuine interest in their tenant farmers and their neighbours, and their expulsion nearly a generation before had brought poverty and sickness and bewilderment to the countryside. Now, after all these years, this man, who for all his ignorance of simple things lived rather like a monk himself, was bringing back their prosperity. When he might have rested, or ridden into Evesham for a market-day gossip, to see a company of strolling players and have a convivial evening, he pottered instead among the flowers he was planting near the house, trimmed vines and borders, and laid out a knot-garden from a design he had got from his sister in Cheshire.

She sent a list of herbs, too, which no household should be without, she said, and he cherished the neat, closely written pages, as fair as the Queen's own, among his deeds and receipted bills, and referred to them often as he worked:

Basil, whose seed cured infirmities of the heart; whose root, held in the hand with a swallow's feather, would relieve the pains of a woman in childbirth.

Wormwood, an antidote against poisonous mushrooms; and from which could be made a conserve (recipe enclosed) which cured dropsy, and prevented drunkenness; and whose leaves, laid among garments in chests, would keep away flies and gnats.

Rosemary, whose early flower brought the bees and improved the honey; and which was good to have in the house in plague-time; and whose leaves and flowers eaten with bread and salt every morning improved the sight; and whose seeds, drunk with pepper and white wine, would heal jaundice; the woody parts being good for toothpicks.

Nigella, boiled with vinegar and water for toothache.

Sweet balm, which was good however used, restored cheerfulness and rejoiced the heart.

Garlick, which must be sown in the wane of the moon, and which would keep birds from young fruit if bunches of it were hung on the boughs. Angelica root would remove the smell from the breath if chewed soon after.

Parsley, which if cast on the surface of fishponds would rejoice the sick fish.

Periwinkle, whose bruised leaves were good for bleeding at the nose.

Solomon's seal, whose juice wiped out freckles and bruises from the skin.

Cinquefoil, as a drink in pestilent air, or for poison.

Rue, which should be cursed and hurt when planted to do well, and would keep adders and lizards away, but should not be put in plague-time nosegays.

Sage, which should be used in pottage to bring appetite, and which when boiled sweetens the breath.

Anise, hoarhound, hyssop, fennel, ginger; smalache for swellings, and lovage for the stone.

All the small, modest, mysterious herbs for strewing and for physic and for home doctoring, his sister Margaret had listed with their uses. He planted them in an intricate pattern, with low clipped box as a border, and was ready for any domestic emergency.

## II

Before the first summer was out Elizabeth had kept her promise about the portrait. It was a warm, shining day in May. He was down at the home farm, to try the cheese Goodwife Biggs was making from ewes' milk—the home farm lay several hundred yards west of the house—when his serving-maid Cisley came flying with a kerchief over her head, in an incoherent babble of excitement about a fine gentleman from Whitehall who had arrived with a parcel.

With a leap of his heart Anthony guessed what it must be. He turned and almost ran for the house, and was panting when he reached his own front door, where two horses stood. In the vaulted hall he found a handsome lad, something better than a page, gazing up at the traceried window with approval. She had done him honour even in the choice of her messenger. Here was one of his own kind, young, good blood, and his way to make. Propped against the wall just inside the door was a heavily wrapped flat parcel, nearly four feet square. Anthony understood the second horse. The Queen's picture had travelled on it.

"I'm sorry you found no place to sit down," he said. "It's a green country-girl with no sense of what is due a visitor. My own room is furnished, if you will come this way. And perhaps you will stay to dinner?"

The lad's eyes were curious and respectful on him, as he spoke. He was sorry, but he was short of time; he had already ordered dinner at the inn in Chipping Campden, and meant to start for London as soon as the horses were able.

"Some wine, then," suggested Anthony. "I can give you something better than our country perry, anyway."

His visitor thanked him, and then, with a little air of importance, indicated the parcel where it stood against the wall.

"From the Queen," he said.

"I am very grateful to you." Anthony lifted it between his hands and led the way to the west room, where he had made himself comfortable enough with a bed, a cupboard, a small table under the north window for his meals and writing materials, and two plain chairs. He set the Queen's picture unopened against the wall again and poured out a good Gascoigne wine from a stoneware jug into plain pewter goblets. Their eyes met across the brims.

"The Queen," they said gently, and drank.

"If you will have another while I write my acknowledgments—" said Anthony then, and the youth allowed him to fill the goblet again, and disposed his great length easily in one of the uncushioned chairs.

There was no time for composition. The pen shook in his hand as he wrote quickly:

Your Majesty's memory is long and generous. My establishment here is now complete. And my gratitude is greater than your Majesty can know. All that I shall ever have or ever be is at your feet.

A. B.

As he folded and sealed the paper the Queen's messenger got to his feet and was waiting. Their eyes met again in a grave smile as the paper changed hands.

"You will always be welcome here," said Anthony. "I shall hope to see you again when I am—better equipped for hospitality."

"Thank you. Perhaps I shall return and claim that dinner some day."

Anthony followed him to the horses, saw him mounted, gave the bridle of the led horse into his hand, waved him farewell—and did not realize till afterwards that he had never heard his name.

He returned to the little room and closed the door behind him, and knelt to cut the cords that bound the parcel. His eager hands were clumsy with the wrappings, but at last the picture was revealed, in a heavy gold frame. He drew in his breath. The Queen stood there, regarding him gravely with her watchful eyes, dressed in white with jewels in her ruddy hair; one fine hand was caught in the long strand of pearls which fell below her waist, where the painting ended.

A long time he knelt there, worshipping. Then he rose and looked about the room for a suitable place to hold his treasure. The fireplace was hooded, which spoilt the space above it with a slant. His bed occupied the south side of the room. There was only the wall above the cupboard which stood between the oriel and the north wall. He lifted the picture to the top of the cupboard, which was the right height for it, and stood back to admire. Some day he would build a fine mantelpiece to her measurement, and she should preside there in a long room panelled in oak, more worthy of her presence—a great carved wooden mantelpiece, with the frame embedded in the polished oak above it, like a coat of arms. Some day . . .

And so the seasons crept past him, each with its own small disaster or growing triumph. Word went round the countryside that the old priory was owned by an eccentric who was willing to put money into it, who was content to live there alone in two gaunt rooms with a few sticks of furniture acquired at an auction in Worcester; who knew how to nurse his profits and turn them back into the land for more profits on a larger scale. It was even said that he read books at night—books about farming and husbandry. There was much speculation in the inns from Worcester to Chipping Campden as to what such a man might have done at Court, to be thus banished into limbo, and whose powerful enmity he might have incurred. A legend grew up behind his back that he had run afoul of Robert Dudley with the Queen.

It was true that he worked with his hands like a yeoman, and burned candles at night like a scholar. Since his early teens he had been a townsman, at Robert's side. His knowledge of the country was a child's knowledge only. It included divers bird-notes and wildflowers, lore of mole-catching and foxes' earths, such simple maxims as that if the sun set red it would be wet tomorrow, and if ducks trimmed their feathers with their bills it meant that wind was coming. But the serious business of sowing and reaping and dunging, lambing and milking and marketing, was all to be learnt from what primers he could find.

He brought to it a fresh and inquiring mind; not a sceptical viewpoint, but one full of logical questions which often confounded the slow intelligence of his tenantry and left them dumb and exasperated and defensive.

They did not know *why* they did certain things at certain times of the year, like clockwork, except that their fathers and grandfathers had done the same before them, which was surely reason enough. Explanations bored or confused them. These things were thus and so. As well ask why the sun rose in the east, as to demand wherefores concerning the swarming of bees in May, or the well-known murderous antipathy between walnut tree and oak.

Abashed by his own ignorance, and defeated by the taciturn peasant, Anthony wrote up to London to his friend the bookseller. Three weeks later a parcel arrived by the Worcester carrier's cart. There were two books only—all that had been printed, apparently, to fill his need. He laid them reverently on the table in his room to await his evening leisure, and went out to keep an appointment with old Hobden and his two lads at work in the west meadow, and incidentally to learn from them what he might of the setting of hedges.

That evening after his late farmer's supper of boiled mutton with prunes, a washed fresh salad of lettuce with oil and vinegar and salt, and a mug of home-made cider, he lighted candles, for the sky was overcast and twilight had come early, and opened the small quarto at its title page:

## ONE HUNDRED POINTS OF GOOD HUSBANDRY

———

*Set forth by Thomas Tusser, gentleman, servant to the right honourable Lord Paget of Beaudesert*

———

One hundred points of good husbandry
    Maintaineth good household with huswifry.
Housekeeping and husbandry if it be good
    Must love one another like cousins in blood.
The wife too must husband as well as the man,
    Or farewell thy husbandry, do what thou can.

———

*Imprinted at London, in Fleet Street, within Temple Bar, at the sign of the Hand and Star, by Richard Totell, the third day of February, An. 1557. Cum privilegio ad imprimendum solum.*

———

He read on, fascinated, amused, excited. In quatrains which were sheerest doggerel, he found many of his problems didactically dealt with, and much sound advice even where he had never felt a lack of it, as—

Leave Prince's affairs undescanted upon,
    And tend to such doings as stands thee upon;
Fear God and offend not the Prince or his laws,
    And keep thyself out of the Magistrate's claws.

And—

> Though love be in choosing far better than gold,
>> Let love come with somewhat, the better to hold.

Month by month through the year, in simple, limping rhyme, Tusser laid down the law of the soil. Wet land, he said firmly, or over-dunged land, or new-broken land was not good for wheat. Anthony made a note of this. Cattle won't eat straw, he was warned, if they taste hay first. What worser for barley than wetness and cold, exclaimed the book in March, and added philosophically—

> Yet true it is as cow chews cud,
>> And trees at spring do yield forth bud,
> Except wind stand as never it stood,
>> It is an ill wind turns none to good.

In May he was exhorted to—

> Get into thy hop-yard for now it is time
>> To teach Robin hop on his pole how to climb;
> To follow the sun as his property is,
>> And weed him and trim him if aught go amiss.

Hops. He would try them. Sir Thomas Baskerville, down Worcester way, grew them, and brewed his own beer. You put them in about October, he had heard, and dunged them in February when you cleaned out your dovecot for the purpose.

47

The sun in the south, or else southly and west,
  Is joy to the hop as a welcomed guest;
But wind in the north, or else northerly east
  To hop is as ill as a fray in a feast.

Under July he read with interest—

While wormwood hath seed get a bundle or twain,
  To save against March to make flea to refrain;
Where chamber is swept and wormwood is strewn,
  No flea for his life dare abide to be known.

Reluctantly he tore himself from Tusser's thin, blackly printed pages to examine the other book briefly, before he went to bed. This was Andrew Boorde's *Breviary of Health*, and while it lacked Tusser's insouciant charm and captivating jingle, its sober prose was at once trenchant and illuminating. Boorde warned his reader particularly against dust, which bred sickness, and laid anxious stress on the cleanliness of buttery and kitchen and especially the dairy, which latter the cat must on no account be allowed to enter, the mice there being best caught by traps. "Use to have a fire in your chamber to waste and consume the evil vapours," he advised, which seemed extravagant but sound. "Lie not in such chambers the which be deprived clean from the sun and open air." (Anthony glanced complacently at his own north light and the lovely oriel which admitted the warm yellow rays of each descending sun.) "Have a merry heart, for pensifulness doth hurt the stomach," cautioned Boorde,

48

and Anthony rose at last, a little stiffly from bending in an east wind, and prepared for bed with a smile on his lips, for life was genial to him these days, and his stomach served him well.

Temptation to browse nightly on the wisdom of his two authors was sometimes resisted in favour of his accounts, which he kept minutely for his very life. The inside cover of his account-book carried a neatly copied verse of the estimable Tusser's, which never failed to cheer him with a sense of companionship even when the balance sagged in the wrong direction.

> Once weekly remember thy charges to cast,
>     Once monthly see how thy expenses may last;
> If quarter declareth too much to be spent,
>     For fear of ill years take advice of thy rent.

With home-made ink concocted by his willing young wench Cisley on a basis of oak-apples and beer, he recorded the sometimes alarming fluctuations of his little hoard.

| | | |
|---|---:|---:|
| Thread, and mending a kettle . . . . . . . . . . . | | 6*d.* |
| Well-bucket . . . . . . . . . . . . . . . . . . . . . . | | 12*d.* |
| 3 pair of harness and 6 halters . . . . . . . . . . | 2*s.* | 6*d.* |
| 6 milking cans . . . . . . . . . . . . . . . . . . . . | 2*s.* | 6*d.* |
| a butter churn . . . . . . . . . . . . . . . . . . . . | 3*s.* | |
| Carriage of books from London . . . . . . . . . . | | 6*d.* |
| Hobden, for hedging and felling the coppice . | 38*s.* | |
| 2 Hobden lads, 2 days work . . . . . . . . . . . . . | | 8*d.* |

| | | |
|---|---|---|
| Cisley, wages ........................ | 6s. | 8d. |
| a Thatcher, for 5 days work ............. | 5s. | |
| Boy to help the shepherd 4 weeks ......... | 2s. | |
| The rat-catcher ....................... | 2s. | 6d. |
| Setting 3 horseshoes ................... | | 9d. |
| Sand for scouring the pewter ............ | | 1d. |
| Taps ................................ | | 1d. |
| 2 cheesecloths ....................... | | 9d. |

The opposite page read quite cheerfully sometimes.

| | | | |
|---|---|---|---|
| 5 calves sold at Chipping Campden ...... | 21l. | 5s. | 6d. |
| Straw .............................. | | 3s. | 6d. |
| Wheat sold at Pershore and Evesham and to private buyers, 4 bush. at 18d. .... | | 6s. | |
| 5 quarters at 12s. 8d. .............. | 3l. | 3s. | 4d. |
| Tenants' rents ...................... | 19l. | 5s. | 3d. |
| D. Biggs for wood money ............. | | 6s. | |

Long before it was time to engage a surveyor, his writing-table was deep in his own carefully drawn up plans for the new wing. Every sheet of paper which bore an idea, a hasty sketch, an impression, an ambition, however wild, was preserved against a final weeding out, a coming down to brass tacks and shillings, when the work could actually begin.

He had roamed the countryside looking at the outsides of other people's houses from all angles; he had gone to immense trouble and exercised great diplomacy to obtain a sight of their insides, noting here a staircase, there a mantelpiece, somewhere else a window of the right shape. He formed revolutionary ideas such as that the best chamber should face south so the sun could come in. And when it was protested to him that the south wind was unhealthy he explained that according to Tusser the best land for tillage was land falling full south or south-west, and that the view from the windows on that side would be far the best. He argued that if crops grew best with a southern exposure it surely followed that human beings would flourish too. And he quoted Jeremiah to the effect that from the north dependeth all evil.

His manœuvres included the establishment of closer relations with his sister Margaret, who lived in a smart timbered house in Cheshire, with fine pargeted ceilings and a broad wooden staircase which he planned to copy, with embellishments, in his own new wing. Margaret's husband was increasingly prosperous in his extensive dairy farming, an amiable, rather ignorant man, whose credit would be helpful and whose practical suggestions Anthony was determined to sidestep whenever possible. His own drawings and ground plans had become so precious to him after months of solitary dreaming, that he had decided most venturously to proceed with only a master mason and carpenter to carry out his wishes. A proper surveyor would interfere in his most cherished designs. And he meant that the house should be built exactly as he wanted it, without reference to superstitions about the south wind or other old-fashioned nonsense.

His plan was to rebuild the ruined south wall of the

old refectory to form his dining-room alongside his repaired kitchen, with bedrooms and servants' attics above; and then to extend the south front westward in a new wing with an entrance hall containing the open wooden staircase with its generous landings and carved handrail and balusters. A library with a door cut through into the old vaulted hall would come next to the west, through which you would reach the grand new parlour which was to be the home of the Queen's picture, with his own bedchamber above it and another storey above that, to remain unfurnished indefinitely, until he had the money— Margaret persisted in referring openly to the latter as the nursery floor.

On the large ground-floor parlour he lavished all his love and care. It was the reason for the whole wing which enclosed it. Where he himself slept really did not matter much. But the room where the Queen's portrait was to hang must be perfect to the last detail. He was willing to go slowly and spend wisely. He expected to be years at the finishing, once the walls of the new wing were up. Except for the Queen's room, he was not impatient. But the design for that, down to the pattern of the panelling and the shape of the window-panes, was already complete in his mind when the master mason and his men arrived. Thereafter his green sod was overlaid with raw timber for the scaffolding, and rutted with the wheels of wagons bringing stone and slate, and the sound of hammering was ever in his ears.

# *1565*

IT was a warm sunny morning in July, and the palace
at Richmond was at its best, with a riot of roses in the
gardens that ran down to the river.

The Queen sat on cushions on a white stone bench, a
little apart from the noisy group of lords and ladies clus-
tered under the sloping roof of the tennis court, watching
a game between the first peer of the realm, the young
Duke of Norfolk, and the new Earl of Leicester, who was
Robert Dudley. Mary Radcliffe and Lettice, Countess of
Essex, attended her, and Lettice's eyes as they rested on
Robert were possessive and tender.

Elizabeth had been Queen for nearly seven years, and
it had changed her, hardened and sharpened her. All the
eligibles in Europe had courted her, and she had humoured them all—except Philip of Spain—up to a point.
Beyond that point, no diplomacy of ambassadors or
statesmen could move her. She protested always that she
had no wish to marry, and even Cecil had almost begun
to believe her. Even Robert Dudley.

For all those years Robert had dangled more or less
cheerfully after the Queen, receiving honours and benefits
gracefully, wearing his responsibilities as favourite lightly.
The unsolved death of his wife in 1560 had eclipsed his

prominence momentarily with the ugliest of rumours. Amy, who never came to Court and whom Robert neglected, no one could deny, was visiting friends at Cumnor and was found dead one night at the foot of a stone staircase— dead of a broken neck. The Spanish ambassador was among the first to spread the story that Robert Dudley and the Queen knew more about it than met the eye. The Spanish ambassador, intent upon his innuendoes, was not clever enough to see that Amy mysteriously dead with suspicion of murder constituted a far greater barrier to Robert's ambitious devotion to the Queen than Amy innocently alive in the country, childless, and divorceable. The Queen and Robert, always cleverer than De Quadra, could see. And to Robert Amy's death in those equivocal circumstances spelt the utter ruin of his secret hopes. The inquest at Cumnor brought a verdict of accidental death: Amy had been unwell, she was giddy, and she fell. But Robert knew he could never be consort now, without proving to the world's satisfaction that he had deliberately removed his wife from his path to the throne.

The knowledge irked him unbearably in the ensuing months, and made him irritable and arrogant and very difficult to get along with, and the Queen's temper was never mild. There were quarrels, scenes, reconciliations. The plotting for various foreign marriages went on, the Queen spoke with increasing frequency and fondness of her own treasured virginity—and Robert was still the favourite.

But now Robert, tethered by an old loyalty yet

thwarted by the Queen's growing caution, had begun to look about him. His eye fell on lovely Lettice Knollys, Countess of Essex. Lettice was a minx, and not overly devoted to her husband who preferred the country to the Court. Robert pointed out to Elizabeth that his supposed flirtation with Lettice was confusing to the Spanish ambassador, at which Elizabeth entered the game with zest and pretended a tender interest in several other courtiers. The Spanish ambassador wrote home that the new Earl of Leicester was out of favour at last, and the negotiations for the Austrian marriage, a project very dear to Spanish diplomacy, moved forward with more confidence.

Finally the joke had begun to lose its savour. Robert's attentions to Lettice were no longer merely for the edification of Spain. Elizabeth suspected that Robert sought Lettice's company because he liked it more and more, and there was a veiled complacence in Lettice's downcast eyes and fluttering smile.

Robert lost the game to Norfolk with grace and good nature. Lettice said he wasn't trying. Lettice said his foot slipped. Mary Radcliffe, already spare and spinsterish in the service of the Queen, gave·her a sardonic look behind Elizabeth's back as the two players approached the bench. Mary saw through Lettice. Elizabeth appeared not even to look.

"For shame, Robert, you've let him beat you again!" cried Elizabeth. "Lettice says your foot slipped."

"No, I didn't slip." Robert's amused eyes met Lettice's in a brief flicker of private understanding. "Just bad luck, that's all. Body of God, it's a warm day!" With an ease which bespoke habit and intimacy, he twitched the handkerchief from the Queen's fingers without so much as a by-your-leave, and wiped his face with it. "Never mind, I'll take my revenge tomorrow!"

"My lord!" cried Norfolk, rigid with horror. "How dare you do such a thing? How dare you commit such sacrilege, here before us all!"

"Such as to play you again tomorrow and beat you?" smiled Leicester in feigned surprise.

"The Queen's handkerchief!" spluttered Norfolk, pointing, and Leicester looked from him to the handkerchief in his hand and back again, impudently. "You are wiping your face with the Queen's handkerchief!" cried Norfolk, beside himself.

"It's cleaner than yours," said Leicester, and Elizabeth laughed outright.

"Not since you have touched it to your filthy face!" exploded the Duke.

"I'm not dirty, Norfolk—only hot." And he passed the square of lace and cambric across his brow again.

Norfolk seized his arm and the handkerchief fell to the ground between them. Their words came fast and flaming.

"My lord!" cried the premier Duke furiously. "I will not countenance this gross insult to her Majesty!"

"My lord, when her Majesty desires your interference she will ask for it herself!"

"I have said before, and I repeat it now—for anyone

to hear! The Earl of Leicester will not die in his bed if he does not give over his preposterous pretensions to her Majesty's favour!"

"If ever the Earl of Leicester asks the Duke of Norfolk's opinion of his conduct, he would be better dead!"

"My opinion, sirrah, is the opinion of half the world!"

"It is certainly well known that the Duke of Norfolk cannot think for himself!"

"Your lordship was always dexterous with words—ay, even when all the evidence is against you!"

"Evidence?" repeated Leicester, dangerously quiet of a sudden, and Elizabeth leaned forward, watching keenly, with a look of cynical amusement curling her lips.

"Ay, even when the evidence points to *murder*—your lordship can talk your way out!"

"Say what you mean by that!" Leicester was savage now.

"I mean just what you think I mean! The mysterious death of your wife five years ago—"

Leicester struck him with his open hand across the mouth.

"Robert!" It was a little cry from Lettice, stilled on the next heartbeat.

There was a moment's dreadful silence. A blow had been struck in the presence of the sovereign, a heinous sin.

In the silence Elizabeth rose slowly, impressively, holding it for their embarrassment as they became aware of her, while they still stood staring angrily into each other's eyes. And then Leicester bowed formally to the premier Duke.

"My lord—I will meet you when and where you wish."

Norfolk bowed formally in return, as Elizabeth's voice cut in.

"I have had enough of this," said the Queen awfully, and they turned to her, losing stature before her like chidden schoolboys. "There will be no duel. I forbid it."

"I crave your Majesty's indulgence," said Norfolk. "Your Majesty saw the blow struck, with your own eyes. And by ancient law a blow given in the presence of the sovereign—"

The Queen turned from him impatiently, addressing a page who had come to stand silently beside her, awaiting her notice.

"Well, what is it?" she demanded of the boy, who showed her a ring lying in the palm of his hand. "Not now. Wait," she said, with only a glance at it, and the page remained where he was.

"I need not remind your Majesty," Norfolk was pursuing his point obstinately, "of the customary penalty imposed on those who so far forget themselves in the presence of the sovereign as to—"

"Oh, but, Madam—" Lettice came forward desperately, her cheeks quite white under the rouge. "It was an unforgivable insult—any man of spirit would have struck him—"

Elizabeth looked her up and down with satirical surprise, until she quavered into silence and fell back a step, her eyes going helplessly from one to another of the tense faces of the little circle. Leicester signalled to her to be silent, and Elizabeth intercepted the signal with displeasure.

"Your Majesty," continued Norfolk pompously, "out of consideration for yourself, I waive the just claim of the penalty for striking a blow in the sovereign's presence—I refer to the loss of the offender's right hand—" (Here Lettice gave another cry.) "Instead, I ask only the satisfaction of crossing swords with this—this upstart!"

"Body of God, how the rooster crows!" jeered Leicester. "No doubt I shall keep my right hand at least as long as the Duke of Norfolk keeps his head!"

"You heard what I said—both of you," Elizabeth reminded them coldly. "There will be no duel. Do you understand? I will not have it." Her grey hawk's eyes went sternly from one to the other of their flushed, sulky faces, and dropped again to the page. She seemed preoccupied. "Let me see that again," she said to him in a lower tone.

He extended his hand with the ring in its palm. She took it from him slowly, her brows knit with the effort to recall it as a token. Suddenly her fingers contracted over it—that Spanish jewel of Philip's—she remembered now.

"But, Madam—your Majesty's pardon—" It was Norfolk still. "Am I to stand a blow from the Earl of Leicester and do nothing? I beg your Majesty to consider—"

Elizabeth seemed to eye him with amusement. Her mood had changed abruptly, and she regarded their quar-

rel now as beside the point, a silly schoolboys' squabble.
Her eyes were bright, her fingers tight over the ring. She
wanted only to be rid of them now, and she bent all her
charm and all her authority to clearing the air and getting herself free of a tiresome situation.

"You want to hit him back, is that it?" she inquired
with mock indulgence, and struck Leicester a playful buffet on the ear with her own hand. "There. There's your
blow for a blow! Now are you satisfied?" They were not.
She watched them merrily, her fingers closed round the
ring. "I should be very angry with you both—but see, I let
it go, and so must you. I forgive you. *This* time! But no
more brawling, Robert, for shame, it might be a guardroom! And you, my lord—it was a childish quarrel altogether. How hot you both are!" She patted Norfolk's
cheek lightly. "Such a pretty game of tennis—so evenly
matched too—and what a pity to spoil good sport with a
misunderstanding!" She beamed at each of them in turn
as they stood sullen, unconvinced, on either side of her.
"Two great lords, bickering like silly children!" she
beamed, herself a fond nursemaid, and joined their hands
and held them together. "What was it all about, anyway? There, now we are friends again! Mind you, I want
no more of this! Lettice—take them away and give them
something cool to drink—perhaps it was a touch of the
sun! Mary—have some rugs and cushions brought out on
the lawn—there where it's shady. Let's have some music
—cakes and wine—let's have a picnic, down on the lawn!
You two big ninnies—!" She gave them each a rough

clop on the shoulder. "Get along with you—I'm sick of the sight of you! Go away!"

Rather sheepishly they obeyed her, and Lettice hung on Leicester's arm as they went. Mary, with Norfolk at her elbow, paused.

"Are you coming, Madam?" she said.

Elizabeth had opened her hand and was looking down at the ring and smiling. She spoke without raising her eyes.

"Presently." And she added, as Mary still lingered— "Wait for me on the bench at the other end of the court."

Mary's eyes were puzzled as she turned away with Norfolk.

"Where did you get this ring?" Elizabeth demanded of the page.

"A gentleman just rode in with it, your Majesty."

"What does he want?"

"He told me to give that to your Majesty, and ask if he might speak with the Queen."

"Bring him here," said Elizabeth.


## I I

That spring of 1565 had been to Anthony Brand the loveliest of all the seven he had spent in Worcestershire. It was neither late nor early, neither too dry nor too wet, the buds and leaves and flowers, the lambing and the planting, were all accomplished according to the most exigeant ideas of the most painstaking farmer. And by April, the house itself had bloomed.

At the beginning of that month the workmen had begun to thin out, their jobs all done, and on May Day he saw his turf replaced and watched the last of the wagons down the lane with the last load of defacing remnants. The wing was there, a little new and bare-looking in the chilly wind of an overcast twilight, empty as an eggshell inside—but finished, and with the roof on and the glass in, and the chimneys ready for the fires.

Incredulously in the early dusk of that May Day he walked round it, really alone with it for the first time since it was begun, with no one coming back tomorrow to hammer and chip and measure—they were all gone, and it was his. His mind was busy with ways to make the Queen's picture feel at home in it. Her place was ready in the oak overmantel, an empty square with carving round it, supported by carved oak pilasters framing the stone of the fireplace, the recurring design a flattened four-pointed flower. The panelling of the room was in the new square style without the linenfold, and the ceiling was of moulded plaster in relief, called pargeting. His builders had been somewhat scandalized throughout, but he had known what he wanted. The south window was a deep square-cornered bay with long round-headed lights and diamond leading. The sunlight falling through it made a lattice shadow on the bare floor boards.

His new furniture had already come down from Worcester and was standing in the vaulted hall: a mag-

nificent court cupboard, carved and panelled and inlaid
with box in a flower pattern; a massive oak draw-table
with bulbous legs; four X-chairs with shaped, uphol-
stered seats of red velvet, very luxurious, one with arms,
and a stool to match; a really impressive bed with a canopy and carved tester, much handsomer than the one in
the little west room; and an old chest, somewhat shabby,
with linenfold carving, to hold his linen. There were
two raw pine-wood boxes with straw sticking out of the
cracks, one of which contained two pieces of good silver—
his first; and the other four frail Venetian glass goblets
with gilt on them—these last unbridled extravagance.

His eye ran over the modest assemblage with pride as
he barred the door for the night. Within a few days now,
when the fires had dried the rooms a bit, everything could
be put in place, and then the inside of the house must be
left till after the weeding and shearing. He had a lad to
help with the garden three days a week now, at a penny a
day, and his mind was bent on growing flowers, as well as
herbs and vegetables. The south windows through which
the eyes of the Queen's portrait would gaze day after day
should look on a terrace of gay blossom, carefully chosen
and planted to vary and continue their display as the
summer waned.

Inquiry among his few friends about the countryside,
and an interview with the great Baskerville's head gardener, who gave himself the airs of a butler at least, had
yielded a rather long list. People were generous with last
year's seed, and a row of small packets neatly labelled had

accumulated in his cupboard during the winter. Cuttings and roots and shrubbery were harder to come by, and must be purchased wisely with pence from a fraction of the wool money set aside for that purpose.

During the cold evenings of the past winter, after a day's pruning and grafting, or the mending of fences and hedges, he would shut himself up in the oriel room with his lists of flowers, working out his terrace garden. The growing collection of random jottings amused him hugely as he went over them one by one, getting drowsy before the log fire.

Nasturtium blossoms, he had noted down, add fragrance to a lettuce salad.

Gillyflowers, red, white, and carnations—set in spring, and harvest in pots, pails, or tubs, or for summer in beds. Gillyflowers sovereign against the plague. Also angelica.

Elder flowers boiled in gruel make good fever drink. Their smell will drive away serpents.

Marigold's leaves powdered will cure toothache.

Hollyhocks crave husbanding and tilling. Their juice mingled with oil heals wasp sting.

Bay-trees planted about the garden will keep away thunder and lightning.

To have red apples you must plant rose-trees or mulberry-trees near to the apple-trees.

Sweet-William. These plants are not used in meat or medicine but esteemed for their beauty to deck up gardens and the bosoms of the beautiful. *Tusser.*

64

Blue columbine. Small leaves shaped like birds, and flowers with little hollow horns.

Bachelor's buttons. Lark's foot—blue. Pansies, or heartsease. Pinks, of all sorts. Snap-dragons—tall. Velvet flowers, or French marigolds—very beautiful. Violets, yellow and white. Eglantine, or sweet brier. Jessamine arbour, made with willow poles. Canterbury bells. Quince trees to back hedges surrounding knot garden . . .

He chose his roses and his hollyhocks and young bay-trees singly and with care, as a man chooses jewels for his mistress, and like jewels, they cost more than he could afford. He dreamed of a garden seat, a sundial, and even a fountain, in prosperous years to come. His ambition drifted wistfully toward a pleached walk, and perhaps a maze. Later. It would all come later.

By that midsummer of 1565, when things had come into blossom, he became slowly obsessed with a desire for applause from somewhere. He wanted to show the house, to point out its beauties to sympathetic eyes, to hear it praised and envied and admired. It was too glorious a thing to keep to himself any longer. It was a dream come true. To pinch himself and prove that it was really there he must display it to someone.

He sent off a trusty servant with a letter to his sister Margaret in Cheshire, begging her to return with the man and make him a visit. He explained with pride how there were now two beds, the new one with down pillows and curtains of painted stuff. And she might have his own new upper chamber, as he had got used to the oriel room where he still carried on all his business affairs. He promised her that she would not starve in his house, and added that she might even find herself very nearly as comfortable as at home.

Margaret was enchanted, and her husband was always indulgent. She arrived at the end of June, when the early meadows had been mown and the shearing was well under way; riding pillion behind the servant in a twitter of excitement, with her luggage on a led horse. She brought as gifts cuttings from her own yellow roses, a set of linen sheets and pillow cases embroidered in her exquisite stitchery, and a fat Cheshire cheese from her dairy.

She was an excellent audience, and went over the house with him minutely from the servants' attics above the nursery floor to the undercroft of the old vaulted hall, and the new kitchen with its latticed game-cupboard and spacious ovens. The house smiled at her benevolently with the sun streaming in all its windows on to the fresh plaited straw matting on its floors. There were fragrant nosegays of marjoram, rosemary, pennyroyal, lavender, thyme, and mugwort in all the rooms. He had a log fire lighted for her in the big parlour in the cool of the evening, with juniper thrown on the flame, and the new chimney did not smoke.

The Queen's picture looked down at them gravely from its place above the mantel, her white dress glinting in the kind south light from the bay window. After supper Cisley the serving-maid brought in a jug of fine Rhenish wine and the new Venetian goblets, and set them on the table, as her orders were, and went out again, gazing backward at the master's sister in her blue gown with its embroidered kirtle and sleeves, and the jeweled caul to her hair.

"Glass!" said Margaret with pleasure, and turned a goblet in her taper fingers so that its gilt lines caught the light.

With hands that shook a little he poured out the wine and handed a full goblet to her. This was a ceremony he had long planned in secret, and its solemnity was to him a sacred thing. Raising his own goblet to the portrait—

"The Queen," he said simply, and drank.

"God bless her," murmured Margaret, with warmth. "She has given you something Robert hasn't got, Anthony—your freedom. And I wish she could see what you've made of the place. But for her you'd still be trailing round after Robert and his new earldom. Who knows, it might have been you mixed up in that dreadful business at Cumnor instead of Blount."

"They had no reason to believe that Amy's death was other than an accident," he said quickly.

"They have not been able to prove that it wasn't," she admitted.

"Naturally they haven't! Robert is no such monster as to connive at the murder of his wife! Besides, he was fond of Amy in a way—she was harmless enough, God knows—only stupid."

"Mmmmmmm," said Margaret.

"He would never have married her in the beginning if she had not been so pretty, in spite of her wealth and his father's command. Northumberland always chose his sons' brides. But Amy was pretty, Margaret, you know that very well."

"Yes, Robert never could resist a woman's face," she murmured. "So far as I know, he has never even tried!"

"Robert was very young when he married," he reminded her doggedly. "It was a long time ago—while little Edward was still on the throne. He came to the wedding, do you remember?"

"A long time ago," she repeated, turning her empty glass in her fingers unseeingly. "Yes, we were all young then, weren't we? And poor Amy was so in love with him. I was sorry for her."

"Poor Amy was an empty-headed little fool! She might easily have got herself into some sort of trouble at Cumnor—something we shall never know about—something which had nothing whatever to do with Robert, perhaps—just to spite him."

"Well, if she meant to spite him she could not have done better than to die as she did," sighed Margaret. "Half the world believes he had her murdered."

"I don't."

"Nor do I. But he had neglected her—for the Queen. And now I hear he neglects the Queen for Lettice Knollys."

He stirred restlessly in his chair and glanced up at the portrait as though it heard.

68

"You get all the gossip up in Cheshire," he complained. "This is an innocent part of the world. We don't hear such tales on Cotswold."

"You only say that because you live with your head in a hole," she told him. "Everybody but you knows about Lettice—everybody but you and possibly the Queen, who is like you and doesn't want to know."

"Meg, I can't have such talk in my nice clean room," he objected, half angry. "Robert and the Queen are old friends, but—"

"Oh, I know, I know, and once he saved her life!" she conceded wearily. "Or rather *you* did. She knows it was you, as much as Robert. I was thinking she must be pretty sick of Robert by this time. And that's why I wish she could see what you've done here. It would please her to see that every man isn't Robert. She's made him Earl of Leicester with half a dozen rich houses, and he throws her money about with both hands and makes love to Lettice behind her back. But you've done something with what she gave you—something she'd be proud of if she knew."

He was gazing at her, his face shining.

"Do you think so? Do you think—" His eyes travelled lovingly round the room, still bare and raw-looking as it was, still smelling of freshly cut timber and new masonry. "She asked me to come back some time and tell her—it isn't finished yet, of course—I hadn't meant to go so soon—"

"Go now," advised Margaret. "Go now and let her

have a look at you. Let her know you're not like Robert. She's unhappy, Anthony. Go now."

"Unhappy?" he said, the light gone out of him. "How do you know, down in the country? How can you be sure, when you've never even seen her? What makes you think she—"

"I'm a woman too," she reminded him. "I don't have to lose a lover to Lettice Knollys in order to pity the Queen."

*Unhappy.* The word knocked at his heart all night. Robert was playing the fool, was he? *Go now*, said Margaret. His breath came quickly. See her again—so soon? He had still so much to do, before the house was finished. But perhaps she would like to know that he was not a pauper these days. Or had she forgotten him entirely? He cherished the small, companionable weight of her ring on his finger—the Spanish jewel which had never known an honest man before it came to him. She would remember the ring. . . . He would have to have new clothes, if he went to Court. . . .

It was a warm day in July, when he rode through the low red brick gate at Richmond. The trim chestnut mare under him had been born and bred and broken on the home farm and carried itself proudly, having never known unkind usage. His clothes, from a Worcester tailor, were well made and became him, with a fashionable starched ruff and padded sleeves, a short cloak in the newest style, and a blue feather in his beaver hat.

# 1565

## III

The gardens of Richmond Palace that July morning were very different from the dark little room in the Tower where he had beheld her last. He found her taller, more stiffly clad, and her watchful eyes were harder and less friendly. There was rouge and powder on her face, her lips were a thin red line, her hair was crimped unnaturally and dressed with jewels which swung and twinkled in the sunlight. She rattled with pearls and dazzled with diamonds. In that first moment that their eyes met before he made his bow, he called her stranger in his heart and longed with a sick disappointment to turn and run away. She stood holding his ring in one thin white hand, dwarfed by its own jewels, and waited for him to speak.

"Your Majesty—more than ten years ago, while your brother was on the throne, it happened that I was able to do you a service. At the time of your accession you rewarded me—most handsomely—with some land and a house near Worcester, and—and—" He faltered miserably. What was the good, after all? "But perhaps your Majesty has entirely forgotten—"

"My memory for service rendered is more than ten years long, Anthony Brand," she said harshly then, but there was amusement in her bright, searching gaze that never left his face.

"Even my name!" he said, astonished.

"I wrote it on the deeds myself—so that Cecil need not know. I was very new then, at being Queen. I used to think I could keep things from Cecil!" Her laughter was a little strident. "I know better now! Well, and what have you done with my picture? Where is it now?"

"The old priory which stood on the land was in—disrepair. I have built a new wing on the south side, with a large ground-floor room panelled in oak. I have come to tell you—"

"That you have run out of money, is that it?"

"Your Majesty—I assure you—I would not dream—" For a moment he stared at her, speechless and outraged. Then he gathered himself together, with white lips, and made another bow. "I am sorry. I am wasting your time. By your Majesty's leave, I will go now."

"One minute." She threw out a detaining hand, surprised and puzzled by the change in his tone. "Why did you come, then?"

"It doesn't matter," he said wretchedly.

"But it does. I don't understand. Come here." Her thin white hand was still extended toward him. He paused unwillingly, beyond its grasp, his eyes on the ground. "Why did you come?" she repeated.

"If I don't want money from you," he said, not looking at her, "you don't understand. I suppose that's natural enough nowadays. I suppose greed is in the very air you breathe, here at Court. Merciful God, is that all you look for from a man? *Pillage?*"

72

For a moment she gazed at him, and his eyes blazed back into hers, his head flung up.

"What do you want, Anthony Brand?" she asked quietly then.

"I want nothing of you—your Majesty," he answered stiffly. "And now may I go?"

"No." She came a step toward him, unconvinced, sceptical still, but curious, like a child. "You shall not go till you have told me why you came."

He stood before her heartstricken, both hands twisting at his hat, his lips tight with strain.

"Just to tell you the house is finished," he said inadequately. "To tell you the house is yours. To tell you the house is there, as lovely as I can make it, as perfect as a house can be—your gift to me—my shrine to you—" The words broke, and he looked away from her, toward the river. "You see, it's of no consequence, my coming. I bring you nothing—I ask for nothing—I am no courtier, I'm just a country lout you had forgotten—"

"Had I?" she queried gently, and his eyes returned to her, puzzled in their turn.

"No—that's right, you hadn't."

"You came just because you wanted to see me again?" she persisted, trying to understand.

"No, I—I was almost afraid to see you again. But—I wanted you to know about the house. I hoped you might care to know that it is finished at last, and that the home farm is tidy and flourishing, and already supports the place—and that the tenantry are all good folk, prosperous, and loyal. When I saw you last it was as you said yourself just now—you were very new at being Queen. I—remembered you like that. We were—both of us—very inexperienced with your queenship. You asked me to come back some time and tell you how I got on—and I promised that I would. And then I suppose I lost touch with things down there in the country, building the house. I forgot how much time was passing—"

"Time?" she echoed sadly. "Have I changed so much?"

He looked at her gravely—fearlessly—in the merciless sunlight.

"Very much," he said. "And yet—no."

Their eyes held. She took another step toward him, so that her hand fell on his sleeve.

"Tell me about your house," she demanded simply.

"It is beautiful only because of you—built to reflect your own beauty as it has shone on me twice—three times."

"Then it's my house too," she said, pleased.

"That's what I came to say."

"Tell me more. Tell me how it looks."

He was tempted.

"You have time to listen?"

She nodded. He began diffidently, but lost himself in the telling, under her grave, watching eyes, the mockery all gone from them now, and the slight weight of her thin hand on his sleeve.

"The new wing faces south," he began, "with a great

many windows to let in the sunlight. It is grey Cotswold stone, no timber, and the trees grow lovingly round it, and it stands with its feet in flowers because the terrace is planted so that bloom froths up against the stone. Even the roses know that it becomes them—roses don't care much for red brick, did you know? The ivy is beginning to take hold too, and the past wet month has made the grass like green velvet—" He fumbled inside his doublet and brought out a carefully folded paper which he spread between his hands. "I can't draw very well, but I thought— I brought this to give you an impression—those are the windows of the big room I call the Queen's parlour—your picture hangs there, above the mantelpiece. The carved oak in that room is the most beautiful of all, I matched each piece myself—the room would be fit to receive you if ever you should come that way—"

"But you speak of the house as though you were its lover!" she broke in, fascinated. "Your wife will be jealous."

"I have no wife, your Majesty."

"This glorious house—without a mistress?"

"You gave it me," he said bluntly. "It belongs to you."

"I gave you all that?" she wondered, watching him. "And much more."

Her fingers tightened on his sleeve as he stood looking down at her.

"I think for once I have been—over-generous, Anthony Brand."

"Now you are like the last time," he whispered, and stooping swiftly he laid his lips against the fingers which rested on his sleeve.

When he straightened she took the paper from him and held it between her own hands lovingly.

"My house," she murmured. "A refuge from all this. So that when I am tired of being Queen I can shut my eyes and say, 'Now I am in my shrine, and it is quiet and peaceful, and nobody quarrels or is angry, and nobody wishes me ill—' "

"You will do that?" he said, entranced.

"Often." She dreamed a moment at the paper. "Grey stone, with its feet in flowers. And a toy farm with the smell of hay and horses, and fat fowls underfoot—were there lambs this spring?"

"An even dozen," he told her with pride.

Elizabeth glanced round the gardens of Richmond with a sigh.

"Who would be Queen, if they could live in that house with a man like you to worship—" she was beginning, and broke off with a sharp sigh, as her eyes came to rest on the place where the others waited for her on the lawn. She folded the paper small again, and she did not return it to him. "There's Cecil, hanging about with things for me to sign," she said. "I promised him the hour before dinner. Shall I marry the Austrian after all? They are trying to keep it from me that he is a wry-neck. Don't look like that! One must keep the ambassadors busy somehow!" She was Queen again now

76

—a little strident, a little satirical; the soft mood had gone with that sight of Cecil. "So my picture is sole mistress of your house, and I keep you company there until you find a wife! Mind you get one soon, Anthony Brand! What would become of the house if you died and left no son? I must have a roof over my head, even after you are gone!"

"I suppose I must marry some day," he agreed, as though it had never occurred to him before.

"Yes, for the succession!" She smiled obliquely, and jerked her head in the direction of Cecil. "God knows I hear nothing else these days myself! You for the lovely house, Anthony—I for England. You will wed some pretty, fond West Country girl, a good housekeeper. And I—"

"Not the Austrian!" he cried involuntarily.

"No, not the Austrian," she smiled. "He is deformed. And not the Spanish heir, he is mad. And the Swede is mad too, had you heard? Oh, yes, quite mad, with murderous rages."

"But you *can't*—"

"I don't like foreigners, do you?" Her voice was hard, but quiet. "English heirs are best. And yet—even Englishmen can be faithless!"

"Elizabeth—" he whispered.

She turned to look up at him, still with that crooked smile, keeping a hard grip on herself.

"Go back to Worcestershire," she said. "I want to think of you living there, with a family growing up round you—not rotting here at Court and getting like the rest of them. Go back—and tend my shrine. The picture over your mantelpiece will never grow old and sad and bitter—like me. Go away—*now*—while you still love me!" she finished wildly, with a strangled sob, and he slipped to his knees at her feet, one of her hands caught to his lips. The ring was in her other hand. She opened her fingers and looked down at it. "The ring— yes, take the ring again. And when your son is grown, if I am still alive, let him bring it back to me. I shan't keep him long." She put it on his finger and he kissed both her hands again.

"God keep your Majesty," he said.

"God?" She raised him to his feet. "Yes, God keeps me, for England. And so long as England is safe, Elizabeth doesn't matter—to him—very much."

"Elizabeth is England," he said solemnly.

She was staring at him with a long farewell look.

"Elizabeth is a woman," she said, and turned away abruptly and then paused, looking back at him over her shoulder. "Has it got a name, your house?"

He shook his head mutely, his eyes on her.

"Call it—Queen's Folly," she said, and kissed her hand to him and left him.

He watched while she collected Mary Radcliffe and Norfolk from the bench by the tennis court and passed on across the green lawn to where Cecil waited in his sombre clothes. Then he made his way blindly to his horse in the courtyard and rode away.

## 1587 - 1588

TWENTY-TWO years the house sat there, its long
sweet shadow creeping across the grass in the summer
afternoons, its windows glowing warm and comfortable
in the winter twilights. And always its beauty and its
acres grew, with the devotion of the man who owned and
served it.

Ivy slowly clothed the pinkish newness of the south
wing, not yet weathered to match the priory grey. He
was warned that ivy was not good for the stone, but he
only smiled, and trimmed it back from the windows. The
flower beds on the terrace flourished, and peonies, honey-
suckle, and golden laburnum—lately come from the
mountains of central Europe—were added to the yearly
list, which was pored over anew each winter by the fire,
when the small neat packets of seed from the year before
were got out and sorted and counted and apportioned
each to its proper place like a game.

Gradually his domain extended its borders westward
into the fertile valley land where fruit and corn grew
fatly, and ran up into the sheep-walks on the hills behind the house. And as his circumstances grew more ease-
ful and his rents and profits increased with each slow
purchase of land and stock and labour-saving tools, so

his outlay could be more generous. He wanted to grow a great many things that were not essential, or even useful, which he desired for their beauty only. And each year his winter planning became less of an agony of elimination and self-denial.

The garden seat and the sundial had materialized. The fountain was still a matter for earnest thought and discussion, and he was still in search of the right design, for he viewed with horror the small stone birds with water spouting from their open beaks which adorned the centre of Margaret's Cheshire rose-garden. Also his mind still dwelt wistfully on the maze, and he had begun to collect patterns.

A master of the fashionable new art of topiary work now came at regular intervals to clip the privet and yew and box—the same man who sculptured the green peacocks and pheasants and geometrical shapes which dotted Sir Thomas Baskerville's broad lawns near Worcester. He thought sometimes of acquiring some real peacocks for the terrace, but Margaret said they squawked and advised cultivating swans for eating instead. He had no proper setting as yet for swans and did not care much for their meat.

The young oak and willow trees he had planted when he first came had done well. The orchard itself was said to be really remarkable, and the soft Worcestershire air allowed him to grow apricots and almonds as well as all the usual things. Columbine grew daintily in the grass between the trees, and he was contemplating a pleached

South Front, 1588.

Edith Thrane

lime walk for setting out next season. Also he heard they had vineyards in Gloucestershire, and he vowed that once he found the right piece of land he would buy it and plant vines himself, if only for vinegar.

In his kitchen garden the new Virginia potato had made itself at home, and he preferred it to parsnips. Asparagus did well for him too, and was known to be very wholesome for everybody, if not too much boiled. Cucumbers he considered suitable only for mules and asses, but he set onions under each fig tree to kill the vermin to which it, as an outlander, was subject. He had now one of the finest assortments of herbs and salad plants in the county.

The house had been more lavishly dressed inside, as well, with the careful furnishing of the dining-room and upstairs rooms, the slow acquisition of carpets and hangings. The bed had been long since removed from the oriel room to the nursery floor, for in 1567 the house received its mistress—a dark handsome girl whose dower included the fifty acres of young orchard adjoining Anthony's boundaries on the southwest.

Catherine was a willing bride, for all she knew the orchard had first brought him wooing, and she studied to please the grave, self-contained master of her new home. She had been well brought up to wifehood by her mother, and was accustomed to the still-room routine of flower-waters and remedies and conserves. She was not too clean-fingered to inspect daily the dairy and the milking and the hen-house. The presence of the cat among

the churns and wooden cream bowls never failed to fetch
the dairy-maid a box on the ear. And yet she was a kind
mistress, in her rigid way, and tender enough when her
maids were ill or in trouble. If the child set to mind the
tawny brown hens was lax in the freshening of straw in
the nests, or the refilling of drinking-pans three times a
day in hot weather, or the scraping of perches, it felt
the weight of her hand. She herself helped the chicks
out of their shells and sprinkled them with rosemary
against the pip; and she promptly discouraged any talk
of artificial incubation as being heartless and unnatural.
Under her personal supervision the candles were made—
white tallow with cotton wicks for the master's rooms,
and others of kitchen fat with rush wicks which smelt
for the servants' use. Soap too was made on the place,
smooth, scented yellow tablets better than could be
bought in Worcester town. She went her rounds nightly
to see that candles and fires were extinguished, and the
washing brought in from the hedges. Her store cupboard
and larder were checked weekly with her account-book,
and there was no pilfering by her servants. She made
exquisite Turkey-work, which was a kind of tapestry, for
cushion covers and upholstery; and her own embroidered
sleeves and Anthony's cambric shirts and the hangings of
the beds were all enriched by her tireless needle. The
New Year's gift which pleased her most was a printed
book, the first of its kind, which gave new patterns for
embroidery and *point devise* lace, ordered by Anthony
from his bookseller in London. She treasured it even more

than the silk stockings sent by Margaret the same year. She and Margaret got on well enough, and exchanged visits and stitchery patterns, but Margaret's unaffected warmth and exuberance always made her feel stiff and uncomfortable, like a grown-up at a children's party.

Anthony was kind and patient, and generous to her wishes always, unstinting in his praise of her housewifery, and they lived together in harmony. But sometimes she wondered if he loved her, and then wondered why he should not—and then her thoughts would fly back to certain things she had heard before her marriage and chosen to ignore, and her eyes would turn to the picture over the mantelpiece in the panelled parlour. In 1568 a daughter was born, and they named her Elizabeth, after the Queen. Five years later another girl was born, and died, and after two years came a son, named Nicholas for her father.

The child Elizabeth had her mother's dark hair and eyes, and the same embarrassed reserve in the presence of her Aunt Margaret's lightmindedness. She grew up in her mother's shadow, learning housewifery, doing beautiful needlework, bestowing a dutiful but lukewarm affection on her father. Before she had reached her teens she took upon herself the preparation of the fresh nosegays which were kept in the bedrooms and privies, gathered March violets before sunrise to preserve their virtues intact for the making of a syrup for pleurisy and colds, and brewed the bitter primrose draught which the whole household drank each May. Later she attempted the cowslip ointment which was said to remove freckles, and was laughed at for her pains. They bought her a virginal when she was twelve, and she had a weekly lesson from a music master who rode over from Evesham, and learnt to sing—

> Philon the shepherd, late forgot,
>   Sitting beside a crystal fountain . . .

and—

> O sleep, O sleep, fond fancy . . .

in a high sweet voice which was remarkably true.

Nicholas, who had his father's fringed grey eyes and air of humorous gravity, was more of a problem. He outgrew his drums and hoops and hobby horses at a very early age. Both children had been able to recite psalms in Latin and their Paternoster before they were out of the walking-cage. But at five Nicholas took to reading the Bible. This alarmed Anthony exceedingly, and a tutor was got in to teach him Cicero, Virgil, and Horace, with a bit of French and mathematics on the side. Anthony had a small tempered sword made for him, and crossed it ruthlessly every morning on the terrace with his own slim Toledo blade which had been blooded in Flanders while Spanish Philip was Mary Tudor's husband. At eight Nicholas was given a half-broken young horse to ride, and was expected to finish the job for himself. Within a month the animal was all but following him up stairs to bed.

84

When he turned ten he received a new and longer sword, and the question of his schooling arose urgently between his parents. Catherine wanted him to go to Oxford as her two brothers had done. Nicholas had heard from a groom of a fencing-school near Corpus, and begged hard to go. But Anthony, who had once contemplated Shrewsbury with equanimity, turned obstinate. Oxford was too far away, the other side of Cotswold. Good-for-nothing Court dandies went there, he said. It was a hotbed of politics, gambling, verse-making, and unmanly vice. He went up to London himself and returned with a new tutor and literally a cartload of books. Nicholas was to be taught at home.

The library shelves filled fast after that. With the exception of Turner's new *Herbal* and Hyll's *Brief Treatise on Gardening*, which were for Anthony's own use, and *A Proper New Book of Cookery*, which was a present to Catherine, the books were bought supposedly to exercise and improve Nicholas's mind. And yet, besides Pliny and Livy (in English) and Plutarch's *Lives*, and the Earl of Surrey's translation of Virgil; besides Stow and Holinshed and Fox's *Martyrs*, and a volume of Mr. Caxton's first edition of *The Canterbury Tales* which was all of a hundred years old and had woodcut illustrations of the characters—some very odd books crept in and were lodged on the upper shelves without a word to anybody. There was a thing called *The Court of Venus*, translated from the French, and another called *A Hundred Merry Tales*. There were Castiglione's *Courtier* and Seneca's *Plays*.

Aesop's *Fables* were all right, of course, and Lord Berners's translation of Froissart was passed into the schoolroom at once. But what about *The Book of the Maid Emlyn*, who got drunk at taverns and threw things, and went through a great many husbands with confusing rapidity and carried an onion in her handkerchief to stimulate tears? Likewise the *Widow Edith*, who was alleged to be wealthy and was certainly of conspicuous charm; also *The Proud Wives Paternoster*, which Catherine hid in her work-basket for very shame, until it was good-naturedly rooted out by Anthony and restored—when he had quite finished with it—to the top shelf whence Nicholas, standing on a chair, had plucked it. Nicholas had considered it, as far as he got before his mother pounced, much more interesting than *Utopia*. But he consoled himself before long, undisturbed, with Malory's *Morte d'Arthur*.

## II

For twenty-two years Elizabeth Tudor had ruled England, and kept the peace by hook or by crook, and England prospered amid a general optimism and a boundless personal devotion to the sovereign. Leicester had his ups and downs in the royal favour, his supremacy threatened now and then by Hatton, Sidney, Raleigh, Essex—and by his own marriage to the opportunely widowed Lettice. But somehow the mysterious bond between him and the Queen survived.

Norfolk's fate bore out that hasty tennis-court proph-
ecy of Leicester's—he had lost his head on the scaffold
for treason after the detection of one of the many plots
connected with the captive Mary Stuart. Cecil and Walsingham directed, or attempted to direct, Elizabeth's
capricious foreign policy in a troubled world, and Walsingham's spy system had become a byword in Europe
even before it brought Mary Stuart to the block.

From long residence abroad, Walsingham had acquired
intimate friends scattered advantageously all over the
Continent, and his confidential correspondents included
a member of the College of Cardinals itself, and a secretary to the French ambassador, to say nothing of supposed converts in Jesuit seminaries and itinerant mer-
chants who made a habit of overhearing conversation
between English exiles abroad. "Knowledge is never too
dear," said Walsingham, and he thought nothing of paying for it out of his own pocket if nobody else would buy
it for him. There were always Catholic mutterings at
home, and Spain was hostile, and the Netherlands
seethed, and the French marriage negotiations dragged
on. But set against the massacre of St. Bartholomew's in
Paris, and Alva's excessive cruelties in Brussels, not even
the tragedy of Mary Stuart at Fotheringay could make
London seem anything but sane and safe and rather gay.

After the assassination of the Prince of Orange in 1584
Elizabeth stood alone as the royal sponsor of Protestantism, and half the civilized world was united against her
as a heretic and usurper. Plots against her life were

hatched again and again, only to be betrayed or thwarted
by Walsingham's army of spies, while her own sublime
disregard of the most elementary protection for her person drove her statesmen nearly frantic with apprehension. Always accessible to the lowest of her subjects, she
walked about her palace gardens alone or with only a
maid for company, and on her progresses round the countryside would stop to chat with anyone who caught her
attention at the roadside. Perhaps she made a bravado of
this lack of precautions, but it was in the time-hallowed
tradition of the Tudors, it came naturally to her for she
was without personal fear in any form, and it made for
an almost worshipful populace.

Bereft of their leader and ravaged by the bloodstained
rule of Philip's new provincial governor, Parma, the
Netherlands wished to throw themselves under Elizabeth's protection, but she was too wary—she sent money,
sent an inadequate army under Leicester with totally inadequate supplies, but she refused the sovereignty of a
territory which would bring her into still more open
conflict with Philip of Spain.

In 1585 the invasion of England by a coalition of Catholic armies was openly discussed. There were rumours
and false alarms that Parma had landed at Newcastle,
or that Guise would strike at London through Sussex.
Beacons were laid ready, and drilling went on in the villages, in preparation for the worst. It was a certainty
that Philip was building at Lisbon the mightiest fleet the
world had ever seen, which was to render England de-

fenceless and facilitate the landing of Parma's army from Flanders.

The summer of 1587 was a tense one. Philip's terrible expenses at Lisbon made it imperative that he should get help from the Pope, as for a crusade, and the Pope could not be hurried. Elizabeth, grumbling at her own expenses, only half prepared, delayed arming herself more fully in the hope of buying Parma off. And Parma's men lay under canvas on the hills round Dunkirk in inclement weather with orders to move at an hour's notice.

Even Worcestershire was not too remote for the general excitement. Farmers and ploughmen and horsebreakers gathered in knots to discuss the latest rumour in the ale-houses; dairy-maids chattered hysterically of Inquisition horrors; and children were frightened into virtue by promises of what the Spaniards would do to them if they didn't watch out.

Anthony Brand was aware, while he supervised the mowing of the first crop of hay, that the peaceful sunny days of England might be numbered; that the careful harvest of his plenty might be only to feed the Spanish oppressor; that the very land on which his eyes dwelt in loving ownership might be taken from him to become the spoil of the Church from which in King Henry's time it had been wrested.

And in the back of his uncomplicated mind, in the depths of his simple nature, a small, cold kernel of determination was forming; the Spaniards might pillage and burn, but if he was given a choice, if by embracing the Spanish creed he could avoid being dispossessed of this shrine of his own making—why quibble with the Church, when his secret worship was held here under his own roof? He would go to the stake to preserve Queen's Folly from mutilation, yes. But go to the stake for an abstract idea of God, when one could best serve Him here, under His blue sky, tending the fruits of His earth—no.

It was a determination which shamed him in a way, and yet he knew that he would hold to it. His wife, he was sure, would choose martyrdom with an air of righteousness very hard to bear, and would reproach him for the sin of idolatry. But he, for the love of what belonged to him, was prepared to forsake the religion in which he had been bred. Between two betrayals he would choose what seemed to him the lesser one, in order to cherish to the end of his life the treasured symbol of his love for the Queen.

Therefore as the summer dragged on, he became a little more withdrawn into himself than usual, with the tremendous weight of his decision, and work went on round the place with no relaxing of effort and care for the coming year, which was so full of uncertainty for everybody.

## III

On the Queen's birthday each year her health was drunk with ceremony in the house which was her shrine. September 7, 1587, was a gay, warm, sunny day after a week of damp and chill. Promptly at three o'clock in the afternoon, the new serving-maid Joan carried the tray with the silver-mounted jug and the Venetian glass wine goblets into the Queen's parlour and set them on the big table that stood opposite the portrait. There was much better glass in the house, but these were the ones from which the Queen's health was always drunk.

She found old Adam already in the room with a stepladder. Old Adam had served Anthony's father, and had gone with Margaret into Cheshire at the time of her wedding. She had sent him down from there some years ago, because his chest was bad and he was coughing his head off, and Anthony thought that the mild Evesham-country air might keep him alive a little longer. He was now eighty-three, and never coughed at all. He had made for himself certain duties about the place, and it was as much as anybody's life was worth to interfere with him. Adam could remember Henry the Eighth as a young man, and was a loyal subject of the Queen, but his theology had got a trifle mixed with all this chopping and changing. He was crooning to himself, a thin wheezing thread of sound, as he placed the ladder with care against the edge of the mantelpiece, a bit of sacking between it and the wood for fear of scratches.

> "When I have in mine purse enow,
>     I may have both horse and cow,
> And also friends enow—
>     By virtue of my purse,"

he sang, for he had no illusions left, and the psalms had
begun to elude him lately.

"Master's outside on the terrace finishing the garland,"
said Joan, "and young master Nicholas is with him. I've
brought up the wine for the toast."

> "When mine purse begins to slack,
>    And there is nowt in my pack,
>  They will say—'Go, farewell, Jack,
>    Thou shalt non more drink wi' us,'"

sang old Adam, and thought again how women talked
too much and always said what everybody knew.

"Doesn't my silver look nice?" said Joan, a friendly
soul.

Having placed the ladder to his satisfaction, Adam
gave a disparaging glance at the silver, which was never
so bright now as in his young days when it was properly
polished.

"Years do seem to be gettin' shorter," he complained.
"Seems like only yesterday we was all drinkin' the
Queen's health on her last birthday—and here it is come
round *again*. We're gettin' old, Joan, all on us. Even the
Queen."

"The master's not old!" protested Joan, shocked.

"Nigh twenty years since he married. *I* remember that
day. The likes of you wasn't born yet."

"*She's* not worn very well!" said Joan, with a toss of
her fair head.

"Very handsome woman she was, when she first came

here," insisted Adam. "I can remember her as a bride, I can."

"That was a frosty wedding night, I'll wager!" cried Joan.

"That's none of your business," he rebuked her severely. "Though anyone can see with half an eye you'd follow him from here to Land's End in your shift! Anybody can see but the master, that is!"

"That's not true!" shrieked Joan, flying into a young helpless passion of futile denial. "You've no right to say such a thing, Adam, right out, in the house! Suppose somebody heard you! Do you want me to lose my place, all because you can't keep your silly old mouth shut—"

She was gone out of the door in a whirl of skirts, half blind with tears, followed by his high, senile chuckle.

He went to the bay window which looked out across the terrace, mounted carefully the single shallow step, and laid his old eyes against the diamond-shaped panes. Anthony and Nicholas sat on the grass together, their heads bent over the flower-studded garland which lay across their knees. The girl Elizabeth moved among the rose-bushes beyond them, with a basket and shears. A pretty thing, thought old Adam, a very pretty thing, if only she were not so much like her mother. He sighed vaguely, as he often did when Catherine came to his notice, and thought of the old days in Cheshire, where the mistress always had a jolly word for everybody, and could see a joke. That saucy girl Joan, with her foolish heart in her eyes each time she saw the master—she was right, though—a man liked a little laughter in his bed. . . .

"Father," said Nicholas into the silence which had fallen between them, "why do you never go to Court?"

"It's been too long now—twenty years—I shall never go again."

"But you've seen the Queen, father? You must have seen the Queen?" insisted Nicholas.

"Yes," said Anthony gently. "I've seen her." His children had never heard the story of the midnight ride from Greenwich to Hatfield, which with many men would have been a fireside tale for the last two decades. And the reason, if he had faced it, was that he had no desire to discuss the Queen before his wife. He supposed that Nicholas was old enough now to be trusted with it. . . . "It was a long time ago," he mused.

"Was she beautiful?"

"I thought she was."

"She's old now," said Elizabeth jealously from among the rose-bushes.

"She's the same age as I am," her father admitted. "Fifty-four. She and Robert Dudley and I are all the same age. Odd, isn't it."

"The Earl of Leicester?" said Elizabeth, and her eyes grew large. "Did you know him?"

"I served him when I was a boy."

"While he was the Queen's lover?" Her voice rang clear in the quiet air, and his head came up with a jerk.

"Who told you that?" he demanded sharply.

"Mother says there was a lot of scandal once."

"Of course there was scandal," he acknowledged impatiently. "The Queen was a young woman, unmarried, gay, and a little heedless. If it had not been Lord Robert it would have been somebody else. People had to have something to talk about, I suppose!"

"Then there was nothing in it after all?" she asked, disappointed.

"Does it matter—now?" he cried in exasperation. "What if there was? He was a fine man—still is, for all his enemies' tales. And it's a lonely business, being Queen."

"She might have married," said Elizabeth, her mother's daughter.

"Who was fit to marry her, outside of England? And if she'd married an Englishman we'd have had a civil war, and she knew it!"

"Father," said Nicholas, "tell us about when you saw the Queen."

And so it had caught up with him at last, in his son's question. He looked at the boy sitting with grave eyes on the grass beside him—the small, straight shoulders, the strong, small hands, the long straight legs and supple pose. It was thanks to her that Nicholas sat there like that, dressed in a blue satin doublet with cambric at his wrists and throat, confident, secure, with a goodly heritage to come. Yes, it was time Nicholas knew what he owed to the Queen.

He began at the stables the night Edward died, and

he finished with his own dash away from Hatfield under the hot stars, and that one light in an upstairs window as he looked back. It was a tale to delight a child in any case, and Nicholas, who had always worshipped his father, sat spellbound.

"And you never knew what was written on that bit of paper?" Elizabeth asked from the roses.

They had forgotten her.

"I could guess," smiled Anthony. "The little King died that night. But she stayed where she was, and they never got their hands on her in London."

"And she was beautiful then?" harped Elizabeth jealously.

The girl was so like her mother. He answered with the kind of automatic evasion which kept his intercourse with Catherine friendly and unembittered.

"You're wearing the new pink gown," he said, smiling. "How nice you look among the roses."

"In honour of the Queen's birthday!" She pretended pettish boredom through her pleased vanity. "Would *she* think I look nice?"

"Would you like to go to Court, child?" he queried, and his eyes were wistful on her youth. He had spasmodic doubts about being able to find her a good enough husband, as things were in the country.

"And be a maid of honour?"

"Perhaps."

"Mother wouldn't like it," she said primly. Her basket

was full now. "The rain last night hasn't done my roses any good," she remarked.

Her roses. Because once a year she clipped them for the silver bowl on the Queen's birthday. He rose and gathered up the garland.

"Go and fetch your mother, Bess. We'll drink the toast now."

She departed with her basket and shears, walking well, with her head up and Catherine's gliding step.

"I'd like to go to Court," said Nicholas unexpectedly.

"You?" said his father, surprised but pleased. "Your job is here, my son. The house will belong to you one day."

"Is the house more important than the Queen?" inquired Nicholas, anxious to learn.

"The house," said Anthony, and his eyes travelled lovingly along the sunlit length of it, "the house *is* the Queen."

Nicholas stood up slowly, attached to one end of the garland in Anthony's hands, and crossed the lawn beside his father to the door in the south front through which Elizabeth's pink gown had disappeared. In silence they entered the staircase hall, where a long sunbeam stretched from the threshold to the bottom step; they passed through the library, and came to the Queen's parlour. Adam was waiting by the ladder, hatless, in his blue smock.

It was Nicholas's privilege to brace his small strength against the bottom of the ladder as Anthony mounted

97

it to lay the garland round the frame of the Queen's picture. When it was in place Anthony paused a moment, his hands resting either side of the frame, as though on the Queen's shoulders, his eyes on a level with hers. For a moment it almost seemed as though he would bend forward and kiss the painted lips. Then he descended slowly, his face secretly illumined and a little sad.

"Will that be all, master?" Adam inquired after a discreet pause.

"Yes, Adam—take the ladder away now," he answered absently, still with that secret look of some glimpsed glory.

The old man shouldered the ladder, which was too heavy for him, balanced it bravely, and shuffled out of the room.

"Then you saved the Queen's life," said Nicholas, awed, now that it had come home to him.

"She's always said so," admitted Anthony, and his eyes went back involuntarily to the portrait.

"Was that why she gave you her picture?"

"She gave us all we possess, Nicholas. You are old enough to begin to think of the future. Your future, whatever it comes to, is here with the house. Your life, when you come to live it, is bound up with the life of the house. You are not to leave it in other hands. You must tend it yourself. You must marry, so that when the time comes that you can do no more for it, your son will go on in your place. You understand all that?"

"Yes, father."

98

"The house is her home, remember that, and we are her stewards. She will die one day—before you do. But the house will still belong to her. You will remember that?"

"Yes, father."

"For twenty years I have drunk her health in this room on her birthday. I should like you to maintain that custom as long as—" He broke off, listening, and Joan ran in, breathless and staring.

"Master, there's somebody come from London—a soldier, I think he is—he says his name is Carey."

"You left him in the old hall?"

"Yes, master."

"From London!" cried Nicholas, his eyes shining, and followed at his father's heels to welcome the visitor.

In the vaulted hall they found a man of middle age, heavier than he liked to be, with a fine grey head and humorous eyes. He stood gazing up at the tall traceried window with approval.

"The place has changed since I saw it last," he said as his greeting, and Anthony recognized with amazement the lad who had ridden down over Cotswold with the Queen's picture more than twenty years ago.

"You again!" he cried, and held out both hands. "Welcome to Queen's Folly! This is my son, Nicholas. Is anyone seeing to your horse? Nicholas, shout up Adam or Jock to stable the horse—"

"If he's allowed to drink," said Carey, "that will do for now."

"Adam's there," Nicholas reported, looking out the door, and shouted, "Give him a drink, Adam! That's all now!"

"I hoped you had come to claim that dinner I owe you," Anthony suggested cordially.

"No," said Carey with his gentle smile. "Not this time."

"Another glass of wine, then!" Anthony's hand fell on his shoulder and turned him toward the library. "We go through here now, to the new wing. I had to have a door cut—" He listened with satisfaction to Carey's compliments on the new wing, and Carey, when he reached the Queen's parlour, bowed to the portrait as though it was his hostess. "We were about to drink to the Queen— our annual birthday ceremony. Will you join us?"

"With pleasure."

While Anthony poured the wine, Carey pulled off his gloves with a glance about the quiet room as though full of regret. Then he burst his bombshell.

"I have brought you a message from the Queen," he said.

"From—?" The wine ran over into the tray.

"Do you think we might—have a talk?" asked Carey, and glanced briefly at Nicholas who stood beside his father at the table.

Anthony's free hand found the boy's shoulder blindly, his eyes never leaving the visitor's face.

"This is my only son. He is old enough to hear."

Carey drew a folded paper from inside his doublet and gave it to him.

"Her own hand," he said.

Anthony took the paper incredulously, stared down at it, and raised it to his lips before breaking the seal. He read the short message it contained—glanced up at Carey, and read it again.

"Come to London—" he read dazedly. "—see Walsingham—plots against her life—need of the love I once bore her—but what does it mean, I—"

"You are rather out of touch with things here in this little paradise, aren't you," said Carey, and his gaze rested almost with pity on his host.

"Yes, I—that is, I haven't been to Court—I—thought never to see her again—"

"You know, of course, that Leicester has gone back to the Lowlands to try and settle things there."

"Yes. I was glad to see him justified in that matter."

"He isn't—yet. Leicester has made a fool of himself more than once—but he and the Queen are still good friends, in spite of his marriage, in spite of everything. And she is as anxious to see him triumph over his enemies at home as to have him beat Parma abroad."

"I'm glad," said Anthony simply.

"So am I. He has been cruelly misjudged. I am authorized to tell you that this means you will be sent to Flanders to help Leicester."

"Help him?" repeated Anthony without comprehension.

Carey glanced again at Nicholas, and then went on grimly.

"They are carrying on secret negotiations with Parma. Walsingham has some scheme of winning him from the Spanish cause. So that if and when Philip launches the Armada at England he will find Parma's land forces divorced from the ships."

"A bribe? But surely there is no bribe in England big enough to weigh against Philip—"

"Parma does not want to spend another winter under canvas with his men. They are unhealthy and mutinous enough as it is. They desert almost as fast as new regiments can fill in. Parma has lost patience with Philip, so they say. The whole thing is this: they are worried in London—and they must have a man they can trust—" Again he glanced at Nicholas. "Might I suggest—"

"You can say what you like before him," said Anthony, gripping his shoulder.

"—a man they can trust with their secrets," Carey continued unwillingly, "no matter what may be done to him."

"You mean," said Anthony, and his eyelids flickered once, "in case I am taken by the Spanish—"

"Exactly," said Carey.

Then Catherine entered in a swish of silk, with Elizabeth immediately behind her, and there were introductions.

Anthony turned to her, his mind awhirl, his heart beating thickly in his chest. He was torn two ways—between the Queen, where he had thought all his allegiance lay, and the house which had come to embody his love for her. His wife, as she stood there in her plum-coloured gown, in her graceful dignity and a dark beauty which came of serenity and self-control, had no part in the tug-of-war taking place within him. To leave Queen's Folly now, perhaps never to see it again, was an agony he had never even contemplated before, a renunciation which went beyond the human ties he had formed there, beyond even the pride of fatherhood. And for once, in a flood of pain that was almost physical, he neglected to be tactful.

"Catherine, I have had a message from the Queen. I am off to London at once."

"Will you be away long?" she asked with composure, while one hand stole up to her throat.

"Yes. I am going to join the Earl of Leicester in the Lowlands."

"I don't—understand," said Catherine, with a glance at Carey and the children which implored the privilege of privacy.

"War is upon us, madam, and the Queen needs every loyal man." Carey endeavoured to justify his own presence apologetically.

"War?" she whispered in horror.

"With Spain. It is certain now that Philip plans an expedition against England within the year. The Crusade is being preached from every pulpit in Spain. Every noble Spanish family has contributed sons to the army. The most powerful fleet Europe has ever seen is gathering in the Tagus, and Parma's army in Flanders is being constantly reinforced—"

"Invasion?" said Catherine, dry-lipped. "The Inquisition—here, in England, at last? My God, will Philip *never* die?"

"He is not old, madam," Carey reminded her, blinking. "Only ailing. Anyway, our Elizabeth was never better! She thrives on trouble, always has. It makes her seem immortal!"

Anthony had stood where he was, immovable, while his eyes went slowly round the sunlit room, caressing it as a lover's gaze rests on his mistress and travels from the topmost shining curl to the tip of a small slipper and back again. At the sound of the Queen's name he looked at Carey again, and his shoulders straightened with resolution.

"Will you stop for a meal," he asked quietly, "or do we ride at once?"

"I don't want to hurry you, but if we could sleep at Oxford tonight—" Carey smiled at him with admiration and understanding. Wives, Carey seemed to say, could not be depended upon to comprehend these matters at once.

"Bess, call Joan or someone—tell them to saddle my mare. Put my night things and a change of linen in the saddle-bags, and pack up some food for the road."

His daughter ran out of the room on the errand, white-faced and silent.

"Anthony—" Catherine began incredulously, "—you

can't mean to go like this—wait till morning—wait—"

"If Philip has made up his mind at last there is no time to lose." He picked up the jug of wine. "We'll have the toast anyway, before I go."

For a moment she watched the red wine rise in the goblet to the brim—his hand was not quite steady. In that moment she was sure of all those things she had only wondered about, obliquely, in the chinks of her busy days, while she strove to please him. She had tried so hard to please him. All that a woman could do to bind a man to her she had done, she thought. Early and late she had tended his possessions, trained his servants with endless care, studied his habits and his wishes in order to anticipate if possible his desires. She had schooled herself to figures and economy in her housekeeping, used his money wisely, asked but little for herself, and yet was always well dressed, neatly coifed, even-tempered. Never had she allowed a caprice of her own, a mood, or an indisposition to interfere with his inclinations. Docile and uncomplaining always, she had borne him children, even a son. And what had she had in return? Kindness, yes, patience, and praise—he gave his dogs the same. Creature comforts aplenty, indulgence, even—that was no more than his children received from him. She could not have told in words what it was she had always lacked from him—but she saw now by the tremor of his hand that the dearth she had always felt was real and not her fancy. There was something apart from her—a claim upon him which was greater than hers, and it was taking him from her at last. Sheer despair engulfed her, so that she cried out against it, like a drowning woman who yet knows there is none to hear.

"But, Anthony—after all these years, you would leave this house—your son—your family—your *life*—and fly off on this wild goose chase, at your age—"

He answered her as usual with the humorous twist which deflected anything approaching a domestic impasse, and kept their intercourse always pleasant and friendly, if at times a trifle artificial.

"My dear, we owe the house to the Queen—my son will preserve it for her—and as for my age, I am the same as the Queen and she is immortal!" He handed Carey a full goblet of wine. His lips were smiling now, his eyes were hidden behind their lashes.

"Anthony, I'll not be treated like this—I'll not bear it!" she cried desperately, for she saw in a flash all her years of dedication to efficient wifehood, all her smothered longings and unasked questions, her very birth-pains cast aside as worthless compared to this secret thing to which she dared not even give a name. "I've borne a great deal, but I will not be treated like this! What will become of us here? If you go you'll never come back, you'll be killed, sacrificed, buried in some nameless grave like hundreds and hundreds of others—"

"I'll come back, never fear," he said steadily, and put a goblet of wine in her hand that received it automatically while she tried to catch his eyes and failed. He gave one then to Nicholas, and repeated gently, returning the boy's wide gaze—"I'll come back."

They faced the portrait, and he lifted his glass—she saw the familiar grace of the gesture on his part, and the unconscious shadow-movement from Nicholas, with a shudder.

"The Queen!" he said.

"The Queen!" they murmured after him.

But Catherine did not touch her lips to the wine.

## IV

Elizabeth stood in the long golden light which streamed through a window above the river at Whitehall. She was dressed in white satin, quilted and sewn with pearls. Her intricate ruff framed her sharp pointed chin becomingly, and her reddened lips tried to smile at the mirror she held in one long white hand. Her wig was too bright in the sunlight, and her face under its rouge and powder was sallow and lined about the eyes which gazed back at her from the mirror clear as a girl's, wise as the Sphinx. She raised her other hand, pushed forward a crimped lock of flaming hair against the hollow of her cheek. . . . A moment more she looked at herself steadfastly, in the cruel light, and laid the mirror gently face down on her dressing-table.

Twenty-two years.

And he? Grown stout, perhaps, forgotten his manners, wearing country-made clothes—a little gauche, perhaps, at being routed from his rusticity—a family man by now, with his wife's kisses still warm on his lips, with fatuous stories of his babies for conversation—perhaps a little ashamed in retrospect of the fervent boy who had stood before her with his soul in his eyes and stammered praises of the house he had built to her glory—perhaps forgetting too that time was not kind to a woman who had the cares of a nation on her shoulders, and no one to turn to at the end of the day for solace and laughter and love-making—perhaps beholding with a shock the ruin of the face which looked at him from that portrait which hung over his mantelpiece—perhaps drawing back at his first sight of it, pitying, looking away—yes, in the very first moment she would know, when his honest eyes met hers —he was no flattering courtier to spare her feelings— twenty-two years—thirty-four, since that night at Hatfield—he would find an old woman, an unlovely old woman, to send him out to his death. . . .

The door behind her opened. She did not turn her head.

"Secretary Walsingham, Madam," said Mary Radcliffe's voice.

She nodded wearily, her back to the door.

It was Walsingham's idea that had induced her to send to Worcestershire for Anthony Brand. Someone who would not be recognized, said Walsingham. Someone who had not been at Court, and whose name meant nothing. But someone they could trust. . . .

"Your Majesty—the man is waiting in my closet,"

said Walsingham at the door. "Will you see him now?"

The Queen's knees bent under her. She sank slowly to the stool beside the dressing-table, and the jewels sewn to the skirt of her white gown rattled on the wood. She leaned one elbow on the table, and hid her face with her hand.

"Say I have gone to Richmond," she said.

"But, Madam, I understood—"

"I am not well, Walsingham."

"Your Majesty!" His voice was charged with instant alarm. "Is it serious?"

She shook her head, as it rested on her hand.

"See him yourself—give him your instructions—and my blessing. Say I am at Richmond, too ill to return— say he is not to wait. Get rid of him, Walsingham. I will not see him."

Into the narrow, somber face of the Secretary came a sudden look of comprehension. Not much could be hidden from his womanish intuition and practiced mind-reading.

"I understand, your Majesty," he said, and bowed.

"Walsingham."

"Your Majesty?"

"Be very—kind to him."

"I will, your Majesty."

The door closed behind him.

Elizabeth sat still, her face hidden. Tears were slipping down her fingers to damp the starched ruffle at her thin wrist.

Left alone in Walsingham's private room, Anthony Brand stared thoughtfully at the floor and waited, the blood drumming in his ears. On the ride up to London he had heard from Carey the frightening facts which England faced only half prepared. After thirty years of diplomacy and wiliness, of bullying and shilly-shallying, Philip of Spain had made up his mind. His puppet, Mary Stuart, was dead, and her son's fidelity to the Church was questionable. James of Scotland was more likely to annex England for himself than for the glory of God. But Philip, a humble servant of God, would conquer it in His name, and bring the erring nation back by fire and force into the arms of the Church.

Clinging still to the precarious peace she had contrived to preserve so long, Elizabeth had sent a Commission to Ostend to confer with Parma on terms. Philip was content to let these negotiations drag on while his laborious preparations went forward at Lisbon and Cadiz, while Drake and Walsingham chafed in London. Anthony had learned with horror that Philip was also content that Elizabeth's death "by natural causes, or otherwise" should be openly discussed by his spies and henchmen, "in God's service"; and that Philip wrote complacently to his ambassador in London of "the principal executions," which were to include Cecil and Walsingham. "The Cause is God's own," he concluded piously, "and we must hope that He will prosper it." Walsingham viewed such communications with grim humour—thanks to his army of spies, most of the correspondence between

the Spanish ambassador in London and his agents came
under the Foreign Secretary's eye sooner or later. The
conspirators were netted, one by one, as they gave themselves away to the watchers in Walsingham's pay. They
were lodged in the Tower, racked, questioned, and com-
pletly foiled, until finally even the ambassador himself
was ejected from England for plotting to murder a sovereign and a woman.

Philip's ships, said Carey, were making ready to sail.
Parma was at Dunkirk with his restless, dwindling army.
Winter was coming on, with high seas and strong winds,
and the Spanish ships would be overloaded for bad
weather. Walsingham was well served for information
in Madrid and Rome and Paris. The Armada could not
hoist anchor at Lisbon unbeknownst to him. But Parma
was harder to anticipate. Apparently he could not move
until the Armada was actually on its way—but could one
be absolutely sure he couldn't? Stanley and Yorke, both
English Catholics in Leicester's service, had deserted to
Parma and betrayed their commands into Spanish hands.
Stanley was believed to be at Nieuwport now, organizing
a company of English renegades and Irish Catholics who
were to join Parma's army of invasion. What were Parma's plans in Flanders?

Beyond that Carey could not go. Walsingham would
begin there, he said. Walsingham had some scheme. Walsingham knew what he wanted done.

*Spying.* The word lodged itself unwillingly in Anthony's brain. To fight, yes. To serve Leicester at the

head of a troop of half-trained mercenaries, to die of
wounds or thirst on a battlefield, or like Sydney after
Zutphen—why, yes, if she required it of him. But—
*spying*. There were lackeys and valets and pages for that
sort of thing; men who accepted purses, men who listened
at keyholes and read private papers and betrayed people
who trusted them, men who died disgracefully. She could
not mean to ask him to turn informer, it was too dirty
a trade. And yet—he knew that he could not refuse her.

Her image rose before him, as it looked down at him
from his wall at Queen's Folly—white-clad, level-eyed,
thin, and somehow gallant. He realized with a chill that
she would not look like that still. It had been twenty-two
years, he reminded himself. Well, he had changed a bit
himself. He glanced down at his silk-clad legs and the
gleam of his scabbard and hilt—his chin was conscious of
the starched edge of his new lace-trimmed ruff. What was
it she had said once—*you could turn into a country bumpkin*. He wondered if he had, and if the work of his
Worcester tailor would pass muster at Court these days.
He knew that his doublet was of conservative cut, but it
was of the best Genoese velvet, with silver buttons. And
she, with her slender waist a man's two hands could
span, would be wearing one of those newfangled farthin-
gales, an ugly thing at best.

The blood hummed thickly in his ears. To face her
again after so long. To school his features not to betray
his feelings if he found her changed, as he was bound to
do. His fingers sought the chain of the miniature of Nich-

olas which he wore round his neck. She would like to see his son. Nicholas would save them, perhaps, in those first dreadful moments when they faced each other, strangers, after a quarter of a century. . . .

Secretary Walsingham returned, noiselessly, in his velvet house shoes.

"The Queen has taken to her bed with one of her headaches," he said gently. "It is nothing alarming, but she will not be able to see anyone today." And he added, because he had been bidden to be kind—"I myself was not admitted. She sent a message by a lady-in-waiting to say that her blessing goes with you on this mission. You must leave London tonight." He settled himself at his writing-table with a sigh, and his long, deft hands were busy among his papers. "And now to business," he said, and his eyes looked deeply into Anthony's. "Somewhere about Nieuwport you will find the man Stanley—Sir William, if you please—who betrayed us at Daventer. He has recently returned there from Spain, where his reception was not, I believe, as cordial as he had expected. It is not unlikely that he has a slight grievance, along with his small Spanish pension. You will sympathize with his point of view." The Secretary's unwavering gaze held Anthony silent during a significant pause. "The Government of England," he continued, "has no time now for vengeance on traitors. Instead of cutting Stanley's throat you will become his friend—his most inseparable and trusted friend," repeated the Secretary with gentle emphasis, as Anthony stirred in his chair. "I have here a packet of let-

ters which will introduce you to his favourable notice. The
man who was to have carried them across the Channel is
no longer—able to do so. The seals are quite intact, of
course, and you have a delay of only five days to account
for. Here are copies of the contents of those letters, with
which he will doubtless expect you to be familiar. Here is
a cipher which you will memorize and return to me before you go. Here is a list—not a long one, but it will
serve—of channels through which you may communicate
with me. The confidence of the man Stanley is your pass-
port to Parma. I need to know more about Parma. I need
to know—"

The cool, passionless voice flowed on.

## V

Autumn gales howled through the Channel and tore at
the flimsy canvas shelters of Parma's men camped round
Nieuwport and on the hills above Dunkirk, presumably
still ready, on Philip's orders, to start at an hour's notice.
Parma had collected countless flat-bottomed river-barges
and a few armed hoys to transport his troops, and several
large boats for landing-parties. But the Spanish fleet must
hold the Channel while he passed over with his men. The
ill-provisioned English garrisons held on at Ostend and
Flushing, their presence there an embarrassment to Parma's embarkation arrangements. Philip commended the
weather to God and said that to expect harm from the
elements was to show want of faith in the Almighty.

Parma had his instructions in full from Philip, with every detail accounted for, as was the King's way. The Armada, wrote Philip, would sail up the Channel to Dover Straits, *avoiding* an engagement with the enemy on the way, and come to anchor off Margate, giving notice to Parma that it was ready to protect his passage. Parma would then embark his army, take Margate, and cut the English communications. Philip even forwarded his instructions on high: "As it is all in His good cause," he wrote, "God send good weather." The one thing Philip seemed to leave entirely out of his calculations, but which occurred forcibly to everybody else, particularly Parma, was what England might be doing in the meantime.

Everybody but Philip wanted peace now—even Parma, even the Spanish admirals, even Leicester. Elizabeth was so sure that some sort of peace could be salvaged by the Commission at Ostend, or that Parma would ultimately desert Philip to her own advantage, that she took no interest in fitting her ships that lay idle at Chatham and Plymouth, thereby driving her admirals and councillors to distraction. There was no uncertainty in the minds of Elizabeth's defenders that the Spanish would come. The only question was how soon, and where they would strike first.

At the end of that year a well-known Flemish merchant arrived unobtrusively in London on business, and immediately sought audience of Walsingham. There was no difficulty and no delay. He was admitted without question to the Secretary's closet. He laid a heavy ring on the writing-table and stood back, his hands clasped under the hanging sleeves of his furred gown, his eyes studiously averted.

Walsingham took the ring in his long, yellow fingers—his thumb nail found the spring and the shallow stone hung loose on its tiny hinge. With the point of a quill pen Walsingham prised out the sliver of paper wedged in the cavity. Its message was in cipher. Walsingham unlocked a chest, took from it a small hand-written book, and began to decode. There were only three words when he finished: *Margate. January. Brand.*

Walsingham laid down the pen and rose with a single movement.

"Wait here," he said briefly to the Fleming. "This goes to the Queen at once."

From that hour there was feverish but efficient activity in the English shipyards. Crews were recalled, provisioning was rushed, caulking and masting went forward briskly, and all at great expense because of former laxness. Within the next few weeks, which were fraught with peril, England was prepared.

Once more, nothing happened. On the eve of his unwilling departure on the great enterprise, Philip's greatest admiral, Santa Cruz, had suddenly died. He was very old, and worn out with Philip's orders. For England it was a respite only. Medina Sidonia was put in command, and the loading of Philip's ships and stores was resumed. But even Elizabeth believed at last that the time was coming in spite of her, and that she must be ready.

The winter was a bitter one on Cotswold. At Queen's Folly the routine of the seasons went on, under the supervision of the capable Hobden and his lads. Slaughter time came and went, the chimneys were cleaned, the fuel housed, the roads gravelled to mitigate the winter mud. The garden was bedded with straw against the frosts, the beehives were turned up and sprinkled with sweet wort. Pruning, grafting, dunging and ploughing began, the first lambs arrived, much too soon. In February Nicholas went out to follow the mole-catcher with his usual interest, and noted with satisfaction that the hens were laying again and that the new cabbage plants looked sturdy and would do well even in the severe weather. Then in a half-gale the hop-poles went up, and a few days later the calves were put to grass. The May weeding was accomplished, sometimes in a pouring rain, shearing began late and with misgivings, cheese-making went forward.

And still the Armada had not come, though there had been several false alarms, and still there was no word from Anthony.

Leicester had returned from the Lowlands in the previous autumn—people said as no great hero, but the Queen's welcome was warm and he had been put in charge of the army which was to defend her person at home. The English fleet under Drake and Howard were tossing on boisterous seas off Plymouth, afraid to seek shelter in the harbour, which lacked a breakwater, for fear they could never get out again. They hoped to take the Armada in water and force an engagement beyond the mouth of the

Channel, secure in their own superior seamanship. Beacons were kept ready in a long chain across England, to flash the call to arms.

Meanwhile on the farms the early hay was cut in inclement, blowing weather, and could not be stacked for damp. The time for reaping wheat and corn was near, when a shortage of hands was anticipated. There were gales from all quarters, and shifting hurricanes. The oldest fisherman on the coast round Plymouth could never remember such a season. It was said in England that Philip's ships were unwieldy, and could not manœuvre in a high sea; and that Parma's dreaded army depended on flat-bottomed scows for transport across the Channel, and to be safe must have a surface like a mill-pond. This was some consolation for hay that rotted where it lay, and sodden kitchen gardens whose radishes came up spongy and whose peascods were flat and small. For it began to seem that God might not be on Philip's side after all.

At last, on the twentieth of July, the first beacon flared on the Lizard headland—the Spanish sails had been sighted. One after another the warning fires sprang up across the countryside, and the village musters flocked to their posts.

With apprehension and despair Nicholas saw his harvest hands and farm lads march away. There was no one left to get the corn under cover and take the grist to the mill; no one to clear the land for the autumn ploughing, which must begin soon. How was he to get the orchard harvest in, when there were only enough maids for the milking and dairy work and garden-picking? Manfully he shouldered his precious responsibilities; rose at dawn and helped to tend the cattle, worked in the fields with the old men and boys no older than himself to save what they could of the wind-whipped grain; nagged his sister Bess to keep the flower garden tidy; noted with gratitude that his mother pinned up her skirt and filled the hen-house water-pans herself and brought in the eggs. By nightfall he would topple into bed too tired to wonder about his father, too numbed with physical exertion even for nightmares about what might be happening in the Channel.

Gradually the militia men filtered home again and took up their tools. The Spaniards had not landed. There wasn't going to be an invasion, or a war. Drake's ships had done the business in the Channel—Drake and God, with His winds. The Spanish fleet was scattered, drowned, broken, drifting. England was safe. Things must be got into shape at Queen's Folly before the master came home.

# VI

And so September seventh came round again.

The tray with the Venetian goblets and the jug of wine were in their place on the table. The ladder was propped beneath Elizabeth's portrait, and Nicholas was at the top of it, stretching to drape the garland in its accustomed way, with Adam below to steady him. At last he descended, and drew a sigh of achievement.

"There. I'm afraid it doesn't look quite as well as usual."

"Reckon she's satisfied, master Nicholas."

"I hope so. Father wouldn't want us to skip a year, just because he couldn't get back in time. Mother said it didn't matter, but I feel better to do things just the same as he did."

"Ay, you're very like the master. Takes me back, it does."

"Did you know him when he was as young as me?"

"Ay, I've known him since he was a baby."

"And Robert Dudley too?"

"Oh, ay, but he's the Earl of Leicester now. He wouldn't remember the likes of me."

"Adam—did you ever see the Queen?"

"Ay—once."

"I wish I could see her—just once."

"Reckon she wouldn't look like that any more. 'Twas years ago now, that was—years and years."

"Was she like the portrait when you saw her?"

"Ay, but handsomer. I was in the crowd outside the Abbey at the coronation. Your father got me the place. And I saw her come along the strip of blue carpet, with her head up and her eyes shining—must have seemed like a miracle to her, after what she'd been through. She gave thanks to God that day, if ever a woman did. 'Twas a great sight—England'll never see another day like that, not in a thousand years—sunshine, breaking through the clouds, she was—" He drew the back of his hand across his eyes. "Seems a long time back, somehow. Will that be all, master Nicholas?"

"Yes, thank you. No—Adam—wait—you're sure there's no more news in the village?"

Adam paused, resting the weight of the ladder against the edge of the mantelpiece, his eyes avoiding the boy's. Oppressed with a dim foreboding these days, Adam dreaded news in any form—no one knew what they were talking about—even the Queen up in London was not sure yet exactly what had happened—or was she?—it was all rumours—all nonsense—they would never really know what had kept the Spanish out of England until the master came back to tell them—until . . .

"No news," he sighed, half to himself, "except they say it's all over in the Channel. Some of the Spanish ships is beating north—they'll have to go clean round John o' Groat's and Ireland, seems like, to get back to Spain. We've fair scotched 'em, I'm thinking. So you see," he added, striving for futile comfort in this desolation of uncertainty, "Parma's army in the Lowlands wasn't any use at all."

"But Leicester came home months ago, they say."

"Ay."

"But Leicester wouldn't—he wouldn't just leave my father there alone, would he, with no way to get back home? Leicester wouldn't do a thing like that?"

"Might be Leicester wouldn't have the say," explained Adam cautiously. "Might be your father wasn't with the army—off on a job of his own, like."

"You mean like an ambassador?"

"Maybe."

"Ambassadors have to travel alone sometimes, don't they?"

"Sometimes."

"But my father is such a good swordsman that he would be quite safe alone, wouldn't he? That is, anything up to a dozen Spaniards, Adam?"

"I should say up to a dozen, ay."

"Are the Spaniards good swordsmen, Adam?"

"Ay—but your father fights Italian style. That beats 'em."

"Mother's been crying again," said Nicholas restlessly. "And that frightens Bess, and she cries too. You do think he'll come home soon, Adam?"

"Ay—soon. We must hope," said Adam, not looking at the child. And as Nicholas said nothing more, Adam shouldered the ladder and, bent double beneath its weight, escaped to the stable yard and his own silent forebodings.

Nicholas drifted forlornly through the library and out of the south door on to the terrace in the late afternoon light. A murky sun was sinking toward a black cloud bank high in the west. There would be another storm tonight.

His mother and Bess had vanished into the upper part of the house, though they knew it was time for the toast. It occurred to him that Bess had not gathered the Queen's roses for the silver bowl. He went back into the house and fetched a pair of shears and a basket from the little west room off the vaulted hall, where such things were kept, and set to work on the rose-bushes, his mind running back to last year when he and his father had made the garland together on the grass nearby, and he had heard for the first time how two messages were carried to Hatfield instead of one.

The full blown roses were spattered with mud from the heavy rains of the last few days. He chose the opening buds of that morning, and meant to snip away the dead blooms later—Bess would not keep the faded flowers trimmed, though he could never see what she did with her time, and the gardener's boy could not be everywhere at once, especially just now when they were setting out strawberry plants. His basket was almost full when Joan ran out of the door with a scared face, calling his name.

"Master Nicholas! Come quick! He's here again—the man who came last year—he's come back—he's in the Queen's room—"

Sir James Carey again? Alone? Nicholas's heart began to beat very fast, which he could not quite understand, as he hurried across the grass to her, the basket full of roses in his hands.

"Tell my mother he is here," he said composedly, wondering why he felt so short of breath when it was Joan who was flying up the stairs as though the devil followed.

As he crossed the threshold of the hall the edge of the descending sun touched the top of the cloud—the warmth and colour of the September afternoon was snuffed out by a chill little wind from nowhere which rattled the leaves of the climbing rose round the door. The Queen's parlour seemed bleak and grey when he entered it, to find Carey standing under the portrait looking up at it.

Nicholas paused on the threshold, and the fingers which gripped the handle of the basket were damp and cold.

"Is it all over? Will my father come home now?" he demanded without greeting, and he was panting as he stood there.

"Good day, Nicholas," said Carey gently, punctiliously, sparring for time, trying not to flinch as the child approached him gracefully across the carpet, the basket of fragrant bloom in his hands—the scent of the roses reached Carey's nostrils, heavy in the sudden twilight which had come to Queen's Folly. "May I—see your mother?" he asked, inadequately.

"Joan has gone to tell her you are here. Have you brought us a message from my father?"

Carey looked down at him a moment, and then took a restless turn round the table, slapping with an empty glove at the back of a chair as he passed, his spurs jingling in the breathless silence that possessed the room.

"No, my boy, I'm afraid I haven't," he said at last.

"We thought—he might be able to write to us now that—" Nicholas's voice broke with eager, obstinate hope against the frightened hammering of his heart. "Has the Queen had news of him?"

Carey had no answer ready.

"Run and tell your mother I am here, like a good lad."

124

"She knows. She will come." Nicholas reached the other end of the long table and set down his basket carefully and stood beside it, leaning on the polished wood. "But there wasn't any fighting in the Lowlands," he argued breathlessly. "They said—they said Parma's army never moved at all—so he—my father couldn't be—dead—"

With his eyes fastened on Carey's face, with Carey's eyes looking back unwillingly into his, Nicholas slid along the edge of the table to a stool and dropped on it. Then his head went down on his crooked arm on the table without a sound.

Carey started toward him and then hesitated. Nicholas was turning the corner into manhood in that moment. There was no comforting him any more like a child. He must bear his grief alone, and master it. Carey shivered in the greying room, and wondered why the woman could not give the place a fire on a day like this. His dislike of Catherine Brand flared up as he stood gazing down at the small bowed shoulders of her son. Praise God, he was thinking, no son of his own was left to her. A hard, dutiful woman, without the gift of laughter, he thought. A man liked a little relaxation sometimes. . . .

Catherine entered quickly, followed by Elizabeth. Both were white-faced, and he noticed how much alike they looked, and felt another pang for the child growing up in their shadow.

"What is it?" demanded Catherine, before he could speak. "What have you come to tell me?"

"Madam," he answered without the formality of a bow, "I bring you the Queen's sympathy for the death of a gallant man."

"I knew it," she said through set lips. "Somehow I knew the day he left here that he would never come back." She stood a moment, looking at the floor in front of her, controlling herself. More than wifely sorrow at Anthony's death, she felt a surging fury that it must be so, a blind resentment against the circumstances of her bereavement. It was such a wanton twisting of his destiny and hers that he should have died as he did—violently and needlessly, and before his time. Grief for the man who for years had been the core of her existence might come later. Now she felt only that she had been robbed. She rounded on Elizabeth, who had begun to cry softly into her hands. "Don't blubber, girl, or else go to your room!"

The tense air of the twilit room seemed to start and shudder at the harsh words. Elizabeth crept to the table and sank into a chair across from Nicholas, sobbing into her hands.

"How did it happen?" Catherine asked then, and her voice by a great effort of her will was low again, and so steady as to be almost too casual.

"I am not yet at liberty to tell you the details," said Carey stiffly, wishing only to be gone.

"Torture?" The word came sharply, taking even herself by surprise.

"No. It was a soldier's death."

"That is a great comfort!" she said ironically.

"It should be, madam," he agreed with perfect courtesy, expressionless. "I can only say that he was not thrown away. He did his part where he was, and we here at home have profited by his courage. The Queen extends to you her sincerest condolences."

"The Queen should be inured to widows' tears by now!" she cried with scorn.

"You can afford to pity the Queen, madam. The Earl of Leicester died suddenly of a fever three days ago."

"Another woman's husband!" said Catherine coldly.

"You are bitter, madam. I hope it will pass. I hope you will rear your son in pride of his father's memory, and in loyalty to the service of the Queen."

"Words—words!" She brushed them aside. "My husband is dead. For her. The Armada has been defeated and England is safe again. The children can weep. But the Queen has been served!"

Carey gave it up.

"If you will forgive me, madam—I must return to London at once."

"It was kind of you to come here again yourself," she conceded stonily.

"I did what I could," was his stiff reply. "I considered myself your husband's friend—and I had a concern for his boy." He rested a moment's pitying glance on Nicholas, bowed, and turned to go.

Nicholas pulled himself erect by the corner of the

table. His cheeks were streaked with tears, but he was not crying now.

"I think my father would wish us to drink the usual toast, sir," he said clearly, "before you go."

"I should be delighted," said Carey, returning to the table, and—

"No!" cried Catherine at the same moment.

As though he had not heard her, Nicholas lifted the silver-mounted jug. His right hand shook, and he laid his left beneath the lip of the jug to guide it to the brim of the goblet, while Carey stood watching him with a rueful smile as he had watched his father a year ago.

"Come, Bess," said Nicholas firmly, and set down the jug to hand a full goblet to Carey. "Your wine, sir—"

"I tell you *no!*" cried Catherine. "The toast will not be drunk today!" And before Carey could take the goblet from Nicholas's fingers she dashed it to the floor between them.

They stared at her vehemence. Carey was the first to recover.

"Your mother is naturally upset," he said quietly to the boy. "Doubtless it will pass."

And with a last, encouraging smile for Nicholas he bowed again, most formally, and went.

The darkening room seemed to listen till the clink of his spurs died away. Then Elizabeth sobbed once convulsively, and Nicholas turned his eyes from the empty doorway to his mother's face. She stood with her back to the light which was fading from the big window, but

he realized that she stood erect and rigid, a woman outraged but not stricken. There was a dark stain on her
skirt where the wine had splashed as the glass fell—the
fragments of one of those Venetian goblets his father had
prized lay at her feet. Impossible to ask for comfort from
a mother who defiled his father's memory with senseless
anger at the Queen. Nicholas lifted his own glass.

"The Queen," he murmured, and drained it manfully
and set it down and faced his mother in the listening
room.

"I forbid it," she said very low, with controlled rage.
"From now on this wicked idolatry will stop. I forbid it.
It's worse than papistry—it's devil-worship!"

"You wouldn't dare to say such a thing if my father
were alive!" he cried, becoming angry too.

"For years the Queen has been mistress of my house,"
she went on, beside herself. "For years I have been made
to feel like a—concubine! He drank to her on our wedding night—to *her*, not to me! I'll swear he bedded her
that night, not me!"

"Mother!" cried Elizabeth in horror. "Are you jealous
of the Queen?"

"Jealous of her?" repeated Catherine softly, with a
dreadful twisted smile. "Well, why not? She's only a
woman—or else a witch. Yes, she casts an evil spell—
she steals men's hearts and mews them up in her noisy
virginity. Say she is chaste in body—I can well believe
it! That way she is a nation's paramour! 'The Maiden
Queen'—alone, and sore beset, and only a feeble woman

on a great cruel throne! Bah! That way she creeps into men's dreams, invades their prayers, lies in their beds between them and their lawful wives! No man's—and every man's! That is her way. She smiles, and looks into their eyes—God, how I have heard rhapsodies about her eyes, and no two men agree about the colour of them! Doubtless she changes it at will, to suit their separate fancies! Sorceress! Witch! Circe! And a thousand thousand times a whore!"

"Mother, what are you saying?" gasped Elizabeth on a frightened squeak.

"All the things I've never dared to say before! All the things I've wanted to say for twenty years, yes, while he still could hear me, too! All the things all the wives in England long to say, from Leicester's down to—me!"

"Then I'm glad he is dead and cannot hear you!" cried Nicholas passionately.

"Ah, you're too young to understand," she said, staring at him with a slow, hostile look. "Too young, thank God, ever to fall under that spell now. And she is too old, at last. They say she is painted purple and wears a wig. They say—"

"I don't believe it!" he denied stoutly.

"No, neither would your father! Well, praise God you are too young to go to Court and dangle after her like Oxford and Essex—"

"I do not wish to go to Court," he interrupted with dignity. "*He* said my place was here, with the house.

Besides, I can see her here, every day—and I shall drink her health each year like this, for him."

"God in heaven, am I to go through it all again, with my son?" said Catherine wonderingly. "It is magic—black magic! I have borne enough! Bess—call Joan! Call Joan, I say!" she repeated sharply, as the girl stood staring. And when Joan came—"Tell Adam to fetch the ladder here at once," commanded Catherine. "And let us have the candles quickly; it's gone dark."

"Mother, what are you going to do?" asked Nicholas, who was after all only a child fighting utter panic and desolation.

"You'll see," she said grimly, and began to pace the floor in a narrow orbit, feverishly, talking to herself. "It's monstrous. One would think the woman was some sort of goddess. For a lifetime she has had all the crowned suitors of Europe at her beck and call, and she refused them all —not one was good enough for her Majesty! No, she must dress in white, and leave her virgin bosom bare, and smirk and sigh and languish at them—raise false hopes and dash them down again, always making sure that they would bounce! Denmark, Sweden, Spain, France, and Austria—Frederick, Eric, Carlos, Alençon, Charles—Tom, Dick, and Harry, let them all come, and bow and pay her compliments and make her lavish gifts—she dearly loves a gift! Let them hope their youth away, and when they marry let their wives be second choice, and be sure their wives will know it! There is black magic in the

Queen, that clouds men's reason! But not my son! No, by God, *not my son too!*"

A cold draught came down the chimney, bringing a smell of dead ashes into the room which mingled with the pungent odor of the spilt wine soaking into the carpet round the fragments of glass. And now, with a silent dribble of fine rain down its many window-panes, the house itself was weeping.

Adam stood uncertainly in the doorway with a ladder. Joan slipped past him into the room with lighted candles which she placed on the table nervously and returned to close the door—her mistress always chid her for an open door—and then lingered uneasily just inside it because she had not been dismissed.

"Bring the ladder here, Adam," said Catherine curtly. "I want you to take down that picture."

They all stood speechless. Under Catherine's compelling eyes Adam advanced waveringly and propped the ladder against the mantelpiece.

"Mother, you can't do that," gasped Nicholas incredulously. "The picture has always been there!"

"Don't stand staring, girl!" Catherine turned on Joan, who stood against the door as though paralyzed, her jaw a little ajar. "Help Adam with the ladder!"

"B-but, madam—the m-master—" began Joan, stunned.

"Your master is dead. Lend Adam a hand."

Too stricken for tears, Joan got herself to the ladder, and leaned against it for her own support. For her the world had come to an end, if Anthony Brand was no longer in it to give her an absent-minded smile or a kindly word when she put herself in his way. She clung to the rough wood giddily, her eyes half closed, her teeth clenched on sounds which, when they came, would be scarcely human in their hopeless grief.

Adam crawled slowly up the ladder and unhooked the Queen's portrait. The garland fell awry and dropped to the floor with a small rustle and thud in the silence. Adam crept back down the ladder, cherishing the picture, and turned at the foot, resting a corner of the heavy frame on the floor, the Queen's serene face turned outward, watching them. He found his voice with difficulty.

"Wh-where shall I put it, madam?"

"In the attics."

"Mother, you must be mad!" Nicholas wrenched himself out of his own paralysis of horror. "Adam, put it back! I command you to put it back at once!"

"You are too young to give commands, Nicholas," said his mother coldly. "*I* am to be obeyed in this house now. Adam, do as I bid you."

"You shall not do such a thing in my father's house!" raged Nicholas, desperate with the helplessness of a child in the grip of its elders' will. "It's treason! You could be put in the Tower! I shall never forgive you! *He* will never forgive you! I can't stop you now, but when I am a man, this house will be mine, and then the picture will go back! *I swear it will go back!*"

His wild words rang in the stark air. The room was

eerie in the candlelight, which threw great shifting shadows in its corners, the tall, rain-washed window blueblack against the storm. Almost before he had finished speaking, the door into the library swung open without a sound, showing the dark room beyond. The girl Elizabeth stood and watched it, frozen, for no one had touched it from either side. And while she stared, fascinated, with widening eyes, a thin queer light seemed to gather in the library and a cold wind from nowhere came to set the candles guttering. . . .

"Look!" shrieked Elizabeth, and covered her face with her hands, and—"*Father!*" cried Nicholas to what he saw in the emptiness beyond the open door. With a rasping scream Catherine dropped to the floor in a swoon.

Anthony Brand had come home.

*1651*

# II

## *1651*

NICHOLAS'S grandson Peregrine Brand was sitting late over his accounts, in the Queen's parlour.

The outer doors of the house were barred for the night, and the hangings at the windows were drawn against the last gleam of summer daylight, for even though Cromwell was supposed to be in Scotland with his army, and ill at that, one could be sure of nothing any more, after nearly ten years of civil war.

The room on which Anthony had lavished so much love and care had changed with the growth of the family's fortunes, but the Queen's picture still looked down from above the mantelpiece. When Catherine awoke from her swoon that night it was back in its place, and Adam was gone with his ladder. No one spoke of how it had got there. She blamed Nicholas for that, to her death, and never knew, for no one cared to tell her, that Adam had not even waited for orders, for it seemed to him that he had them when the face of his dead master looked in at the door. Catherine died the year Nicholas came of age, a silent, bitter, tragic woman, hugging her resentments; died while Elizabeth was still on the throne, flirting with Essex and Raleigh.

No one spoke, either, of Anthony's return, except when

Nicholas explained the Presence to his bride, and taught his son Richard to regard it as a perfectly natural phenomenon. And later in his turn Richard calmed his own bride when she fled screaming from the diffident apparition of a man dead, as she well knew, for nearly forty years. Richard's son Peregrine from his childhood accepted without question the fact that the builder of the house had been unable to forget it in a foreign grave, and viewed his periodic passage through the beloved rooms with a humorous sympathy. Anthony never made a noise, he never interfered, his expression was melancholy but in a way content. Even the servants got used to him and ceased to associate the sight of him with untoward events. He was lonely, and he had come home. It was simple enough.

Most of the original furniture which once seemed so grand and which witnessed the first toast to the Queen had gradually found its way into the nursery and the servants' rooms. The table was now a magnificent gate-leg, with spiral carving. The high-backed chairs had cushioned seats and cane insets and exquisite carven heads. A new Turkey carpet was on the floor, and the window hangings were of Mortlake tapestry in superb warm tones. There had been a great deal of good silver once, making a fine display on the buffets and side-tables, but that had nearly all gone to help the King.

It was more than two years now since the Parliamentarians had martyred King Charles and declared a commonwealth. In the early days of the war when Rupert came to Worcester with his Cavaliers and met Essex there, and when the King had turned to fight at Edgehill, the countryside roundabout Queen's Folly had swarmed with soldiers. Then the actual fighting drew away to the north and east, or down into Cornwall, and even the battles of Naseby and Cropredy had been at a safe distance.

But last summer the dead King's eldest son had come to Scotland from his exile in France, and signed the Covenant, and on January first he had been crowned at Scone as King Charles II. Cromwell, returning hastily from his butcheries in Ireland, marched north against him. The battle of Dunbar went to the Roundheads by a blunder of the young King's general. Charles withdrew to Stirling, Cromwell occupied Edinburgh, and there was no telling what the next move might be.

So it had all begun again—the anxiety and the waiting, the heartburning and the pity and the terror, of a war where a woman's husband might be fighting against her brothers, and one's nearest neighbour was likely in his zeal to betray a lifetime of friendship.

In spite of sequestration, fines, and imprisonment, the great houses of the West were still loyal to the Crown, and prayed that Charles II might come safely into his own again. By its isolated position, hidden in a fold of the hills more than twenty miles from Worcester and surrounded by its own broad lands, Queen's Folly escaped billeting and pillage, sometimes barely by the width of a field or the height of a hedgerow to hide its chimneys.

Its contribution to the King's cause in the past had been generous and prompt. All its spare income and most of its silver plate and a large part of its fat produce had been sent to the King at Oxford, to be used as he saw fit. For years it sent him everything but soldiers. And tonight Peregrine Brand, only son of the only son of the only son, was working out not for the first time what could be spared (without starving the land and stinting the crops) to place at the disposal of the young King when he came, as he must do, to England.

Household books and bills and rent rolls were in a dozen orderly piles on the table before him, and his head rested on one fine hand, its fingers thrust upward through the dark hair which fell in long soft waves to his shoulders. He was almost of an age with the King, who had just turned twenty-one in Scotland, and his stripling slenderness was clothed in cavalier satins, with lace to his lawn collar and cuffs. The Brands regarded with horror not unmixed with derision the ugly utilitarian costume and laughter-destroying doctrine of the Puritans. It was not merely a sentimental loyalty which bound them to the Stuart cause. It seemed to them that the Commonwealth spelt the end of the glamour and gaiety and beauty of life.

His mother entered the room through the library door, with a lighted candle in her hand. There was only the one entrance to the big parlour now, for the narrow door which Anthony had cut through the wall of the little west room had been closed in the first year of the war—con-

verted with a sliding wainscot panel into a fairly commo-
dious hiding-hole in the thickness of the wall, large
enough for two men at need. While Essex was at Worcester this secret chamber had held all the remaining silver,
and food supplies for everybody in the house, because no
one knew what would happen in those days. Now it contained only a few family treasures on a shelf, and a small
store of unperishable food in case of emergency, for Isabel was nervous again since the young King had come to
Scotland.

She was a fair, handsome woman, a little plump, very
young to have so long and grave a son. She wore a pale
summer silk with lace collar and cuffs, and her hair was
in Henriette Marie ringlets about her face. Her eyes were
blue and candid, her full, sweet mouth had a permanent
droop. A good deal of the time she unconsciously resembled a smacked child who is not sure where it went wrong.

She glanced over her shoulder nervously into the dark
room behind her, and reached the comfort of Peregrine's
company with an audible sigh of relief.

"Peregrine," she began at once in her soft, plaintive
voice with a slight lisp, "it's time you were in bed,
chuck."

"Is it, mother?" he answered with a weary civility, and
gave her a brief smile, and went back to his figuring.

She came up to him, rustling deliciously, and the scent
of orris powder that always hung about her met his nostrils. She laid one fond, ringed hand on his shoulder and
leaned to read what he had just written: *To the gelder,*

*for gelding 5 swine, 6d. For mending the coach harness, 18d. To boy bringing news of the King in Scotland, 9d.—*

A little shudder ran through her. She set her silver candlestick on the table and seated herself round the corner from him, idly picking up several papers and laying them down again on the wrong piles, at random. Patiently he restored each to its original place as she passed on to the next, and neither of them noticed.

"Have you nearly finished?" she asked fretfully, for she wanted to talk and felt lonely.

"These are the July accounts," he explained. "Father left home in such a hurry I've had to straighten things out the best I could."

"Must you do it all tonight?"

"He'll want to know how things stand when he comes back."

"I suppose we're on the safe side?" she queried uncertainly, and he glanced at her, surprised.

"If you mean, are we solvent—yes, we are. Why?"

"I don't know. So many people seem to be ruined these days. And rows of figures terrify me. I'm always afraid that when you start adding them up you'll suddenly find we haven't got any money at all."

"That's why we do it every month," he told her, amused. "To make sure we still have some. Which brings us to the kitchen-book," he smiled.

"Oh, but, Peregrine—"

"Come along, mother—where is it? Hand over."

"I don't see why your father makes me keep it when

142

it never comes out right anyhow—" she muttered, and went unwillingly to fetch a paper-covered dog-eared book from a cabinet by the window. "I'm sure I try to put everything down—like your sixpence for gelding swine!" she added, and wrinkled her nose in distaste. "But it's much more difficult than you'd think, Peregrine, when I am in the buttery or up in my room, and some fool of a girl comes with a story, and I give her money, and then the book is down here at the other end of the house—"

He took it from her reluctant fingers gently, and opened it. It looked like a child's copy-book, blotted with ink and tears. In between spasms of conscientious listing of small expenditures would come a recipe or a memorandum of local gossip or a stitchery pattern only half drawn and very badly at that.

*For yeast to bake withal, 2s.*, he read. *For two little glass bottles of orange flower water, 14s.* And then—*To make Puff-Paste: Take a quantity of fine flour, four whites of eggs, a little rosewater or other cold water, mould your paste together or beat it with your rolling-pin, for the stiffer you make it the better, then roll your paste forth and lay your butter on in bits; turn it up of both sides and so do it four or five times and then make it up. You may lay a bit on a little paper and so set it in the oven to see if it rises. You must be sure to beat your butter with a rolling-pin till the water be very clean forth of it.*

There followed some notes regarding the intricacies of "rosemary stitch" and an incomprehensible diagram of the same. After which, suddenly recollecting itself, the book resumed soberly: *For a box of garden seeds sent from London, 15s. To a poor widow woman, 2s.* And then—*Syrup from clove blossom to be used as a sauce for puddings.* . . .

A tactless grin spread slowly over Peregrine's face as he turned the untidy leaves.

"But you haven't made up your totals at the bottom of each page as I told you to," he said. "It's easier that way, to do it as you go. And what do all these blank spaces mean?"

"I can't keep running to the book every time I part with a farthing!" she cried, exasperated, and looking ready to cry. "I know that I've spent something, you see, and I always mean to fill it in later, but then I can't always remember—"

"*To the smith, for making a wire for a curtain,*" read Peregrine aloud, and looked up with interest. "What curtain was that?" he wanted to know.

"Oh, Lord, don't be like your father and question me on every single item!" she implored peevishly. "One would think tenpence really counted in this house! You both say we've got enough money, so what does it matter?"

"Well, I only wondered," he murmured apologetically, for the Brand men were not mean, and he began to make up the totals. "Father doesn't care how you spend the money," he tried to explain, his head bent over the page. "That is, he doesn't mind that it's spent—but he likes to

144

know what it went for. And it's only good housekeeping, mother, to—"

"How well you've caught it!" She was gazing at him balefully. "When your wife's time comes, whoever she is, she'll lead just such another life as mine!"

"Poor mother—" He reached to pat her hand, laughing and kind, the image of his father. "Does she have such a horrid life?"

"Housekeeping," she repeated with quiet but deadly resentment, her fingers unresponsive beneath his touch. "The place—the farms—the cattle—the tenantry—worldly goods—sacred Queen's Folly! Nothing else matters, does it!"

"Well, after all, mother, the farms support us—the cattle feed us—the tenantry serve us—the roof keeps us dry—"

"No! We run the farms with daily care—we feed the cattle—we tend the roof, and every stone and cranny of the house as though it were a growing, ailing child! You sit up nights with it—your father is out of his bed at dawn to see that it shall want for nothing during the day. The house eats us all alive, consumes our days, one by one, makes slaves of us all, and sits here smug and smiling in the sun, like a well-fed courtesan!"

"Mother, I don't see what you're grumbling about!" he said, very much surprised. "If there was a gay Court in London and you were missing balls and fine clothes and flirtations like they have in France—well, yes, then you might get bored with Queen's Folly. But God knows,

London's no place to be these days, with the Puritans stalking about it! Wait till the young King comes into his own—and then perhaps you will lack something here!"

She glanced over her shoulder at the door.

"Peregrine."

"Mmmmmmmm?" He had started figuring again, on her smudgy pages.

"Peregrine, I tell you the house is up to its tricks again."

"Tricks?" he repeated absently.

"I saw that Thing again just now—in the old hall."

"Oh, you mean Anthony," he said easily. "Yes, he was here a little while ago."

"Where?" she asked with apprehension.

"There—in the doorway—as usual."

"What did he do?"

"He never does much of anything, does he? Just looked at me, and went away."

"I don't believe you mind him a bit," she shivered.

"No, why should I? He's my great-grandfather. Poor devil can't rest, that's all. Doesn't mean any harm."

"Do you think there's anything in what your father says?"

"That Brands must die at home if they want to stay in their graves? Hard to tell. Grandfather Nicholas is all right, anyway. He never left the place for a day!"

"It must have been awful for his wife," she muttered,

staring toward the doorway. "To have to go on living here—with That."

"Serve her right. She tried to change things here, because he was dead. She must have hated the old Queen—" He glanced involuntarily at the portrait over the mantel-piece, and her gaze followed his.

"So do I," she said, very low.

"What?" He laughed, but indulgently, as all Brands laughed at their womenfolk. "She was dead before you were born!"

"Not in this house," she muttered, her eyes on the portrait.

"I wish she was alive now! She'd settle old Ironsides fast enough! He'd never have cut off her head! She'd have had his first!"

"You're wrong to belittle the dead King, Peregrine. He was a good man. It's high time his son avenged him."

"Well, give young Charles a chance, mother—he's no older than I am!"

"He's been dawdling up there in Scotland a whole year—"

"Don't think for a minute that he's enjoying himself amongst the Presbyterians! He's tried to get away, as you know very well, but they've kept him like a prisoner till lately. Now that they see the army will never fight without him to lead it, things may be different. Father hopes young Charles will invade England soon. Hundreds—thousands—will rally to him here if he does!"

"More fighting?" She shrank back in her chair.

"I suppose so. You can't have it both ways, mother."

"Where will the fighting be this time?"

"Wherever Cromwell tries to bar Charles's way. Probably up north."

There was a silence, with the scratch of his pen, while Catherine's thoughts turned backward to the other war, and the miraculous rise of the man Cromwell whom, like all simple-minded Royalist wives, she blindly hated. The executions were the worst, she thought—Strafford—Laud—Montrose—the King himself—to cut a man off in full vigour, with one stroke of the axe, while his blood still sang with youth and his wife still yearned for the clasp of his arms, and his children looked to him for guidance and love. . . . Another shudder ran through her. To hustle a man to his grave just because he was not of the same opinion about things that did not really matter, not as women—who saw so much more clearly than men—lived their lives. What did the principle of Episcopalian government (one of their grand phrases) signify, what did it matter how often Parliament met or how elections were held, what was the Prayer Book, after all, or the Covenant, or treason, for that matter, if you set them beside the life of a man who was all some woman lived for—or beside the agony of childbirth, or the pitiful helplessness of orphaned children? These were the simple things a woman lived by; concrete, comprehensible things, like pain, or an empty cradle, or one voice out of all the world that your heart leaped to hear. . .

148

"I wish your father would come home," said Isabel with trembling lips. "It's nearly a week now. What do you think is keeping him?"

"Don't worry, mother. He's probably staying close in Worcester, waiting for news."

"They wouldn't—arrest him—in Worcester?"

"What for?" He spread his hands.

"They don't always wait for a reason. I wish he'd come."

"He'll come soon."

"Aren't you anxious about him?"

"I'm trying not to be. They know he's a Royalist, of course—but so are lots of other people! He went to hear news of the King, up in Scotland. He'll stay till he gets it somehow, and then he'll come home, never fear."

"Please God the armies don't come this way again," said Isabel fervently. "You were too little to remember much about the first time—but you know Essex burnt Greenways Hall because somebody fired from the windows and killed a Puritan. Of course Queen's Folly was never garrisoned or used for billeting, by the grace of God, but Cromwell is a terrible man—a ruthless, wicked, terrible man—"

"You like Queen's Folly a little better if there's danger of its being burnt over our heads, don't you!" he teased, and patted her hand again where it lay among his papers.

"Lord help me, it's all the home I've got now," she reminded him wretchedly, for her father had fallen at

Cropredy and two brothers died at Naseby and their estates were confiscated.

"Nothing will happen to it," he said, and his eyes travelled lovingly round the room. "It's got a happy destiny of its own, the way some people are born lucky and some are not. Even when they were fighting quite near to it before, I don't think it was ever in danger. I somehow feel it will go on—still beautiful and safe— no matter what happens to us."

"I'm sure of it," she remarked unkindly.

"That's why I'm going to ask father to let me go north and join the King."

For a moment she gazed at him in speechless horror.

"No, no!" she cried, and caught at his sleeve, and clung, as though he meant to start north that very minute.

"Don't be a coward, mother," he smiled, pressing her tense fingers. "You want a King in London, don't you? Well, I want a hand in getting him there. I'm old enough now, and I'm nearly as good a swordsman as father was at my age. He says so himself. Jamie Crawford is a captain now—only he's on the other side, curse him! I used to beat Jamie regularly at everything when we were children. That's an omen, surely. I should like to see Jamie again, now that he's turned Puritan," said Peregrine with a thoughtful malice, "and beat him again!"

"Your father promised me you would stay here," she cried unguardedly, "even if he went himself! For my sake, he promised!"

"Even if he went himself!" Peregrine stared at her. "Does he mean to go? *Does* he?" He shook her arm impatiently. "Why didn't he tell me? Is that why he went to Worcester?"

"No, no—I shouldn't have said it!" wept his mother. "He will come back from Worcester—he promised me he would come back this time! But he says if the King tries now and fails it may mean the ruin of us all. He says—" She put her head in her hands, her elbows on the table, and sobbed.

"We can't both go," Peregrine reflected, "on account of the house. If only I had a younger brother," he added thoughtlessly, speaking to himself, "to look after the house—"

"The house—the house—the devil take the house!" cried Catherine hysterically, and got to her feet in anger, beating on the table with her two fists. "*What about me?* If the house is safe and has one of you to care for it, that's all that matters to you! *I'm* only a woman! I'm made of flesh and blood, not stone, but I don't count! I'm only a slave, a concubine, to serve the house and its husband and its son!" Sobbing with rage and terror, she struggled on, while he gazed up at her from his chair, aghast. "God help the women you Brands take into your beds, God help your own bride, Peregrine Brand, when it's her turn to come here and learn as I did that she's only a breed-mare for the foaling of sons—always more sons, to cherish and tend Queen's Folly—"

"Mother, in heaven's name, what's come over you—"

He rose, deeply shocked and horrified, to slide an arm round her, and she clung to him, shaking, and strangling on her own tears. "You're overwrought," he said gently, patting her shoulder, stroking her hair, soothing her as he would a child. "It's the heat, no doubt—"

They had not heard horse's hooves outside, and Richard Brand entered the room swiftly, cloaked and booted from travelling, his spurs and sword-belt clinking faintly as he came. He viewed the scene before him with affectionate dismay.

"Isabel, what under the sun?" he was saying, surprised, amused, but scarcely annoyed. "I could hear your voice as soon as I got into the hall! What is going on here—"

She threw herself at him, her tears changing from anger to relief as her arms went round his neck.

"*Richard!* Oh, thank God, you're safe home at last!"

"Yes, of course I'm safe," he said, petting her perfunctorily while his inquiring eyes went to Peregrine over her head. "Come now, what is this all about? I thought I'd find you both gone to bed—"

"I think it must be the heat, sir," said Peregrine, pushing back his hair with a weary gesture. "I feel it myself—and the anxiety—"

"There's a storm on the way," said Richard, brushing aside the anxiety. "I wasn't sure I'd get home without a wetting. Steady, my girl, come and sit down. Peregrine, get your mother a glass of wine."

"No, no, never mind—it's too hot for wine—" Isabel

sat obediently in the chair where he placed her, and strove for a grip on things. "There's been thunder in the air all day—it always makes me nervous. I'm sorry, Richard, I was worried about you, and I—"

"No need to worry, my dear," he said kindly. "I was very discreet."

"Father—was there any news of the King?" Peregrine could not hold back the question any longer.

"Yes, there is news." His father looked at him with suppressed excitement. "Charles has come south by forced marches. He was at Warrington yesterday."

"Warrington!" cried Peregrine in astonishment.

"So near?" said Isabel, very low.

"But how could he be at Warrington already?" demanded Peregrine. "Has he given Cromwell the slip?"

"He's done a mad, dangerous, glorious thing. He's turned his back on Cromwell. Left him behind in Scotland."

"Fled?" said Isabel.

"On the contrary. Look." He snatched up a piece of paper, turned it over for the blank side, and with Peregrine's pen sketched a quick map. They hung one over each of his shoulders. A distant mutter of thunder could be heard, and lightning showed through the cracks between the curtains at the big window. "Look—here's the Firth of Forth, do you see? Here's Stirling at its head—the King's headquarters. Here's Edinburgh, halfway down its southern shore—Cromwell's headquarters. And here is Perth, the key to Charles's supplies. Well—Cromwell crossed the Firth and marched on Perth."

"But that would leave Charles and his whole army between Cromwell and England!" cried Peregrine.

"It would. But if Cromwell took Perth, Charles's supplies were cut off at Stirling. So Charles simply left Cromwell to his own devices and started for the Border with his men."

"But Cromwell will be after him like a bird!" said Isabel.

"Charles got a good start before Cromwell found out what was going on. Lambert's cavalry and Harrison's militia caught the King at Warrington."

"What happened?" asked Peregrine breathlessly.

"Only a skirmish. Charles was outnumbered, and not ready to risk a battle. His men are tired—and he hasn't enough of them. He fell back along the London road first, but now he's turned west—for the Severn." Isabel's hand went to her throat. "Yes, he's moving this way. He'll probably make a stand near Worcester as his father did, hoping for recruits. He counts on it as good staunch Royalist country. I'm afraid he'll be disappointed."

"But the whole countryside will rally to him!" Peregrine cried.

"But they're not rallying. For one thing, he comes with a Scottish army. They don't like that. It smacks of—invasion."

"But in the King's own cause—"

"I know. You see that. I do. But the farm lads and

the villagers who ought to be flocking to him—they see
only Scots—Presbyterians—and cheerless discipline, ser-
mons, and moralities—worse than the Puritans, they say!
And here's another thing—so many people have had such
a hard lesson—fines, confiscation, imprisonment—those
that managed to save something out of the wreck after
Naseby aren't anxious to risk it again. I blame them. I
blame them bitterly for thinking of their own skins at
a time like this. But I can still see—"

"But, father, we've got men!" began Peregrine eagerly.
"We must go to him."

"Certainly I must go to him," was Richard's quiet
reply. "And about forty good lads with me."

"Oh, Richard, no—" moaned Isabel in soft despair.

"Ah, but the boy has proved himself a king, Isabel—
and a soldier! That was brave, to take a chance like
that. To go to Scotland in the beginning was to put his
head into the lion's mouth. And now he's come to England. If he is defeated now—he'll go the way his father
went."

Isabel looked up at him, her cheeks shining in the
candlelight with the slow tears she no longer tried to
wipe away.

"Yes, and what about the men who fight beside him?"
she whispered. "If he is defeated—they'll go the same
way."

"He mustn't be defeated," said Richard simply.

"Father—" Peregrine's eyes were bright; his slim
body was held erect. "Take me with you."

"No." There was no hesitation in Richard's refusal. "Your place is here."

"In case the King goes the way his father went!" Isabel reminded him resentfully. "And drags his loyal officers to the scaffold with him!"

"But Jamie Crawford is a captain now!" Peregrine protested.

"Jamie Crawford is a Puritan!" said Richard in a terrible voice. "Let him do as he likes, until he hangs!"

"Richard, they were playmates!" cried Isabel, horrified.

"I could always beat him, though!" Peregrine insisted. "Remember, father, when you gave us our first fencing lessons, here on the terrace?"

"You've come on since then," Richard admitted with pride. "The Puritans sing hymns instead."

"They know how to win a battle all the same," murmured Isabel.

"I grant you that," he agreed ruefully. "They're closing in on Charles from the north and the east. Even Worcester is no place for Royalists these days—some of them have been arrested. Ammunition is being taken away from those houses known to have a supply. I was right never to prepare Queen's Folly for a siege—it would be under suspicion now. We must trust to its luck once more to keep it safe, as in the dead King's time."

"There, mother, do you hear? He believes in the luck of the house just as I do!"

"Yes, but you'll stay here, luck or not," Richard told

him firmly. "We'll be short of men at harvest time—you must manage the best you can about that."

"Yes, father," said the boy submissively.

Richard laid off his cloak and sword-belt with a sigh, and sat down at the table. Instantly the business of the estate absorbed him in all its important trivialities.

"How's that cow with the cough?" he wanted to know. "Any better?"

"The veterinary has been here. He says she'll do all right. One of the greys has gone lame in the off fore."

"Have you been jumping him again?" Richard demanded sharply.

"No, father."

"You ought to break your neck if you do! Put your own mare at any fence or hedgerow you choose. But don't jump my greys; I won't have it. There's the storm," he added, almost with relief as another roll of thunder filtered into the quiet room. "That will clear the air."

And Isabel, whose nerves were astretch with the dread of marching men and clattering cavalry, thought of the Worcester guns and drew in her breath with a little sob.

"Richard, you've decided to go, I can see that. When?"

"Tomorrow morning." Her fingers went up to her mouth, and she stared at him piteously. He turned from her, already preoccupied, to Peregrine and the papers on the table. "That doesn't leave much time. Have you done the accounts?"

"Yes, father." He handed Richard the papers, one by one, with their neat totals at the bottom. "The dairy

—it's done very well lately. Poultry—I can't think why they're not laying better, it must be the weather. Old Hickson in the east cottage says his roof wants seeing to—"

"Hickson is the most unfortunate man on the place!" said Richard with some irritation. "There's always something wrong."

"Richard—" It was Isabel again, desperately, a soft hand tugging at his sleeve. "Are you going to work here all night? When did you eat last? Can't I get you something now?"

"Yes, my dear, that would be very kind of you." He gave her his charming smile, preoccupied. "Have the maids all gone to bed?"

"I don't mind doing it myself—there's a nice cold steak pie—or I could get you something hot in no time at all—" she offered eagerly.

"No, no, nothing hot on a night like this. Some ale— a bit of ham, perhaps—some bread and cheese—anything will do." His mind was on the papers in his hands, and she left the room with a long backward look, carrying her candle, her fear of the dark rooms beyond engulfed in the new fear which had come home with him.

More fighting, she thought, hurrying through the staircase hall where a draught nearly blew out her candle, and leaving the dining-room door wide open so that she could hear them if they called. Perhaps fighting as near as Worcester—perhaps. . . . In the kitchen she found another candle and another, and set them both alight on

158

the table while she worked. But was there no peace or sanity left in the world so that a man who was willing to mind his own business and keep his family in comfort and safety must be drawn into the maelstrom? If only Cromwell would die, she thought—if only the King had never come to Scotland. . . .

With cold hands that shook she set out a wooden kitchen-tray with half a loaf and one of the small new cheeses—he liked to make the first cut in a new cheese—found a cold ham in the latticed cupboard and carved it unevenly because her trembling fingers would not obey her will, arranged the ragged slices on a pewter plate with care, to tempt him—filled two tall silver tankards with ale, and wiped their bottoms with a cloth when her unsteady hands had slopped it. The small cosy sounds she made preparing the food were swallowed up in the brooding silence of the house and the mutter of the on-coming storm. Her tears dripped down unheeded on her lace collar. . . . He had not gone before—there was surely no need for him to go now—one man more or less could not matter to the King—one man to her was all the world. . . .

## II

Before the glimmer of her candle was out of sight he had forgotten her.

"That sick child down on the home farm"—he was saying to Peregrine over their papers, "—is it all right?"

"It died," Peregrine stated simply, and their eyes met.

"Ah, what a pity! The only one, wasn't it?"

"Yes. The mother rather broke my heart."

"You went down there at once?"

"Oh, yes. But there was nothing one could do. She kept saying, 'There's another on the way, but it won't be like my first again.' They're good people."

"Yes, we must look after them," said Richard, saddened. "See that she has everything she needs when the time comes, won't you."

"Yes, father."

Richard became absorbed in the papers again, noting careful totals, marking cattle to be sold, supplies and fuel which must be bought for the winter, trying to save a sum in four figures free for the King's use. But this time, obeying a strange, strong impulse, he meant to take it to the King in person. If the King came to Worcester he would want men who knew the countryside, men who could tell him where its strength and its weakness lay, where he would be safe, and whom he could trust. His father the first Charles had never known whom to trust.

They were all in it now, Richard knew, up to the neck. They had seen now what Cromwell could do in the way of reprisal. If this uprising failed, the whole face of England might be changed forever, with the Puritan rule. It was a last wild throw for the old days, the spacious kingly days with maypoles in the villages, and church-going kept in its proper place, and women dressed

like flowers instead of capped and garbed like scullery
maids. More than the young King's life was at stake
now. It was the life of England they were fighting for,
the England which had given birth to Queen's Folly, and
its happy village industry which had grown up during
the past century at the cross-roads at the end of the lane.
Fourteen houses there were now in Folly village, and its
own ale-house that was almost an inn, with clean beds
and a couple of horses for hire. Simple, thriving, laugh-
ter-loving people in his village—what would become of
them, and their friendly babies, if the Puritans overran
the land with their everlasting thou-shalt-nots?

"Father."

*Canvas to put young bay-trees in, 8d. Lent to the vicar
of Bretforton (to redeem him from the pursivant's hands)
and to be paid again at Lammas, 23 pounds*—doubtless
a bad debt, but the man had an ailing wife—

"Father, will you—be away long?"

"I can't tell." He laid his hand on Peregrine's sleeve
with a brief, hard grip, and gave the boy his whole attention. "Nobody knows. Things aren't going very well
with the King, I'm afraid. Peregrine—you have a right
to speak your mind on this. We were very lucky before,
when the war came this way. We kept out of it, and
lay low, and sent all we could spare to the King. I think
I'm justified in trusting once more to the luck of the
house, don't you?"

"There's no choice, is there?"

"For me, no. But I'm thinking of the house. In case

of a retreat from Worcester, it will be very nearly in their path again. I'm risking its life as well as mine. And it should be yours one day."

"But we've always been for the heir—even when little Edward VI died! Cromwell is a usurper and a murderer!"

"I hoped you'd feel that way," smiled Richard. "We must throw everything into the scales for the King. Every man, every penny, must go to his support. If he fails now there may not be any Queen's Folly anyway, by the end of the year. If he fails—it's quite possible that life in England won't be worth the living."

"You mean reprisals?"

"Yes, that and worse. Remember—if they should come here while I am away, see that there is no resistance from any quarter. Do nothing to provoke them. Keep even the maids and children in hand. Remember what happened at Greenways."

"I will," said Peregrine gravely, and there was a pause, while Richard returned to his papers.

Peregrine sat silent, facing his responsibilities. All his life he had known that the time must come when Queen's Folly would be his solely, to cherish and protect. But that time had seemed a long way off, a charge to come when he was a man in his forties at least, as his father had been when grandfather Nicholas died, only a few years ago. Nicholas was seventy when he died, and he had inspected the farms and kept a searching eye on the accounts right up to the end. For the first time Peregrine was sharply aware of himself in the sequence

162

of Brands, as the last Brand if anything should happen to his father. For the first time he felt inadequate and small, and yet oddly exalted, before his tremendous heritage. The only son of the only son of the only son. . . .

"Father—Anthony's been round tonight."

"Has he?" said Richard, smiling, without looking up.

"It upsets mother."

"I know!"

"I can't imagine being frightened of him myself. I sometimes think he's part of the luck."

"That's the luck up there," said Richard, pointing with his pen at the portrait of the Queen. "Don't ever let anything happen to her, will you."

"No, father."

"We shouldn't do well without her," said Richard seriously. "The half year's wages will fall due soon. We must allow for that." He wrote, at the top of a fresh page—*"To Edward Hobden (gardener) for his half year's wages, due Michaelmas, 4 pounds. To John Cope, (coachman) for the same, 3 pounds, 6s. To Tom Evans, (swineherd) for his quarter's wages, due Martinmas, 6s., 8d. To—"*

"Father. You'll be sure to come back?" said Peregrine impulsively.

"Oh, yes, I'll come back. But you can see, can't you, how necessary it is for you to stay here. There's no one but you to look after the place."

"I suppose so."

"It's not going to be a very gay war, Peregrine. Not

163

like when the bad old kings used to go junketing in France. Civil war is a grimmer business, setting friend against friend."

"You're thinking of Jamie Crawford."

"Yes. I liked his father—killed at Naseby."

"He was on the wrong side," said Peregrine.

"He didn't think so." Richard drew a long breath. "No, it's a dreary business altogether, and the Scots make it drearier. Not much to choose between a Scots Presbyterian and a London Puritan, people will tell you! The only real difference is that the Scots will fight for the King till all's blue because they hate the Puritans so! The King rides with his life at his saddle-bow. If he's taken—" He snapped his fingers. "One good hot battle should decide it."

"Soon?"

"Very soon, I think. So you see, I may be home again before you can turn round. What's this thing—the kitchen-book?" They exchanged smiles over Isabel's efforts. "What a mess!"

"She means to fill it in," Peregrine explained gently, "but then she can't always remember—"

"Four shillings, sixpence," said Richard, "for 'a pound of sweet powders.' What sweet powders would that be?"

"I've no idea!" grinned Peregrine.

" 'To Thomas, for nursing of his child, fifteen shillings,' " read Richard, and his smile faded.

"The one that died."

"I should have been here."

164

"We did all we could, father."

"I'll go down myself in the morning. Aren't there any totals?" he queried, fluttering the pages of the kitchen-book.

"I was just beginning on them when you came."

At this point Isabel returned with the tray, and Peregrine cleared a place for it on the corner of the table. She saw the book in Richard's hands and relapsed into confusion.

"Oh, that," she said. "I'm sorry, Richard, I—I've got a little behind with it again."

"It looks as though it had been slept in," he remarked without animus, and then added, as her lower lip quivered piteously, "Never mind, my dear, I know you hate it, but—" Thunder ripped the air and died away, and a sudden wind lashed against the casements so that the long hangings stirred, and lightning danced continuously in the cracks where curtain met curtain. The candles flickered in the draught from the door Isabel had left open behind her, and she went hastily to close it, and returned as hastily to the table again for the sake of proximity to her menfolk. "This won't do the roads any good," said Richard philosophically, "but it may break the heat. Wind's come up." He lifted his tankard thankfully and let the cool ale slip down his throat.

"Richard—" Isabel touched his sleeve, and sat down beside him, drawing her chair close to his. "You won't be away long, will you?"

"I hope not, sweeting." He gave her his hand, palm

up, in a spasm of tenderness for all women and what they had to bear. "Shall we all go up to London for the coronation?" He was smiling at her too, kindly, bantering, affectionate, but not giving full value to unspoken things between them. It was a way he had.

She clung to his free hand while he drank again, her eyes on the glitter of her rings against his strong fingers, the points of light from her diamonds blurred with her tears and dancing in the candlelight. He hated crying and a fuss, she knew. But she was no Spartan woman, to conceal her love and watch him ride away with a smiling face. She was a poor weak fool, she knew, but she worshipped him, and the touch of his hand could still set her pulses leaping like a girl's. She wondered with a sudden, searing terror what would become of her if ever she beheld him stiff and cold in death, blood stained, perhaps, battle-scarred, mutilated. . . . Or worse—she shivered and gasped in the clutch of her own foreboding —suppose she knew him still alive but condemned to die on the scaffold? For a hideous moment her imagination fumbled innocently at the dreadful pageant of execution, and herself powerless to save him from the fall of the axe. . . .

"Wh-what will they do to Cromwell," she heard her own voice asking shakily, "if the King wins?"

"I can guess," he smiled. "Can't you?"

"That won't bring the first Charles back again," she shivered.

"Charles the Second will do, my dear." Gently he withdrew his hand to cut himself a piece of cheese.

Peregrine stood up, the other tankard held high.

"The King!" he cried.

"The King!" echoed his father solemnly, rising, and they drank, while the thunder roared again over Cotswold on a livid flash of lightning.

But Isabel sat motionless, staring down at the blur of rings on her fingers gripped together in her lap.

## III

For the next two weeks life went on at Queen's Folly the best it could. Old men and boys tended the cattle and struggled with the harvest and the early autumn planting, for a troop of forty-three hands had ridden off with Richard Brand to join the King. Peregrine was out from dawn till dusk, astride his chestnut mare with the white feather on her forehead and one white foot.

The King reached Worcester on August twenty-second with a tired army, most of which had come all the way from Scotland by forced marches, with skirmishes on the way. The city opened its gates to him and saw him comfortably lodged within its walls. For several days he was busy there, inspecting its fortifications which had been proven negligible ten years before, and appealing to the countryside for recruits. Meanwhile Cromwell drew up on him relentlessly with horse, foot, and militia outnum-

bering the Royalists nearly three to one, and installed
himself at Evesham.

By the first of September there was talk in Folly village of a siege of Worcester; then there was a wild re-
port running across the fields of a battle on the Severn
and terrible slaughter of the King's men; rumours of the
King's death on the field, other rumours that he had got
away safe into Wales, still others that he had gone to
London in disguise. But no one seemed to have been to
Worcester, no one had seen the King himself, no one
had any first hand information.

On the morning of the seventh, Isabel sat at her embroidery frame in the light from the big window in the
Queen's parlour, trying to keep her mind on her needlework. Her sweet mouth drooped piteously, and every
now and then she sniffed, the aftermath of a recent storm
of tears because Richard was not there to garland the
portrait for the birthday ceremony as was his custom.
Peregrine had done it instead. They were both still hoping, subconsciously, that Richard would return in time
to take his place for the toast when the wine came in at
three.

Isabel looked up quickly as Peregrine crossed the
threshold. She knew the difference in their step well
enough, but she hoped that his face would tell her at a
glance that there was no need to worry any longer. Instead, he still wore the set, secretive look which concealed
his own anxiety.

"Thomas is back from the village," he said in answer to her questioning eyes.

"Is there news?"

"Nothing definite." He sat down heavily in a chair by the table, so that she could not see his face at all.

"But, Peregrine—what has *happened* at Worcester?" she insisted fearfully.

"Nobody seems to know exactly."

"But we know the King was there! A whole army can't just vanish!" she cried hysterically.

"Mother—" Visibly, he nerved himself to it. "The King's army was wiped out three days ago at Worcester. The Puritans were three or four to one. The Royalists and the Scots were massacred, or they laid down their arms, or they fled." She was staring at him incredulously, her lips aquiver. He struggled on, making flat, cold statements to keep his voice under control. "The King's body has not been found among the dead. He has not been taken prisoner. So he must be a fugitive, and there is a price on his head. One thousand pounds is offered for his capture—dead or alive. It's treason and the block to shelter or succour him. The King is being hunted like a common thief, from ditch to ditch—"

"The King!" she cried impatiently. "I don't care about the King! Where is your father?"

"I've hardly dared to think about him."

"Peregrine!"

"I hated to tell you, I didn't want to, I—it was more than I could bear alone!" He turned in his chair to face

her at last. "It may be days before we can know what
has happened to him. He may be dead—or taken prisoner—or he may be alive, somewhere with the King.
Some of them got away—the ones that had horses. There
are little bands of mounted Puritans beating the country
for Charles—or for any Royalist they can find. The country people are afraid to harbour a fugitive from Worcester. One poor devil was discovered hiding in a hay-loft
the other side of the village—and the farm hands murdered him on the spot, for fear of Cromwell's men. That
wasn't father. Thomas made sure. The lists of prisoners
will be posted. I could ride into Worcester and see—"

"No, no! He said you were to stay here!"

"Are we to sit down and do nothing, then?" he asked
hopelessly, and she leaned her head against her bent arm
on the embroidery frame. "If only I'd gone with him—"

"No, no, no—suppose I lost you both—oh, God, don't
let him be dead—bring him back home, in pity's name—
I love him so—I love him so—" Her voice died away.
She was not crying.

He rose draggingly, and laid his arm about her shoulders. There were no more words for them to speak.

Slowly the sun passed its zenith and began to slip
down the western sky. Somehow they ate another meal,
still silent, served by a maid who snivelled at the sideboard and no one rebuked her.

When the meal was over Isabel returned to her embroidery in the Queen's parlour, for the steady dip and
draw of the needle and long strand of wool seemed to

hold her nerves together. The wine stood ready on the table now. Peregrine wandered restlessly about the house, waiting, waiting. For a long time he stood on the grass at the western end outside the windows of the room where his mother sat. The ground sloped down in a grassy glade, before it met the lower edge of the enfolding hill beyond. He and his father had talked of making a fish-pond there, with a fountain, or possibly a formal garden with a pleached walk. . . .

At last he turned and walked slowly toward the old front of the house, guarded by its ancient yews, and the tidy lane which ran unobtrusively away round a bend to the village and then with another bend joined the road which a mile further on met the Evesham highway. Beyond that lay Worcester and its tragic uncertainties.

As he turned the corner he stiffened and paused, and a little chill ran through him. Someone was coming toward the house, keeping to the shelter of the trees which lined the lane. Someone who stumbled and caught at tree-trunks as he passed, and whose sword was bundled under his arm instead of hanging properly at his side. A man with long hair and a buff-coat—a Cavalier—a fugitive from the battle, seeking shelter, laying a trail perhaps to bring the Puritans down on the house.

That was Peregrine's first thought. His second was of the sliding panel where the man might be safe—safe from the cautious country folk as well as from the Puritans. He must be got into the house quickly before he was seen, however, before he fell to the ground and could not be got up again. Peregrine started toward him, everything else forgotten in a rush of generous pity for a hunted fellow being. Then with a sobbing cry he began to run. The broken Cavalier was his father.

Richard was wounded in the left side, with a clumsy bloodstained bandage showing under his unbuttoned buff-coat. He was hatless, muddy, dishevelled, with a look of death already on his face, three days unshaven. His left arm, almost useless, was bent to hold the sword and scabbard in the dangling belt which the wound prevented him from wearing.

They met silently in the shadow of the great yew a few hundred feet from the corner of the house. In silence Richard surrendered himself to the eager strength of his son's embrace. Together they staggered across the grass and fumbled their way through the door into the vaulted hall.

"In there—" gasped Richard, and Peregrine guided him to the door of the Queen's parlour, his spurs and harness clinking as they went, so that Isabel was on her feet with a stifled cry, and reached his side a second later.

Gently they lowered him into a chair by the table, and Isabel flung herself on her knees beside him, babbling incoherent prayers and foolish words of pity and comfort, while Peregrine poured some wine from the decanter on the table. Richard drained the glass, and Peregrine, braced against the edge of the table beside him, supported him with an arm round his shoulders.

"Is there news of the King?" asked Richard, as soon as he could speak.

"No, father, not here. When was he last seen?"

"I saw him—at the gate—coming out of Worcester. It was getting dark. We had decided to scatter to escape notice—I begged him not to go back to Scotland, they'll turn against him now. But he's not safe anywhere—nowhere but in France—"

"Richard, you must get to bed at once!" wept Isabel. "You're bleeding!"

"Bed?" he echoed grimly. "I've no time for bed."

Peregrine's encircling arm tightened.

"Father, what happened? Where have you been ever since the battle?"

"Trying to get home—travelling by night—"

"On foot?"

"I seem to have crawled most of the way—in ditches —oh, I had a horse for a while—" He tried to smile. "The King gave it me, after mine was killed under me. That was early in the fight. He led four charges himself, but it was no use, Cromwell kept bringing up fresh men. The King saw me go down, and he caught a riderless horse by the bridle and swung it round beside him—I heard him cry, 'Up with you, man, I can't hold this brute!'—and I got into the saddle somehow, and he was gone—" He sagged in the chair, still smiling. "It's a fine long lad, Isabel—I wonder if I thanked him—"

"Peregrine—his wound—make him go to bed!"

"I've no time, I tell you," Richard insisted faintly.

"I've been so long getting home—at first I didn't dare move by daylight—once they followed me for hours— thought I was the King—same height—same kind of coat—finally I lost them—but the horse gave out and I had to leave it—came on alone, as fast as I could— time getting short, and so much to do—Peregrine—"

"I'm here, father."

"Want to talk to you—Isabel, set somebody to watch the road—the county's thick with Puritans—they're searching the barns and houses—go keep an eye on things —don't let them take us by surprise—"

"But, Richard—"

"Please go—must talk to the boy—" And when she had gone in a swift rustle of silk—"More wine," he said, and drained the glass again. "That's better—got to keep my wits a little longer—"

"Father, don't you think you'd better rest—"

"My boy, I'm dying—only a miracle I lasted as long as this—no, you're not to grieve—your mother will do enough of that—take care of her, won't you—I—I should have been kinder—"

"Kinder! She adores you!"

"I know—that made it harder. Peregrine—when you have a wife be good to her—do the best you can—be- cause whatever you do, it isn't enough. You'll come to see what I mean—try not to let her feel that we—that you love the house more than you do her. See what I mean?"

"Yes, father."

"We Brands—wed the house when we come of age—to cherish and protect. Gradually it grows on us—yes, it's begun with you already—it takes possession of us, till the feel of a newel-post under our hand is like the feel of a woman's shoulder—hard and cool and very precious. And sooner or later our wives find it out. That way we miss a great deal out of a man's life—but the house doesn't care about that. Are you listening?"

"Yes, father."

"We belong to the house, never forget that—never leave it to the care of someone else, outside the family—tend it yourself, as long as you live. And whatever happens, be sure to come home to die." He gasped with pain and struggled on. "You must marry—I wanted a happy wife for you—I hoped for someone who might not be jealous of Queen's Folly, but perhaps that was unreasonable. Anyway,—how about Henry Blount's youngest girl?"

"Jane Blount?"

"She's a very pretty girl—don't you think so?"

"She's very young, father—not more than sixteen."

"That's all the better—bring her here while she's still young and teachable. Your mother will show her the ways of the place. Jane might really come to like it, we can't tell—and she's half in love with you already."

"But I hardly ever see her!" protested Peregrine, humouring him.

"True—but she looks at you when she gets a chance—see her oftener—understand?"

"Yes, father."

"She might be happy here—don't you think so?" He clung wistfully to the idea.

"I can try," said Peregrine.

"That's what I mean—you must try. I've been too careless—it wasn't right—your mother's a dear soul, Peregrine."

"Father, you mustn't regret things—mother wouldn't have had you different."

"I know—she's loyal—always was—but be good to Jane, won't you."

"Yes, father."

"Teach your son to love and care for the place as I've taught you—begin when he's only a baby—let him make friends with the tenantry, give them a chance to know him, as they know you—I used to take you round the cottages on my shoulder before you could walk—they look to us, you know—we're all they've got to look to, these days—we must father and mother them all—teach him that."

"Yes, father."

"And show him how to use a sword—make him sweat at it while he's little, you can't begin too soon—we're a long way from the old Court brawls and secret duels—but it never does a man any harm to be a good swordsman—you can hold your own with the best—you can teach him as I taught you—can't you—"

"Yes, father."

"I wanted to see him—"

176

His head fell forward on Peregrine's arm, and the boy leaned above him, cherishing his weight, his cheek against Richard's hair, dry-eyed, but with an agonizing ache in his throat that made speech impossible. He knew without argument now that it was too late for surgeons and bandaging and nursing to save the life that was slipping away with each laboured breath. His father would die here within the hour, in his arms, while the portrait of the great Queen looked on. It was too late now to get him up the stairs to his own bed and what comfort there was left for him. Too late for anything but promises, and soothing words, and a quiet waiting. The constriction in his throat was like a strangling hand.

"Is that cow all right?" asked Richard faintly, and Peregrine found that he could not answer. "You won't forget to have them mend the stile into the south field—somebody will get a bad fall if it goes on as it is—those people on the home farm—make sure she has everything she needs when the new baby comes—and you'll always remember the Queen's birthday, won't you—"

Isabel ran in, white-faced.

"Richard! They're coming! A dozen Puritans, along the lane from the Evesham road—you must hide—Peregrine, we must get him behind the panel—quickly!" She tugged away the chair to the right of the mantelpiece, pressed a spring, and the panel slid back. "Quick, Peregrine, I tell you there's no time to lose!"

"I led them here," Richard was saying sadly to himself. "They followed me home—I was wrong to come by the road—but the fields were—confusing—the fields were—so wide to cross—the hedges—I couldn't get through the hedges—I never meant to lead them here—"

Peregrine lifted him to his feet, and with Isabel on the other side they got him through the narrow opening. Peregrine swooped after the sword left lying on the table and handed it after him. Isabel slid back the panel, Peregrine replaced the chair.

"What shall we do?" she quavered, too frightened now for tears.

"Sit there, by the embroidery frame. Look as though you had not moved for hours," he directed. "Keep still, and let me talk to them."

She took her place obediently, fumbled a moment with the needle and began the slow, steadying dip-and-draw of her tapestry stitch. Peregrine got pen and ink and an account-book from the sideboard and settled himself at the big table just in time.

There was a crunch of horses' feet on the gravel outside, a shout, a maidservant's half-choked cry of alarm, a man's brusque voice. The two in the Queen's parlour sat still. The faces which they turned toward the door as the Puritan captain strode across the threshold wore just the correct amount of well-bred surprise at the intrusion.

The Captain was a lean, fiery zealot, with the light of a fine fanaticism in his eyes. He was young, in his early twenties, but he seemed much older from campaigning and self-denial. He was severely dressed in a plain buff-coat with a white linen collar, boots, sword, and spurs, and a helmet on his close-cropped hair. The two armed troopers in cuirasses and helmets who followed him took up their stand either side of the door.

"I am sorry to disturb you, madam," he said crisply to Isabel, who did not rise, "but we have reason to believe that Charles Stuart is refuging in this house."

"You are quite wrong, sir," said Peregrine courteously, on his feet behind the table.

"It will be much pleasanter and simpler for everyone concerned," said the Captain, still addressing himself to Isabel, "if you will surrender him at once."

"But surely—" Conviction and relief were growing on her face. "—surely—aren't you Jamie Crawford?"

"I am," he admitted with a stiff bow.

"Peregrine, are you blind?" she cried with an almost hysterical relief. "It's Jamie, all grown up! Lud, boy, how you have changed!"

"Of course it's Jamie!" cried Peregrine cordially. "How was I to know him in his captain's face? Have a glass of wine with us, Jamie!"

"I have come for the Stuart," said Crawford, unmoved by their unwarranted relief.

"Don't be silly, Jamie, the King is not here," said Isabel easily. "Nobody knows where he is."

"If this is to be your attitude, madam, I shall have to search the house. And if I fail to find the man I seek I shall smoke him out by burning it to the ground!"

There was a stunned silence. "And now, madam, will you lead me to the Stuart?"

"Jamie, you must take my word for it," said Peregrine. "My word of honour that the King is not here."

"He is not the King!" shouted Crawford hotly. "Except in Scotland! And he was seen coming this way on foot less than an hour ago."

"That's not true," said Peregrine, still polite.

"Somebody's told you wrong, Jamie," Isabel assured him in her soft, lisping voice. "I've not been out of this room since dinner."

"I can rely on my information. And the Royalist sympathies of this house are well known."

"But, Jamie—"

"You think because I came here as a child," he broke in roughly, "before ever the war began—because you fed me strawberries, madam, and he lent me a horse to ride—you think you'll be let off now! Well, you're wrong!" He swung round on Peregrine. "And by the way, where is your father? My business is with him today, not with women and boys!"

"My father is not here," said Peregrine very quietly, after a moment's hesitation which passed the insult over.

"That means he was at Worcester—doesn't it! I looked for him there, but I didn't see him. Have you had word of him since the battle?"

"No."

"Dead, maybe?"

"Maybe."

"That leaves you and me. And I'm a soldier. Why weren't you at the fighting?"

"My father—wished me to stay here."

"Ah, yes, the heir!" cried Crawford, as though just recollecting. "I've heard about you Brands, and your wicked idolatry of the worldly goods bestowed on your family by that Jezebel, the old Queen! Why, I remember you used to—" His eyes sought the portrait, which looked back at him remotely from its garland, and he stared up at it while his anger and fanaticism grew. "Ah, yes—your customs haven't changed, have they! This is a Royalist house indeed!" He turned on Isabel savagely. "Will you give me the Stuart, madam, or must I take him?"

"But, Jamie, he's not here—" she faltered, thoroughly terrified again.

Crawford's eye fell on the chair where Richard had sat. He bent to look more closely at the cushion of its seat, ran a hand along the polished walnut arm—his fingers came away with a smear of blood on them. He straightened, and flung a command at the troopers.

"Search the house! And if you find nothing—*fire* the house!"

"Jamie, you can't—" began Peregrine, in incredulous horror.

The panel slid back and Richard stumbled through the opening into the room, his sword in its belt and scabbard still huddled against his left side.

"That's a waste of time, Jamie. You see, it wasn't the King, after all."

Everyone stared at him, paralyzed. Crawford recovered first.

"I'm sorry, sir—you'll have to come with me."

"To Oxford?"

"Yes."

"*Richard—!*" sobbed Isabel, for Oxford meant only one thing, but no one heeded her.

"Jamie, will I do instead?" Peregrine inquired quietly.

"You?" said Crawford, astonished.

"My father is—dying," Peregrine explained. "If you want a head for the scaffold in Oxford, you'd better take me."

"No, no!" cried Richard desperately, lurching forward so that the sword rattled down on the table as he leaned there. "The boy is not a soldier—you've no right to touch him, he was not at Worcester—" He struggled for breath, while Crawford hesitated. "He's right, though—I shall never reach Oxford alive—if you can contrive an hour's delay—searching the barns and vicinity—I'll spare you the trouble—"

Crawford stood in the middle of the room, debating. He was young, but not inexperienced in the hard ways of war. In the old days it was true he had been a welcome, pampered guest in this house, and the shattered man before him was old enough to be his father. His father . . . who had died for the cause this family opposed, and opposed with ridicule, which was the unforgivable offence and had led to bitter quarrels and complete estrangement. . . .

"Will you ride your own horse, sir, or one of mine?" said Crawford.

Isabel threw herself on her knees beside him, catching at his swordbelt with frantic hands, for here was the thing she had dreaded most—Oxford—the mockery of a political trial—the block.

"Jamie, in pity's name—is this the boy I loved like my own? Jamie, we were friends once, you and I—we played games in the orchard when you were little—you could always run faster than Peregrine, do you remember, your legs were longer than his then—and once you remembered my birthday—" She was sobbing, her face buried against the rough cloth of his uniform, holding him fast by the belt while he stood uncertain, embarrassed, looking down at her. "Don't do this to me, Jamie —don't do it—it isn't much I'm asking of you—just that he may be left in peace to die here, and not on the road —not on the scaffold—for me, Jamie—or else take me to Oxford too, for I don't want to live, remembering—"

She went on sobbing, clinging to him, till he raised her gently, glanced behind him and signed to a trooper, who brought a chair. Crawford put her into it, and she went on weeping into her hands.

Then with a jangle of spurs in the tense silence, Crawford moved to the table and Richard faced him across it. For a moment they looked into each other's eyes and

Crawford read death in Richard's. His gaze dropped briefly to the bloodstained bandage and returned.

"And I have your word of honour there's no other man from Worcester hiding here?"

"You have."

A moment more the Captain stood, reconciling his Puritan conscience with his humane impulse. His was not a sentimental creed. Then he saw a way to score a point both ways, and still not carry with him to his grave the dreadful guilt of Isabel's hopeless grief.

"Very well," he said slowly. "I'll take my men and go. But first—" Fanaticism flared again in his eyes. "—first I'll purge this house of its pagan worship of a dead Queen! It's the next thing to Papistry—it's worse than Papistry, because the woman was a whore! Have down that picture there!" he cried to the troopers. "Have down that graven image and take it out into the stable yard and burn it!"

*"Not while I live!"* Richard's voice was once more miraculously the firm, confident voice of an able-bodied man. It needed only a few steps backward for him to stand against the mantelpiece, his right arm flung out along its edge protectively even while it supported the weight of his racked body.

The advancing troopers halted in their tracks, nonplussed.

"Well, what are you waiting for?" Crawford demanded of them angrily, to cover his own realization that he had irretrievably blundered. "Shove the table

184

over and up with you, you can come at it from there!"

"You shall not touch the portrait!" cried Peregrine, darting forward to intercept them.

"Out of the way, milksop!" Crawford reached out and caught him by the shoulder, throwing him back so roughly that Peregrine nearly lost his footing.

"Stop where you are!" cried Peregrine with a force which halted the uncomfortable troopers again. He crossed swiftly to where the sword lay on the table. "By your leave, father—" He drew the blade, still caked with blood from Worcester fight, and replaced the scabbard on the table. "Now, then, Jamie—who said milksop?" There was dead silence in the room. "Would you like to lay off some of the weight you're carrying," he added meaningly, "or will you fight me as you are?"

"Oh, no, Peregrine—Jamie—please—!" begged Isabel, her sobs wrenched off by this new crisis.

Peregrine took a step forward as Crawford did not answer and his voice rose sharply.

"Will you fight me like a gentleman and not a Puritan, Jamie, or will you have a slap in the face as well? Tell me, Jamie, how does one insult a Puritan so as to make him remember that he was once a gentleman like the rest of us?"

They faced each other furiously, two boys who had once been friends, who felt the old bonds of common everyday things tugging at their new quarrel—of laughter shared and good-natured trials of strength, of stolen fruit and secret childish escapades, and the silent companionship of childish weariness at the end of glorious summer days with a dog in the fields. Their eyes held for a long, heart-breaking moment, while each put that behind him and chose instead the bitter reality of their manhood.

"Clear the room!" said Crawford briefly, to the troopers.

He waved the table back toward the mantelpiece where Richard stood, and Isabel rose hurriedly as one of the men approached her chair. Crawford removed his helmet, sword-belt, and buff-coat, and drew his blade. Peregrine tossed his own coat to Richard, braced against the mantelpiece, his face a mixture of pride and sadness. Isabel was viewing the preparations with terror.

"Richard, they mean it—they'll kill one another— Richard, for God's sake, don't let them go on with this —they're only babies after all—Richard, they used to play together, can't you stop them—"

"Be quiet, Isabel," he said peremptorily. "And keep back out of their way."

Crawford and Peregrine stepped out into the middle of the room in their shirts, and the troopers backed slowly toward the doorway where they remained on guard.

"Now, Jamie," Peregrine was saying quite calmly, "if I spit you, you take your men and go. The Queen's picture stays where it is, and my father is left in peace. Do you agree?"

186

"I agree," snapped Crawford, and Richard spoke from the mantelpiece.

"Give the order to your men, Jamie—before you fight. See that they understand the terms."

"You heard the terms," said Crawford tersely to his troopers, and they nodded sullen acquiescence.

"And the boy goes free," Richard insisted, "even if he kills you."

"Very well. But if I kill him the whole house burns!" cried Crawford.

The blades came together.

Peregrine was easy, confident, smiling, against his opponent's visible anger. He did not hate Jamie, nor wish to wound him needlessly. Blood must be drawn, he supposed, and he meant it to be Jamie's blood, for Jamie needed a lesson that Puritans could not tramp through other people's houses giving preposterous orders. He knew well enough that in the unforeseen exigencies of a genuine sword duel, where a man might slip or miss his parry, even a simple routine thrust might prove fatal. But when he first crossed swords with his old playmate, the idea—allowing for accidents—that he and Jamie might kill each other seemed utterly fantastic.

The first two clauses went to Crawford, on vicious lunges before which Peregrine gave ground lightly, but in some surprise. Jamie was in earnest. Jamie had lost his temper as usual, and could no longer be depended on even to fight fair. Jamie was never a good loser, as he well remembered. In the old days you always engaged in even a friendly scuffle with Jamie at your own risk, because if you looked like winning Jamie would go berserk and you probably got hurt. Peregrine's smiling lips set a little grimly. For the first time it really came home to him that this was no friendly bout on the terrace with his father standing by to strike up their swords. This completely unreal thing, which his sane, country-bred nature still boggled at, was happening—he was fighting for his life against the Commonwealth. The knowledge was like a cold douche down his spine. He was a split second slow as the blades met for the third time, and Jamie's point ripped his loose sleeve. That steadied him, for Jamie had gone for his heart. Did Jamie think he would stand like a dolt and be killed before his father's eyes, and by a thrust they had both learnt on the same day ten years ago, here on the terrace at Queen's Folly? Had Jamie nothing new to kill him with? Because—it was an exhilarating thought—he had a few new ones to show Jamie.

"He's better than you'd think, father, for a psalm-singing soldier," said Peregrine coolly, above the ring of the steel. "Did you see that? You taught him that, out on the terrace here—*and* that!—come, Jamie, what about a few army tricks? Or don't you learn much fencing in your army? What, the same one *again?*—"

Even while Isabel gasped with horror at the violence of Crawford's attack, Richard was conscious of a dim relief. Propped against the mantelpiece, giddy with his own pain, he stood with his eyes narrowed, the whole of his remaining strength concentrated on watching the bitter fruit of his own teaching. Jamie was fighting as he had always fought even in play—wildly, spectacularly, with a slashing fury. He had learnt nothing about fencing since his boyhood. He still could not entirely control either his temper or his point. His military rapier was heavier than the one in Peregrine's hand, and with it his old-fashioned cut and thrust could wear Peregrine down very soon, tiring him unbearably. But if Peregrine kept his head and relied on his nimble wrist, perfected in neatness and dexterity only last year by a French fencing-master down from London, it was possible for him to end the affair almost when he chose. End it, that is, forever. The French reply to Jamie's somewhat open flamboyant style, if it came, would be no tactful flesh wound.

"Mother, you'll have to move," Peregrine was saying above the hiss and rattle of the blades. "Captain Crawford is coming your way—mind the embroidery frame behind you, Jamie—*and* the stool—he's good, father—he's ve-ry good—"

Both boys were breathing hard now, but it was Crawford who was giving ground. Peregrine had discovered with satisfaction that Jamie's years of soldiering seemed to have done little but increase his brute force. He had gained nothing in that finesse which was becoming the fashion in France.

They turned back across the middle of the room, Peregrine kicking the stool out of his way as he went, and Crawford made a desperate stand, while to Richard's agonized eyes Peregrine seemed to flag. The heavy army sword was having its effect, and Peregrine's right arm had begun to ache from shoulder to finger-tips, but his voice when it came again was still cool.

"Damn you, Jamie, you've drawn first blood—but I can kill you if I must—his guard was always high, do you remember, father?"

Richard suppressed an almost intolerable impulse to cry out to him to save his foolish breath, and to finish the fight quickly, quickly. . . . A better directed thrust than Jamie's would have made that last result in a disabling wound, and Richard's heart had stood still. On what he himself had taught them, they were too evenly matched —but behind Peregrine's superb self-possession there was still the Frenchman with his dainty, dancing-master tactics, his economy of effort, his dexterous wrist and deadly point.

The pain in Peregrine's right arm had become a burning torture, sapping its strength and resilience, making nothing of the prickle of the deep scratch near the elbow which was bleeding freely down his white shirt-sleeve. He could not go on much longer, and there was but one answer to that—Jamie's reckless high guard, his occasionally wide open breast. *I can kill you if I must*—he had heard his own words with astonishment. But it was no longer just Jamie he was fighting, it was the thing Jamie stood for—the iron-clad, wrong-headed, barbarous Cause which had struck down his father and which now threat-

190

ened the house. It was not just that Jamie was being a
fool, he had become malignant.

For a minute more they fought with no sound but
their own laboured breathing, the stamp and shift of their
feet on the floor, the unceasing clatter of the blades. Then
Peregrine lunged in *tierce*, and Crawford dropped his
sword and stood swaying, a hand to his side.

There was a little cry from Isabel, and the troopers
ran to catch their captain as he sagged to the floor. Peregrine waited, his point down, his left hand clasping his
sword arm, panting for breath to speak—

"I'm sorry, Jamie—you were crowding me—"

"Mount the men," gasped Crawford, twisted with
pain, to the trooper who bent above him. The two hesitated, on the point of mutiny, with a sullen glance toward Peregrine, and Crawford stiffened in a last effort
at authority. "You heard my order, damn you—before
we fought—the boy has won—get me to my horse—
quickly—"

He collapsed in their arms, and they carried him out.

Peregrine brought his sword to the salute. He was not
a soldier, he had never been to war, he had grown up
in the country and needless slaughter with a fowling-
piece had never appealed to him. Now he had fought
a duel and, barring a miracle of recovery, he had killed
his man. Like many an older and more experienced
swordsman before him, he felt a little sick.

While Peregrine still stood staring at the doorway
through which Jamie Crawford had been borne feet fore-

most, Richard fell to the floor beside the mantelpiece and lay still. Isabel ran to him and lifted his head in her arms. He was dead. She buried her face against him silently, rocking to and fro in her grief.

Peregrine stood where he was in the middle of the room, looking down at them, nursing his wounded sword arm in his other hand. He and his father had taken leave of each other alone together, with Jamie Crawford on the way. His father had died serene in the knowledge that the house was still theirs, and safe, and that the Queen—he raised his face to the portrait and a small, wry smile came to his lips—the Queen had still got a roof over her head.

*1936*

# III

## *1936*

### COTSWOLD COUNTRY

*THIS historic specimen of beautiful architecture dating from the XVth century, carefully modernized, maintained in perfect order.*

Formerly a priory, with the original vaulting, stone mullions, and trefoiled windows of the period, this small manor house built of grey Cotswold stone is seated within its own estate of 300 acres. Considerable sums have been spent on the property by successive owners. Near a pretty village, amidst rural surroundings, it represents the acme of modern comfort. The gardens are old and sunny, a superb setting for the house.

Beautiful period rooms, original oak
Jacobean lounge, 26 x 35, containing 2 fireplaces
Very choice panelling and mantels throughout
9 master's bedrooms, 7 bathrooms
Exceptional central heating
Constant hot water
Company's electric light and water, telephone
Modern drainage
Rose garden, wild garden, long herbaceous borders
Yew hedges, topiary work
Tennis court and croquet lawn
Walled kitchen garden, orchard in full bearing
Model home farm and dairy

Hunting with the N. Cotswold Pack
A large beat of shooting can be obtained adjoining

TO BE LET FURNISHED FOR THE SUMMER MONTHS OR LONGER

Inspected and confidently recommended by the sole agents, Milder & Waring, —— Mount St., London, W.

April 30, 1936

Dear Mr. Brand—

Re your advertisement in *Country Life*, we have received a highly satisfactory offer from an American lady, Mrs. Temple of New York. All the information concerning references, etc., is to hand at this office, in case you wish to go into it yourself, but we, as your agents, beg to assure you that we are entirely satisfied that you would be placing the house in the hands of a most desirable tenant.

The only difficulty regarding the terms of the usual lease is the period of occupancy, as Mrs. Temple seems very uncertain that she will be able to remain in the house for the full three months required in the lease. She offers, however, a guarantee of three months' rental in the event of her departure before the expiration of the lease.

Mrs. Temple is accompanied by her niece, and they would like to take possession as soon as possible, if you are satisfied, and if the house on inspection comes up to their expectations. They have directed us to say that if it is convenient to you they will drive down to Queen's

Folly from London on Monday or Tuesday of next week.
Assuring you of our prompt attention at all times,

Faithfully yours,

M. A. Milder.

His eyes went from the letter in his hand to the window which he faced across the top of his writing-table, drawn up close beneath it, in the little west room with the oriel. There was a litter of bills and account-books under his elbows, and the gaze he rested on the rolling landscape outside was full of a tender possessiveness— the gaze of a lover on the face of his mistress. From that window to the skyline of the enfolding hills, it was all Queen's Folly land.

Just so Anthony had sat, spring after spring nearly four centuries ago, patiently accounting for threepences, while the first pale primroses and scattered cowslips gave place to the gay golden smear of mustard across the greening fields, and the damask rose, the Lancaster red rose, outside the window laid its first crimson blossom along the grey stone mullions. Richard had sat there in his turn, blessed with a sense of financial security which was part of Nicholas's legacy to him and which had been built up by years of vigilant love and forethought, intelligent economy and a lavish spending at need; plagued at the same time with the intestine wars and the dread of pillage and confiscation.

Richard's son Peregrine at the same oak table had pored over the plans drawn up for the new east wing by an architect from London, a pupil of the great Wren himself; that architect whose classic Carolean doorway opened into a superb panelled drawing-room, running the whole width of the wing with a curving bow at the south end, and a spacious staircase hall at the other. Peregrine had preferred it as an entrance to the chill lofty grandeur of the vaulted hall, and he extended the gravelled drive the full length of the north front and round the corner in a majestic sweep to serve both doors. The new east front faced on a terrace with a balustrade and a formal garden below stretching out to the edge of the grassy hillside, almost as he and Richard had planned it in the lull before the young King came to Scotland.

After the tragedy of Worcester Charles II had escaped to France in disguise, to return nine years later peacefully, in the full panoply of restored monarchy. Peregrine flourished in the gay, prosperous days of the Restoration. He bought splendid silver to replace the pieces sacrificed in Charles I's cause, and handsome new furniture with intricate spiral carving adorned his luxurious rooms. Also—for he was practical as well as beauty-loving—he bought several hundred more of the rich valley acres for orchards. To Peregrine, who went up to London for the coronation, and who afterwards spent one tremendous week at Court in the autumn of 1683, the house owed its more exotic possessions—a scarlet lacquer cabinet on a carved gilt stand, a marqueterie clock and a "seaweed" bureau, a large carved and gilded mirror in the latest ornate taste. Returning from London with

North Window, Oriel Room, 1936

Edith Thane

trinkets for his wife and daughter—coloured silks and silver thread and beads for their embroidery work, the new elbow-length gloves, painted fans, ostrich feathers, and curling tongs—he presented his grandson, then seven years old, with a small walking-sword. And then he had a long, low-voiced talk with his son Anthony, the gist of which was that if the young Duke of Monmouth should try for the throne when Charles died he was not worth a risk.

Anthony the second died the year Queen Anne came to the throne, and his son Richard turned his back on the will-o'-the-wisp of the Pretenders and learned to shrug a philosophical shoulder at the German Georges. Another Richard, a third Anthony, and another Nicholas spanned the century to the Napoleonic Wars—all single-minded well-to-do country gentlemen, fearing God, tolerating the Hanoverians for lack of anything better, and buying more land. They all kept a sharp eye on the account-books, and the little west room where business was done and tenants were interviewed achieved the title of office. This Nicholas's wife, a lovely brunette, was painted in a white satin gown by a young man named Lawrence who had become the fashion at Bath; and her grandson, Richard the fourth, came of age just nine days before the twenty-first birthday of the Princess Victoria.

His grandson, still another Richard, found himself a very wealthy man at his coming of age in 1889, and developed a hobby for planting trees. Then, because he believed like his forefathers in turning back a certain

amount of his clear profits into improvements ranking as
luxuries, he built new stables and raised hunters. In 1913
he went in suddenly for bathrooms, and when he finished
there were seven, and people came from miles round to
take tea with him and make sure of the count. Under this
fifth Richard Queen's Folly had become neighbourhood
news. It was a house where they turned on a tap and the
water ran out hot, day or night. They served ices in the
summer, made in their own still-room. They had a telephone. They drove a motor car. And then, to top it all,
in the summer of 1914, they began to put in central
heating.

When the war had lasted a year, and things looked bad
for its ever ending, the fifth Richard went out to France.
He was wounded at the Somme, came home on crutches,
inspected the books, interviewed what was left of his tenantry, heartened them all, agreed that his son Peregrine
had better join up at once—and died.

Early in 1917 Peregrine the second arrived at Pas-
schendaele. By a succession of small miracles he survived
those muddy weeks of horror, and several other things
almost as bad. At Christmas, 1918, he returned to Queen's
Folly as to Abraham's Bosom. Thenceforth his life there,
the life of all the Brands, flowed past him gently. The
troubled 1920's with their strikes and Labour Govern-
ments and soaring taxes and financial panics merged into
the more prosperous 1930's with the strain shifted to
Geneva, armaments, and Continental complications. He
read his papers and listened to his news bulletins on the

wireless—he knew what was going on in the world; he was never a hermit. But none of it seemed quite real— at least not as real as what was happening in one small fold of the Cotswolds on his own diminishing acres. The Brands had always made their own world. The death of the kindly, bearded man who had been King almost as long as he could remember came home to him bitterly as the passing of an era. He found it rather frightening to be nearly as old as the boyish new sovereign. One more safe and comforting landmark had gone.

He sat now in that little room hallowed by the fears and hopes and victories of his forefathers, fingering the estate agents' letter. He was thirty-nine, and his long, lean body was clad in ancient, well-cut riding-clothes. His mousy hair was greying, his grey eyes were fringed with long dark lashes, and his mouth was the kind to hold a woman's glance. The room known as the office, with its bare stone walls and long accumulation of letter-files, crippled furniture, seed catalogues and farm journals, saddlery, wet weather gear, and children's battered games, was to him the last refuge, the ultimate funk-hole, in his domain. It was here that he faced things. He was facing them now.

First, the bills; bills from people who needed to have them paid. Second, the list of things which needed doing; things that not only hampered his tenants by their lack, but sometimes even endangered the people's health in the event of continued neglect. Third, a list of assets; the red lacquer cabinet, the Restoration chairs—the high back of each adorned with two small carven hands perpetually presenting an exquisite carven crown—the Hepplewhite boudoir set, all the bedsteads, a great many of the books. Fourth, the agents' letter.

He stared out through the window at the fading day.

Very well, let them come, and let them pay the full three months' rental whether they stayed or not. But even then, where was he? To let Queen's Folly to Mrs. Temple of New York was no solution, it was merely a sop to his accusing conscience about debt. By the time she went he would be just as badly off again. He would only have gained one more summer. Well, then—sell the whole library and have done with worry for a while? Have a dealer down from London and strip the unused rooms of their best pieces, enough to make a respectable total and leave a bit over for the winter? He put his head in his hands. He had been through that once, and then it was only the things in the attics and the empty servants' rooms —things his grandfather had banished from downstairs during his improvements before the war—not the things one lived with and was used to seeing every day. Some of the stuff in the attics had been in the house since it was built—the dealers attached a certain value to that. And if he had hated to see Anthony's bedstead sold—the little one that had first stood in this room—if he had grudged the sacrifice of a shabby inlaid buffet and some uncomfortable oak chairs, how was he going to feel when the real treasures, valuable in his own eyes for their intrinsic beauty as well as their associations, began to go?

Of course there was some kind of arrangement whereby old houses like this one, show places, could be opened to the public on certain days of the week at a fixed price of admission. And for this he understood the owners received concessions from the Government as to taxes and repairs, and even paid the staff out of the shillings and sixpences taken in. He was not clear as to details but he had heard of places which had been saved that way. People came down in char-à-bancs and bought catalogues for sixpence and tramped through rooms where all the rugs had been rolled up and all personal belongings had been locked away, while a guide recited the family history and the architectural dates and called attention to especially fine furniture and pictures—and while the owner cowered in some unimportant upper chamber or dodged about the grounds trying to look like a gardener. Several days a week, this would happen. . . . No, no, not yet. Not Queen's Folly.

He took up his pen and wrote a letter to Milder and Waring, saying that he would be very glad to show Mrs. Temple over the house on either Monday or Tuesday of next week. "As before, I shall appear not as the owner, but as the owner's agent," the letter concluded, "and I shall reside at the home farm during the period of the lease." He signed his name and made the letter ready for the post.

Then with the agents' letter and his own reply in his hand he went to find Anne the housekeeper, and break the news to her. This was important, because Anne, who had been born on the place and grew up to be his mother's maid and then his own nurse, was the only confidante he had, and except for a couple of half-grown girls and a cook was the only indoor servant.

## II

Early on Monday afternoon when he was down at the far end of the rose-garden encouraging the pansies set out between the bushes, Anne came down the yew alley toward him, black-clad, her fresh white apron glinting in the sunlight, her hands cuddled one inside the other against a chilly wind. She was a big woman, a matronly spinster, with a broad, sad, lined, and patient face, which lit up incredibly when she smiled.

"They've come, sir," said Anne, as soon as he could hear her without her raising her voice.

"Who?" he asked stupidly, his mind on a suspiciously withered pansy bud.

"The Americans," she said expressionlessly.

"Good heavens, already?" He straightened and threw down his tool. "I'll come up to the house." She turned back toward the south front, and he followed just behind her. "Are they all right?" he queried anxiously, for he valued her opinion in such matters.

"I think so, sir."

"Young or old?"

"Young. Well, maybe forty, for Mrs. Temple. The niece is only a girl."

"Do they seem to want to stay?"

"The niece will stay."

"What did she say?"

"Nothing," said Anne inscrutably, and it was for remarks like this that he treasured her companionship.

He found them in the first Peregrine's spacious drawing-room, standing in front of the fire which Anne's foresight had provided, for he did not have fires himself on mild days in May. As he approached them, introducing himself as the owner's agent, his unaccustomed country-keen nose caught a whiff of perfume; an expensive smell, he thought, shaking hands with them, but of an amazing simplicity. Their clothes also were simple—English tweeds whose lines his untutored eye only subconsciously appreciated. The girl wore a soft brown suède jacket with a green scarf, and Mrs. Temple's sweet childish face beamed out from a red fox frame. Her short hair, so silver fair that it hardly showed the grey, was blown out round a crazy little Tyrolean hat. Their voices were soft, with what was to him a most unusual cadence, a combination of Maryland, finishing school, and a lifelong proficiency in three other languages. He felt, by the time he had finished shaking hands, that he could bear them.

"Is it all like this?" asked Mrs. Temple, with a gesture which took in the perfect room.

"Some of it is older," he answered gravely.

"Well, I may as well tell you at once we've fallen in love with it," she went on, while the silent girl's grave eyes travelled lingeringly from the red lacquer cabinet to the intricate legs of the large oval table, and on to a portrait of the second Richard with his own hair curled, powdered, and tied with a black ribbon, in the middle years of George II's reign. "We really fell in love first with your advertisement in the magazine, or that is, Constance did, but *I* said it was much too good to be true, and that it was bound to be bleak and uncomfortable 'way down here."

"It can be considerably less bleak with the central heating on," he said.

"Does it really *heat?*"

"Yes, really. You can turn it on if you have a week's bad weather in the middle of the summer."

"And are there actually seven bathrooms?"

"Seven," he confirmed gravely. "They're mostly prewar, but there are three in this wing, two in the old part, and one upstairs for the servants. The heating was finished and brought down to date in 1923."

"How on earth did it all happen?" she marvelled.

"The present owner's father was a wealthy man before the war. He put a great deal of money into modernizing the house, making windows open easily, providing constant hot water, porcelain tubs, proper sanitation, and so on. He liked to be comfortable himself, and he was thoughtful of his servants."

"How unusual of him," said Mrs. Temple gently, her eyes very bright and interested.

"Would you like to see over the rest of the house now?" he inquired, disposing of the personal note.

"Oh, yes, please!" They both spoke at once, and stood eagerly like good children waiting for him to lead the way.

"We'll go this way, through the dining-room." He opened the door which Peregrine had cut in Anthony's east wall to link the new wing with the old house.

The dining-room remained nearly as Anthony had left it, with a large draw-table with fat legs, a magnificent splay-fronted buffet carrying a few pieces of old heavy silver, and carved oak chairs with loose red plush cushions in the seats. The mantelpiece was of carved stone, the design a flattened four-pointed flower. Above it the portrait of Anthony's father, painted on wood and wearing a Henry VIII plumed cap, looked down at them mistrustfully.

From the dining-room they passed Anthony's beloved wooden staircase, its dog-gate open and latched back against the wall, its carved handrail and newel posts gleaming from generations of dusters, and came to the library. And it really was a library, with shelves which went all the way round and all the way up, and which held books that had been taken down and dusted and put back in their place twice a year for over three centuries. Some of Anthony's own which had come down in the cart from London for Nicholas's education were still there— the *Courtier*, and Froissart; some had already gone up to London to fetch what they could in sudden emergency— Malory, Mandeville, the *Martyrs;* and some had simply vanished years ago, as books do which are much read by the younger members of a family—*The Canterbury Tales* and Pliny, and Aesop. The shelves were a little thinned in places, with books lying on their sides to fill in, and modern novels were few. But there was reading for a lifetime still.

"What *heaps* of very old books!" exclaimed Mrs. Temple happily. "I shall read them all."

"Some of them have been here since the house was built," he said quietly, and caught the girl's grave eyes upon him in a stare of silent appreciation.

A portrait of the first Nicholas at the time of his wedding, wearing a wide ruff and a tall narrow hat, followed them with its eyes as they reached the door of the Queen's room.

"This is the Elizabethan parlour," said Peregrine, and stood aside for them to enter. "It's the best room in the house for a sunny afternoon. The family always used to have tea in here."

"*Oh!*" said the girl and stood still, blocking the way, till her aunt slid past her, wide-eyed, across the threshold.

Sunlight lay in a diamond pattern across the rather worn wine-coloured carpet. The polished top of Anthony's old refectory table with the bulbous legs mirrored a silver bowl of primroses, arranged by Anne's tireless fingers. A tall vase of blue lupins caught the light from the narrow north window beyond the fireplace, and above the mantelpiece the portrait of the Queen in her white gown regarded them gravely, wrapped in her watchful dignity.

Peregrine was surprised—not that the miraculous

beauty of the room had impressed them at first sight, but that they had reacted to it so wholeheartedly. His eyes rested on the girl as she moved forward like a sleep-walker, and paused, a lattice-pattern of shadow across her skirt, her face raised to the searching eyes of the portrait.

"It's Elizabeth," she said, with awe.

"*Queen* Elizabeth?" Mrs. Temple hurried to her side. "Why, so it is! How young she looks! I've never seen that picture of her before, have you? Where is the original of this picture, Mr. Brand?"

"That's the only one there is," he said simply.

"*What?*"

"It was painted for the man who built this part of the house."

"But how *exciting!* Is his picture here too?"

"There isn't one, apparently. He was killed abroad, as a fairly young man. That's his son in the library."

"Was he one of her lovers?" Mrs. Temple inquired with the forthright interest of a nice child.

"I doubt it," he smiled. "He spent most of his life down here, anyway."

Peregrine glanced round him rather helplessly for more business-like topics. The girl had gone to the big bow window and stood there on the step in full sunlight, looking out at the terrace where the lupins, forget-me-nots, columbine, and primroses were in bloom. She spoke again in her soft voice, breaking the silence which his embarrassment had left.

"Aunt Dolly, let's fix this up today. I want to move in."

"Yes, so do I," agreed Mrs. Temple promptly. "When can we come in, Mr. Brand?"

"Tomorrow," said the girl at the window.

"But, darling—"

"We can get back to Town tonight, pack up, sign the lease tomorrow morning in Mount Street, and come straight back here in time for tea."

"Hadn't you better see the rest of the house?" asked Peregrine, a little dazed.

"Yes, of course," said Mrs. Temple, looking as practical as possible. "I want to see those bathrooms. And the kitchens," she added firmly. "I suppose there isn't an automatic refrigerator?"

"No," he smiled. "But there are various old-fashioned arrangements for keeping things cool."

"No ice?"

"I'm afraid not."

"And I suppose there are no screens anywhere?"

"Screens?" he repeated politely, thinking of coromandels.

"Fly screens. I suppose you have to pop little cheesecloth tents over everything until you're ready to eat it."

"I see what you mean," he said regretfully. "As a matter of fact, there are cupboards with wire netting in the kitchen and scullery, and not very many flies anyhow. The stables are a long way from the house, and very clean." He pressed a bell beside the mantelpiece. "Anne will show you the kitchen, and then take you upstairs. Anne is the housekeeper, an old and very trusted servant of the family."

"Oh, yes, she's the one Mr. Milder said went with the house," she nodded. "He said one couldn't rent the house without Anne to look after it."

"That's true."

"I suppose she'll know where to find extra maids and so forth if we need them."

Anne came in, with a dignity as great in its way as the Queen's own, and they departed with her, Mrs. Temple chattering efficiently about fresh eggs, the butcher's habits in hot weather, and where the milk came from. The girl followed slowly, with a long backward look at the Queen in which they seemed silently to reassure each other, and he was left alone in the middle of the floor.

He sat down on the edge of the big table and got out a cigarette. In all these nine dismal years of letting the house he had never viewed prospective tenants with less animus.

He fell to dividing their three months' rent into the sum of his total indebtedness, and no amount of juggling would leave a single pound over for the fresh expenditures which crowded in upon him. Something more would have to go, in the autumn. Something very good, so that he would have a substantial lump sum on hand for repairs. The last of the old silver—the lacquer cabinet—the big gate-leg table—the best Jacobean bedstead—more books—he drew a long, weary breath. All put to-

gether they would not be enough for the coming winter
and its pressing needs. He could go on, a few more years,
he supposed, getting deeper into debt, stripping the place
of its portable valuables for comparatively small stop-
gap sums until it was no longer fit to let—until he and
the Queen faced each other across emptiness. What then?

The girl's soft brogues had made no sound of a foot-
step before she stood in the doorway.

"Still here?" she said in her odd, muted voice. "We've
seen everything, and still we're crazy about the place.
Not even plumbing that you have to yank up on instead
of pulling down can stop us. We're going to move in tomorrow."

"Splendid," he said, getting off the table, conscious
again of the dim, perpetual surprise these extraordinary
women produced in him.

"So we're leaving right now, in order to pack tonight.
Where's a good place to get some tea along the way?"

"Stow-on-the-Wold—the Talbot," he said without
hesitation, and followed her through the vaulted hall to
the front of the house, where their car waited, Anne and
Mrs. Temple still in animated conversation beside it—
and Anne was smiling!

"Stow-on-the-Wold for tea," said Constance, climbing
into the driver's seat. "Find it on the map, auntie."

Mrs. Temple delayed to offer him her hand, and thank
him for letting them have the lovely house, while the girl
sat dreaming at the wheel with the motor running, only

rousing herself to smile and wave good-by when the car door clicked behind her aunt.

"What a nice man!" said Mrs. Temple very audibly, as the low blue roadster shot away.

## III

It was a coldish May, with spectacular cloudbursts and long, unexpectedly sunny evenings. They had fires most of the time, and drank nightcaps of weak whiskey and water, and found, a little to their own surprise, that they were comfortable and liked living in the country. Mrs. Temple was still somewhat confused as to just how she had got there, in an old house on the far side of the Cotswolds, but Constance was clear enough about it. The house was looking for her, said Constance, and so she came. Her aunt said that was a spooky notion and would have none of it.

But Constance's vivid memory would flick back to the dull April afternoon at the Berkeley when she had picked up a copy of *Country Life* and for no known reason had begun to read the advertisements in the front. *The gardens are old and sunny*—perhaps those half dozen words alone were responsible for catching her attention. There were two pictures, small but very good—a low grey house with pointed gables and trefoiled windows, well-trimmed vines and broad old chimneys. Toward one end of the long façade labelled "North Front" a wide Gothic door level with the ground was set in a deep plain moulding.

At the other a later wing jutted out with diamond-shaped window-panes and tidy topiary work, the gravelled drive curving past and round the corner to what the other picture called the "Jacobean Entrance"—a rather magnificent stepped-up door between stout Stuart columns. Apparently you could choose your period and walk into either the fifteenth century or the seventeenth according to how you felt each particular day. It may have been curious architecture but it was certainly a cute idea, thought Constance, lying back in the deep chintz chair at the Berkeley while the Piccadilly traffic pottered along below the windows of her corner room, and her mind strayed idly among absurdities. "Emily, have the Rolls brought round to the Priory door at ten—James, deposit the Garstin-Ponsonbys at the Jacobean entrance when you bring them from the station—Albert, take Mrs. Temple's bags down to the fifteenth century departure platform—" Constance grinned a secret sort of guilty grin. Unkind, to make fun of the sweet old house.

It certainly had everything, she ruminated, running her eye down the printed list again. Nine bedrooms—seven bathrooms. From her experience of English country houses, old or new, that was a most unusual item. Constance was accustomed to exercise her gentle American wit on what she termed the exigencies of English plumbing. She said that the "line-forms-here" joke was too true to be funny. She said that it was not so much a question of hygiene as of the rights of man. But she said it all in that soft drawl, very different from the nasal whine of

214

what she would refer to with malicious exaggeration as the "o-ould Saouth." America's most casual slang on her lips acquired a curious dignity of idiom.

She was a tall, blond young goddess of a woman, and she had seen her twenty-fifth birthday two months before that afternoon at the Berkeley. She had come safely through the moods and gaucheries of the late teens and knew her own mind. She wore her smooth pale hair in a heavy bun on the back of her neck, and had level blue eyes with a darker ring round the iris. And she was the fifth richest girl in America, though skilful trustees and carefully planted investments had preserved this embarrassing fact from the notice of the newspapers and she was never interviewed or photographed as a dollar princess.

They had come to England in March for Aintree and then stayed on to make a few visits. It was all great fun and the telephone rang a good deal, and everybody was very glad to see her again, and houseparty invitations came streaming in. She was thinking what a nice place London was, anyway, and wondered why one ever left it for less genial surroundings.

*The gardens are old and sunny*—what? Oh, yes, the house. *Seven bathrooms.* One could have a houseparty there in something like comfort. *Tennis court and croquet lawn.* She hadn't had a croquet mallet in her hand since she was a kid. It would be good for the average houseparty to have to play croquet. *Exceptional central heating.* Maybe. But in England nobody ever turned it on because they said it made the rooms stuffy. If this heating was really exceptional and heated, one could turn it on full blast, by golly, and keep them warm whether they liked it or not. Two fireplaces in the Jacobean lounge—that would help. Electric light—no bedroom candles, for once. One could give a houseparty here to end all house-parties, where the female guests would be comfortable in their bedrooms, and could see to put their make-up on and even to read in bed at night, and wouldn't have to wear their furs at dinner. One could—

And then the door clicked behind her and Aunt Dolly came back, and stood rubbing one slim silk ankle against the other on the Berkeley hearthrug.

"As usual," said Aunt Dolly, "I have been buying another knitted jumper. I can't stand this. We're lunching at the Hilliards' tomorrow and they never have a fire in the dining-room. It's something to do with the Church of England, maybe. So I'm going to wear this under my blue suit and they can just pretend it's a silk blouse." She shook out a smart white knitted jumper with covered buttons down the front and long sleeves.

"This cold is driving me to drink Scotch with my meals," said Constance darkly. *The gardens are old and sunny.* . . .

"Got any plans for this afternoon?" queried Aunt Dolly.

"No," said Constance. "It's too far."

"What's too far?"

216

"The Cotswolds. Besides, we'd have to see the agent first."

"What are you talking about?"

"Aunt Dolly, I've got a wild idea. Let's take a house."

"Where? In Town?"

"No. In the Cotswolds."

"What, 'way down there?"

"It's got seven bathrooms."

"Imagine that!" said Mrs. Temple, impressed at last. "You mean there's some particular house you want to take?"

"This one."

Mrs. Temple went to perch on the arm of the chintz chair, and her furs brushed soft and cool and fragrant against her niece's cheek.

"Oh, how sweet!" she said at sight of the pictures, and then she began to read. " 'Rose garden, *wild* garden,' " she read aloud. "I'd love to see a *wild* garden, wouldn't you?" She went on reading.

"It could be done," murmured Constance.

"It could," agreed her aunt, who was always ready to try anything. "It sounds a long way from anywhere. But we could have people to stay, of course, with all those bedrooms, in case we got bored."

May had passed into June, and nobody came to stay and they didn't get bored.

June gave them a superb week of heat which brought the snapdragons and delphinium borders to their prime, and the raspberries turned red before their eyes in the walled kitchen garden. They found a couple of good rid-ing-horses in the home farm stables, and they pottered about the lanes among the hills discovering other lovely houses, though none so lovely as Queen's Folly, they as-sured each other loyally. They motored slowly from vil-lage to village, admiring most of what they saw. Some-times in the evening they would drive through late golden light with dreamy, lengthening shadows to a local cinema fifteen miles away, and come home to make hot choco-late in the large empty kitchen and drink it in front of a fire in the Queen's parlour, with Anne's delicious almond cake. They gardened on their marrow-bones along the herbaceous borders, tactfully overseen by the sole gar-dener who had so much more than he could do nowadays, what with being crippled up by the war and all. They went out with baskets and shears and cut flowers and filled their own vases in the mornings. They played cro-quet, and worked on jig-saw puzzles. They did half-for-gotten needlework which normally they almost never had time to touch, and sent to London for more patterns and wools. They read old books from the library shelves, and read them aloud to each other because they found them too fascinating to keep to themselves. They had tea on the lawn, and lunch in the rose garden, served by one of Anne's half-grown country wenches in a short-sleeved delphinium blue uniform. They kept up a fantastic, never-ending game about those Garstin-Ponsonbys, who were forever about to be asked to tea while the straw-berries, or the raspberries, or the roses were at their best—

who really should have come yesterday, because today
the full blooms of the Richmond rose must be cut away—
who should have seen the lupins last week—whose marigolds had never looked like *this*—and who never, never
came, because they did not really exist at all.

And somehow, hour after hour, day after day, the two
of them amused themselves, and slept like tops, and woke
with a feeling of having a great deal to do, and wondered
where the time went to, and—obviously—were not bored.

In July it rained quite a lot, but the roses were sublime.
Quite suddenly they realized that their three months were
up. They had lived up their full lease, almost without
knowing it. The summer had slipped away, and with it
the Courts, and Ascot, and Cowes. They had cut the Season dead. Constance went out for a morning ride alone
to think it over.

At tea-time she returned, to find Mrs. Temple at the
big table in the Queen's parlour with an enormous jig-saw
puzzle spread out before her. The puzzle covered most of
the table top and was less than half finished.

"Oh, my God," said Constance mildly, "are you still
at it?"

"It's a wonder," her aunt beamed happily. "It's worth
all the time and trouble to get them from America, they're
so much harder."

"What's this one called?"

"The Old Mill."

"It would be," said Constance, drifting away.

Mrs. Temple looked after her with puzzled affection.

If she had been at all a usual sort of aunt, she would have had visions long since of Constance lying in a ditch unconscious after being thrown, or at least a catastrophe of some sort. Instead she had eaten her excellent lunch alone with a good appetite, reminding herself to tell Constance when she came back that they had had new potatoes, if you please. She told herself philosophically that Constance was having a bit of temperament about finishing with the delicious house which had exercised a strong romantic influence over both of them, and she thought what a pity it was that nobody had solved time and space yet so that people had to be continually leaving one nice place to get to another, instead of being able, she ended vaguely, to enjoy several places at once. Perhaps Constance would want to stay on another month at Queen's Folly, which would be very pleasant, the dahlias would be out soon. One might even suggest another month— who cared about Paris, anyway; it had gone rather to pot these days. Yes, why not skip Paris, and spend the time here, where they were settled in and comfy. Provided, of course, that that nice Mr. Brand could fix it with the owner. At this point, over the raspberries and cream, she fell to wondering about Mr. Brand's private life, which was not at all in evidence, and about which they had gleaned absolutely no clues. One could like Mr. Brand very much, she thought, if ever one got the chance. He came and went about the place, conferring with the gardener or with Anne—clad in his old, well-cut riding clothes and a brown tweed coat with pipe-bulged pockets, hatless, friendly but retiring, seemingly unhurried yet always on his way somewhere else, so that he paused, as it were, on one foot, to reply to their greetings and to inquire solicitously after their welfare. He was a man whose departure from her sight no woman could watch totally unmoved, and he often left them gazing somewhat wistfully after his retreating figure, bound on its next imperative errand once he had reassured himself that they were still contented lessees of the property he tended so assiduously. "What does he *do* all the time?" they wondered, and found no answer except that he was always busy and preoccupied in a polite and even leisurely way. It would be nice, they had agreed, to see more of him. . . . When Mrs. Temple returned to her puzzle in the parlour after lunch it did cross her mind that it wasn't much use having a telephone in the house if nobody ever rang up to say whether they would be in for meals or not—and she did say to herself that she hoped Constance would come home in time for tea or else it would begin to get a bit worrying. And when the marqueterie clock in the staircase hall struck four, it was necessary to remind herself that she was not the worrying kind—and then Constance walked in, with no apologies and no explanation.

"Tell auntie where you were at lunch," suggested Mrs. Temple with deliberate affectation, because she didn't usually pry.

"Auntie's got a nerve. I lunched at an inn in a village—I don't know the name of the inn or of the village, and I don't care!" She was wandering restlessly about the room—pulled off her hat and threw it down, and ran her fingers through her hair, and couldn't seem to settle.

"Alone?"

"If I'd been alone, I'd have known where I was, silly."

"Oh." Mrs. Temple thought it out. "I know! You were with our man of mystery!"

"Right. He's not so very mysterious after all."

"How disappointing."

"No—I wouldn't call him that. But all our guesses about him were wrong. It was so easy we didn't think of it."

"Well, do go on. Has he been telling you the story of his life?"

"Yes, I suppose he has," said Constance, a little surprised. "He'd die of chagrin if he knew."

"Did he tell you why half the portraits here look like him in fancy dress?"

"Because they're all Brands. And he's a Brand. The family has lived here without a break since 1559."

"Heavens!" said Mrs. Temple, counting on her fingers. "Nearly four hundred years."

"Yes. You see, he's not the agent; he's the owner."

"But he *said* he was the agent! And he lives at the home farm."

"He lied in his teeth," said Constance with some satisfaction. "He was born here in this house." She sat down at last, on the divan, and leaned back with a long sigh. "It's beginning to straighten itself out in my mind now. You see, we met by accident down by the bridge this morning when I went out for my ride. And we rode along together for a while, and then we got off and sat on a stone wall and talked. And then it was lunch time, and he said there was a nice inn a mile further on. And so we went there and had lunch—and then we rode back. It's the first time I've ever really had a chance to get acquainted with him—that is—we don't seem to see much of him, do we—" Her voice trailed away.

"Well—what all did he say?" asked Mrs. Temple when she had waited as long as she could.

Constance was staring up at Elizabeth's picture.

"Aunt Dolly, that portrait of Queen Elizabeth has hung there, just where it is now, for three hundred and seventy-one years. Let that sink in."

"Why, that was before the *Mayflower!*" said Mrs. Temple after another calculation on her fingers.

"Quite a bit."

"Did he tell you that?"

"Yes."

"Well, what else?" prodded her aunt. "Why did he say he was the agent?"

"I suppose because he was ashamed."

"Ashamed of what?"

"Of not being able to afford to live here any longer, and keep the house full of servants and family as it used to be—rather the way a man is ashamed if he can't keep his wife decently."

"I think that's rather sweet," remarked Mrs. Temple, busy with the puzzle again.

"Yes, I thought so myself," said Constance, with an amused glance.

"Go on—tell me more."

"Well, you see, there isn't any money. Land has been sold, stock and timber have been sold, furniture, some of the books and pictures. But the money always goes. Taxes, repairs, death duties, upkeep, more taxes—the only way he's held out at all during the last few years was by letting it to rich Americans."

"Like us?"

"Yes, if you must. One of them, the last man who had it before us, for the hunting last year, offered him ten thousand pounds for that portrait of Queen Elizabeth. I hope we won't do anything quite as tactless as that before we go."

"And Mr. Brand wouldn't take it?"

"No."

"Well, it's natural that he should want to keep things together, I suppose," admitted Mrs. Temple, realizing there was a silence.

"You know, it's kind of sad," Constance observed almost too casually, without removing her eyes from the portrait. "We Americans aren't so filthy rich any more—though a few of us have still got enough to scrape along on. And it's kind of sad to find the thing I want to do more than anything else in the world—the way I want to spend what money there is still in the family sock—and there's got to be a man like that one in the way!"

"Why? What do you want to do?"

"I want to live here," said Constance with quiet passion. "I want to live here the year round, not just for three months one summer between New York and Paris. I want to fill the stables again, and repair the cottages, and be friends with the people, and put in proper drains at the farms, and save the timber. I want to stop him breaking his heart over the place!"

"You mean you want to buy Queen's Folly?" Mrs. Temple had forgotten all about the puzzle now and was watching her attentively from the table.

"He won't sell."

"Did you ask him?"

"I didn't have to. He won't. Not so long as he can get along by letting it. Not till things are a lot worse than they are now. Not till we're all old and ready to die on our feet," she cried despairingly. "He can hold out that long, trust him!" Mrs. Temple did not interrupt or argue, she never did, but allowed a sympathetic silence to fall. "You know, Aunt Dolly, I could be awfully gone on that man!"

"Could be!" said her aunt, gently derisive. "You are!"

"I guess I am, at that," Constance admitted, unembarrassed. "I guess I must have been, ever since the second time I ever saw him—the night we came down here to stay, and he was standing on the priory doorstep as we drove up in the sunset. He wasn't wearing a hat—and he opened the door on your side of the car and helped you out, and a boy came running round the corner of the house to collect the bags, and—it was a funny feeling I had then, I—I felt as though I'd come home. And now our time is up and our sailing is booked from Boulogne— it seems all wrong, somehow."

"I suppose we could skip Paris," murmured Mrs. Temple, who had no cares and no ties in the world beyond this blond daughter of a dead sister. "Everybody says it's no fun this summer anyway. That would give us another month here and we could catch the boat at Southampton—" She left it hanging there.

"What good would that do, I wonder?" said Constance gloomily.

"We-ell—you could see him some more—" Her aunt bent a tactful head above the puzzle, pushing bits of it around with her finger.

"I did mention something of the sort to him today."

"Did he say we could have the house longer?"

"Oh, yes. He seemed—pleased." She sighed again. "Of course, he needs the money. But even if we did stay another month he might never ask me to lunch again. I suppose we could invite him here occasionally, or would that look as if—" She broke off unhappily.

"I gather your intentions are honourable, Constance?"

"So honourable they creak!"

"But seriously, dear—"

"I am serious," said Constance simply. "I keep telling you."

"You mean you want to marry this practically unknown man and settle down here?"

226

"You put it rather crudely, Aunt Dolly, but I suppose that's about it!"

"What fun!" said Mrs. Temple, enchanted.

"What fun!" echoed Constance wistfully.

"Constance, you've been and fallen in love with a house!"

"I didn't say that," she denied, with a guilty, sidelong glance, and Mrs. Temple gave a burble of pleased excitement. "Oh, I don't know what's the matter with me! He *is* the house! I can't imagine them apart!" She broke off again with a humorous little whimper, suddenly shy. "Dammit, I want them both! I want the moon!"

"Well, I *am* surprised!" said Mrs. Temple, but she didn't look it.

"You're not half as surprised as I am!" Constance drew a long, philosophical breath. "Well, well," she drawled with an effort at levity, "life does go on!"

Mrs. Temple considered her from across the room—canary-coloured jumper, sky-blue scarf, long legs clad in excellent jodhpurs.

"You do seem to fit in here somehow. I've noticed that a dozen different ways. As though you *belonged* here. *You* know—the lady of the manor!"

"Thanks. But has *he* noticed anything of the kind? Oh, no! Not he! The bat!" She smiled tenderly.

"All men are blind," began Mrs. Temple sententiously.

"Yeah," said Constance, jeering at her. " 'What Every Woman Knows!' " She sat quiescent, her head against the back of the divan, her feet stuck out in front of her,

her thoughts adrift. "What a day," she murmured. "We visited one of the farms on the way home, and came through the village. I love to see him with the tenants on the place—they gather round—they don't push, oh, dear, no—but they do sort of *close in* on him wherever he turns up. The kids sort of put out their hands to his clothes, and the babies burst into toothless grins at sight of him. It makes him look very tall and—sort of feudal. He's the master. And you get the feeling of what it means—what it's meant for hundreds of years. And you suddenly feel the way they do toward him—sort of humble and proud at the same time—"

"You have got it bad!" said Mrs. Temple admiringly.

"Haven't I! For better or for worse."

"Forsaking all others?" Mrs. Temple suggested dubiously.

"Forsaking all others," Constance repeated softly without hesitation.

"You mean you'd really be content never to come home again?"

"Where's home? A house on Long Island that father bought ready furnished a few years ago? Or the house in Washington where we lived before that? Or the place in Maryland where we lived while mother was alive? Or the forgotten little dump in Cleveland where I was born? I can't be uprooted—I've never grown fast to anything! Till now."

"Constance, you mean this, don't you? You've made up your mind?"

"Yes, yes, yes, to everything! Yes to Peregrine Brand, if he ever asks me—which he won't!"

"Maybe he will."

"I wouldn't bet on it if I were you."

"But why not? He seems entirely unattached, doesn't he?"

"Worse than that—he seems entirely *de*tached. I know I'm not a raving beauty. I mean, I don't cause traffic blocks in Bond Street. But I am accustomed to a certain—"

"Appreciation," nodded Mrs. Temple.

"—approval, or if that's too strong a word, *acknowledgment*, from a masculine eye. This one looks at me as though I was a tree. No, that's wrong. He likes trees."

"Now that you mention it," said Mrs. Temple with another critical survey, "this agrees with you. You're looking right handsome these days, my girl."

"I've always heard," said Constance, "that being in love improves a woman's looks—at least till she begins to pine."

"Maybe we aren't doing him justice. Maybe today will give him ideas, if he hadn't any before. Maybe next time—"

"No," said Constance sadly, resignedly, with a shake of her head. "In the first place it wouldn't occur to him. And in the second place, I've got money. And in the third place, I don't believe he's woman-conscious anyway. And in the fourth, fifth and sixth places—oh, what's the use?" She sat a moment, relaxed, dejected, staring at her boot-toes. "Isn't it a cute name? Peregrine. He says it's always been in the family. If there are girls, the eldest is always named Elizabeth." Her eyes went back to the portrait above the mantelpiece. "Think of the things she's seen and heard, here in this room. Think of the things she'll never, never tell!"

"Maybe she knows about the ghost!" cried Mrs. Temple.

"Of course she does—don't you, Bess!"

"Constance—did he say anything today about the ghost?"

"No."

"Let's ask him sometime."

"Why? Have you seen it?"

"N-no. But I've heard things."

"You don't hear it."

"How do you know?"

"Well, I only know what Anne told me. It comes and stands there in that doorway—and just looks at you. And then it goes away."

"You—think you wouldn't mind that?" queried Mrs. Temple, with a nervous glance at the door.

"He was a Brand too. Somehow I'm not afraid of Brands."

"Do you suppose he was murdered in that doorway— or what?"

"Heaven knows. Anyway, he belongs to the house just the same as this one does—just the same as the pictures on the walls. All Brands—all loving Queen's Folly to distraction—all rather sweet." She rose restlessly. "Well, now that I've broken down and confessed all—what's to be done?"

"Well, we might ask him to tea, and then—"

"And then you can slip away with a knowing smile and leave us alone together!" Constance supplied swiftly. "Yes, I'd thought of that myself! Oh, what's the use!" she sighed again, and went off upstairs to change.

## IV

Almost without its being mentioned again, the decision to stay another month was taken—perhaps longer, if the weather kept good. This took them through August, which became very warm and bright toward the end, so that September came upon them unawares.

They were so comfortable, and so amused. The central heating, which had been brought up to date in 1923, was not exactly along American lines, but they conceded with sly grins that in its way it was really exceptional—and indulged in wood fires besides. In the same mysterious year the modern overstuffed furniture in bright chintz covers, recently renewed, had gone into the lounges and bedrooms, and it clustered cosily round the fireplaces without quarrelling with the older pieces ranged in a mellow frieze round the walls.

They puzzled a good deal over these post-war improvements. Maybe he was going to marry then, they speculated. And if so, what had gone wrong—or if nothing had gone wrong, where was his wife? Of course things weren't so bad in 1923. But he'd put a lot of money into the place then, for a mere man alone. They longed to ask him, Why 1923? But something in the quality of his unaware uncommunicativeness held them back. It would sound like prying.

Hot baths were as simple as turning on a tap. Their food, largely home-grown, was fit for kings. And since nobody came to stay, and that houseparty which was to make all other houseparties look like primitive polar expeditions never materialized, there was no need for more servants than they had found in the house. "But this is the way to *live*," they would tell each other contentedly, as they sniffed up the warm fragrance of climbing roses in the sun, or sat with their feet up round a fire while rain beat ineffectually at the casements. "All that rushing round people do!" they would say contemptuously.

Their advances to Peregrine Brand were rather like the timid overtures of a child trying to salt the tail of a bird on the lawn. They crept up on him, with casual offers of a cup of tea or a cocktail. Once they picked him out of a hedge beside the road where he was supervising a couple of farm lads at stopping a hole, and took him back to the house for lunch. He seemed grateful, but always a little surprised. "Perhaps he's not in the habit of fraternizing with his tenants," remarked Mrs. Temple. "Unless they can mend hedges," she added reflectively.

Gradually, by the exercise of infinite tact on their part,

the corner was turned into friendship. Even Constance admitted gloomily that at least he no longer shied like a startled mustang at sight of them. He even met the Garstin-Ponsonbys, and accepted their obnoxious perfection in gardening matters without questioning the bitter rivalry it had created. "Mrs. Garstin-Ponsonby never has greenfly," he would announce solemnly when they came upon him bent over the rosebushes with a bucket of evil-smelling liquid on the ground beside him. "Don't let her know I've been spraying!"

One morning they caught up with him in conference with the gardener down where the peach trees grew flat against the wall, and after the usual courtesies he murmured something about running into Chipping Campden about some hay, and seemed to hang, as usual, on one foot in his permanent state of imminent departure.

"Could I go too?" asked Constance in a very small voice.

He looked surprised.

"Of course," he said. "We could have lunch there if you like."

And she wouldn't even go back to the house for her hat lest he think better of his offer and go away while her back was turned.

He drove an ancient two-door Rover sports saloon with a black fabric body and fat balloon tires which threw out the recordings of his speedometer by about one third, so that the game little car had always travelled a great deal further than it got credit for. Its horn-button had disappeared from the steering-wheel and the only way left to evoke its hoarse warning note was by applying a loose end of naked wire from the horn to the metal ignition lever. (He had no idea why this sounded the horn, but it did.) Nothing but sheep or sacks of feed or farm tools ever rode in the back seat any more. Even his dog refused it, and sat up beside him in front like a Christian. The Rover's reserve petrol tank was supposed to exist, but he was never sure that it wasn't turned on at that very moment, and so a large tin of petrol was kept filled in the luggage trunk at the rear—it was quite a trick to project the curving stream of petrol from the tin into the small opening under the bonnet from a necessary height of at least a foot. The engine seemed to use more oil than petrol, and when it was feeling fit would do a good 40 m.p.h. The brakes worked only every now and then, but Peregrine swore the car could find its own way home from Chipping Campden, and the gardener's little boy kept its outside rubbed with Cherry Blossom Boot Polish as water-proofing for sixpence a week.

But her own smart blue roadster was left behind in the garage while she begged jaunts about the country-side with him in the Rover. Several times she enticed him to the local cinema in the evenings, and discovered a new and confusing emotion—parking the sad little car at an angle among the other cars in the village square and sitting beside him in the smoky darkness of the theatre. "Just a farmer's wife on a spree," she thought wonderingly, while the magic feet of Fred Astaire in a sailor suit tapped out a love song on her heart. "I care for this—this is what I want—I'll *have* this, thank you, God—"A furtive glance at his face in the flickering light from the screen showed a small, relaxed smile. He liked it too. He was enjoying himself. Did it never occur to him that she might leave Queen's Folly eventually if he continued to do nothing about keeping her there?

Sometimes he talked to her freely now, usually on their rides and drives about the hills—talked about the people on the farms, their small tragedies and smaller successes; or about the land itself, and what could be done with the little he had left; or about the house, its beauties, its legends, and its needs. He made no secret of the fact that he had not enough money any more to run it properly.

"I was rash enough once," he confessed one day when they had ridden down toward the Vale, and he pulled up his horse on the edge of a steep rise that spread out the surrounding country before them like a map. "I sold that land down there—yes, all that—to an estate builder, mostly. I'd have got more for it if I'd held on another ten years. But I was young then, and I did desperate things. We had new roofs that year—all but the big house, it was all right then—and our cess-pools were seen to, and our wells cleaned out, and our barns tightened up. We bought new tools and an extra wagon here and there. We had a beautiful time while it lasted. But that was our last fling. Since then we've gone very carefully."

"Was that when you did that marvelous job on the heating?"

"Yes. The heating was the big house's present, since its roof could be made to do, with a bit of patching. That and the chintz furniture. But I knew all the time I should have had the roof done properly instead of buying fripperies," he added ruefully. "I knew the time would come when it couldn't be put off any longer. It was my father coming out in me, I suppose. He believed in being comfortable, and he didn't count any improvement in the house an extravagance. It was his pride always to have the latest gadget for Queen's Folly, like the electric light machine, for instance. That's new too, now, the old one gave out, and I'm still paying for it! Of course it all makes the house easier to let, which is fortunate, but that was not in my original plans."

There it was again. 1923. Well, what were his plans then? She waited patiently in silence, but he touched his horse with his heel and they moved on down the slope.

Day by day she pieced together his background, largely by inference, for he did not talk about himself, and rarely came nearer the present than stories of that fifth Richard his father, who did things so very well, and who spent such a lot of money and yet always had more by the time he needed it. The Industrial Revolution which began to pinch so many large landowners in the latter part of the 1800's had somehow passed the Brands safely by at first, and their grandeur continued into the new century. All their capital was not in the land. They had it invested in the right things, bearing interest. They were sound, safe, and snug, and they spoke of making presents to the house as though it were a beloved woman. Peregrine's central heating was a diamond necklace, an extravagant bauble bought by an ardent young lover. And now, like a necklace, it was in pawn—to herself. So that she began to wonder less about some mysterious woman who mysteriously did not marry him, and to doubt instead if he had ever looked twice at any woman at all.

Of the time since Richard's death in 1916 he contrived to say very little. A lot of timber had gone during the war, a lot of land. Richard's death duties had come heavily at the wrong time, taxes had gone up cruelly since then, and expenses had kept pace with them, some old investments had failed. That much she could guess. She had to guess too at the growing bitterness of the struggle to run the place from month to month and year to year. He had reduced its acreage drastically, sometimes by selling the farms to the tenants—and here his personal feelings got in the way, and he made terms that were much too easy, and could never press for payments which fell overdue. He was in debt for necessities, and he worried about the people he owed money to. And Constance, whose fortune had weathered 1929 and come to her more or less intact at least in its potentialities, took to lying awake at night trying to invent a way to increase the rent cheques.

There was never any self-consciousness between herself and her Aunt Dolly. They worked together for Peregrine Brand's undoing—or, as they would remind each other whenever a feeling of guilt set in, his salvation. Each time she returned from an excursion with him, her aunt would rally round with restoratives and leading questions, and get the thing bought down to date, and they would discuss the situation from any new angle which appeared to them.

Therefore, on an afternoon when Constance had been down to Evesham in the Rover to take a balky wireless set to be overhauled, Mrs. Temple looked up inquiringly from the eternal jig-saw puzzle.

"Hullo," said Constance moodily, and sat down beside her and found the piece she was looking for, in silence. At last she spoke out of the depths of her own thoughts, continuing the subject which was never far from their minds. "Of course I might buy up the mortgage, if there is one, and give it back to him."

"Mmm-mmm." Mrs. Temple shook her head decisively. "Pride."

"As you say—pride." She left the table and came to a stand before the portrait, looking up at it. "Did you know it was her birthday?"

"I never knew she had a birthday."

"Most people have."

"Yes, but it was so long ago—" said Mrs. Temple vaguely. "What's the date?"

"September seventh."

"Did he tell you?"

"Yes. It seems the Brands have had a ceremony for

three hundred and seventy-one years. On her birthday they drink her health here in this room."

"How sweet," said Mrs. Temple, touched.

"And one of the things that was eating into his soul today was that this year she couldn't have her toast because we were in the house instead of him. So he's coming in to tea, as soon as he's finished with the gardener, and we're all going to drink it now."

"At tea-time?"

"It doesn't seem to matter what time of day." She brushed a hand across her eyes with a weary, childlike gesture, and dropped down on the chesterfield. "It's so awful to think of his losing the place after all these years. That's what he's afraid of, I know. Suppose it was taken away from him for taxes, or debt, or—it does happen, you know. Half the old estates in England have gone that way. He says he's not the only one. If only I could *do* something! I feel as though I'd been brought here to do something, and I don't know what it is! If only *she* could talk, and tell me what to do!"

"Well, if he can't think of anything, I don't see how you can," said her aunt, being practical. "Isn't there *anything* he can do himself?"

"What do you expect him to do?" Constance demanded unreasonably. "Commit hara-kiri on the doorstep? Rob a bank? Shoot the Lord Chancellor? The English don't charge round *doing* things and making a mess. The English just—sit tight."

"Constance. Don't you think it's a good sign—when he tells you these things, I mean?"

"Maybe. Still, I don't know. He had the blues today. He'd have talked to a fence-post if it had said Yes and No and Why at suitable intervals, and didn't worry him. He'd have preferred a fence-post if it comes to that." She sat leaning back with her head resting against the divan and tears on her cheeks, looking white and tired and tense. "I feel as though I'm letting her down! She counts on me, and I'm letting her down!"

"Constance, I'm getting worried about you. It's as though you were—bewitched!"

"I think I am."

"*Constance!*"

"It isn't just that I've gone to pieces over him. That's natural enough anyway. But the house itself has got me. When I rest my hand on the bannister it's as though the wood was alive and warm. When I wake up in the morning, it's because the room itself has laid a hand on my heart. When I've been away from the house like this, and come back to it—each time its windows are watching for me."

"But, darling—"

"Haven't you noticed it yourself? Or is it just me? Does the house ever seem to you—as though it *listened?*"

"Y-yes," admitted Mrs. Temple, glancing round uneasily. "Ordinarily I don't notice it much. But when you talk like this I feel positively spooky. Of course I shall hate to leave Queen's Folly—like a person I've got fond of. Do you think it will miss us when we go?"

"I'm not going."

"*What?*"

"It won't let me go." She rose and faced the portrait on her feet, her arms outflung in a gesture of hopeless helplessness. "What is it you want of me?" she cried despairingly to the watchful white-clad Queen. "*What can I do?*"

The Queen made no answer. For a moment they gazed at each other, and to Constance the thin painted lips seemed scornful of a twentieth century weakling who could not bend the world to her will. She flung away and went to the bow window and leaned there, staring out at the bright dahlias on the terrace.

"You could tell him, I suppose," said Mrs. Temple very calmly into the hysterical silence. "You could always tell him how you feel."

"And ask him to marry me?" Constance completed the suggestion with a wry smile. "He'd love that!"

"Well, if he's too stupid to see for himself—"

"He's not stupid," she denied without heat. "He's just worried. He's only thinking of the house—not ever of himself. He only lives for the house. He—I guess he doesn't need me too."

"Oh, nonsense!" said her aunt briskly to this defeatism. "Any man gets lonesome! He can't talk to the house, can he? He can't take it to bed with him!"

"Aunt Dolly!"

"Well, you began this!"

"I never began anything of the sort, I only said—" Her voice broke absurdly, and she ended on a sniff. "We've got to stop talking like this, he'll be here any minute."

"*I* say you'd better tell him," said Mrs. Temple relentlessly.

"But, Aunt Dolly, I can't! A girl can't just—"

"Sit tight like the English and you'll lose him!" prophesied Mrs. Temple grimly. "I sometimes think the English have a very special Providence that manages things for them while they do nothing in their own inimitable way. But I doubt if it works for you. I'd take a hand myself, if I were you."

"Shut up, here he comes!" hissed Constance at the window.

"Did your heart turn clean over when you saw him?"

"Yes, and it's not funny. And my hands have gone all wet and cold and my knees feel queer, and I've got all sorts of other symptoms. You don't suppose I'm sickening for something simple like typhoid, instead of—"

"You'd better come and sit down," said her aunt. "Put your mind on the puzzle, it's very steadying."

As Constance whisked into a chair by the table, Peregrine appeared diffidently in the library doorway. He always remembered that it was their house, though he was less formal about it than he used to be.

"May I come in?" he said politely, and added, "Anne asked me if you wanted tea now and I said you did."

He grinned apologetically at Mrs. Temple, who suddenly heard herself saying to herself, *You can't blame the girl!* "Was that all right?" he asked, and she assured him that it was.

"There's something we've been wanting to ask you," she went on cheerfully, for Constance wasn't helping and somebody had to say something. "Who is the gorgeous young man in the lace collar in Constance's bedroom— I mean the portrait."

"Which room is that—the one over this one?"

"Yes."

"That's the first Peregrine. The one I'm named for. That room used to be mine. It's a funny thing—Peregrine built the new east wing, and put his whole soul into it. The upstairs rooms are lovely. But he went on sleeping in the old master's bedroom, over this one. We all do."

"What else did Peregrine do?" They were both paying him the fascinated attention any reference to the traditions of the house always evoked in them.

"He was a fine swordsman, for one thing. He fought a duel, here in this room."

"Imagine that!" cried Mrs. Temple, enchanted. "Because of a lady?"

"No," he smiled. "Much more serious than that. It was because the Puritans threatened to burn the house."

Anne came in with tea, which she arranged on the low fireside table. She was followed by a maid with a tray, on which there were a decanter and three glasses, which she left on the corner of the big table beside the puzzle.

"That's the birthday wine," he said.

"Does the Queen have her own special wine?" Constance asked, eyeing the golden glinting liquid.

"But of course." He seemed surprised. "It's laid down regularly on the coming of age of the heir, with the date of maturity marked on it."

"Everything's so *tidy!*" sighed Mrs. Temple contentedly, taking her place at the tea-table. "You do all these things so well, here in England. To think the first Peregrine drank the same toast right here in the same room—"

"Out of the same glasses," he finished gently.

"Not *really!*"

"And he saved the house," murmured Constance with an affectionate glance round the room. "He risked his life to save the house."

"Well, his father had got his death wound at the battle of Worcester. It was up to Peregrine after that."

"Killed in battle!" Mrs. Temple shivered, pouring tea. "It still has a dreadful sound!"

"As a matter of fact, Richard got home before he died. We always do. All but Anthony," he added as an afterthought.

"Anthony! You mean the ghost? Oh, do tell us—" Too late, Mrs. Temple's fingers went uncertainly to her impetuous lips.

Peregrine only smiled at her consternation.

244

"Anne's been talking, I see. There is a superstition in the family that if ever a Brand is so unlucky as to die abroad, or anywhere away from the house—he won't rest."

"Is it true?" asked Constance, very low.

"I don't know. None of us has done it since 1588." He smiled again, with a certain diffidence. "I thought I might find out more about it in 1917, but—I was let off that. All male Brands are taught three things from the cradle: cherish the house—serve the King—and come home to die."

The simple words lay naked on the air. For a moment, choked by their own complicated emotions regarding the man who spoke them, both women found it impossible to break the unselfconscious silence with which the ancient room in its dignity awaited their next move.

"And the girl who hangs beside Peregrine," said Mrs. Temple at last inadequately, "was she his wife? She looks so young—"

"Yes, Jane was just seventeen when he married her. He had just turned twenty-one."

Mrs. Temple saw her chance. She darted one quick, mischievous look at Constance, who was staring at the wine in the decanter as though it was a seer's crystal. Mrs. Temple beamed at him across the hissing tea-urn.

"Peregrine worked faster than you do, Mr. Brand," she said archly.

He looked surprised.

"Not very much," he said. "In fact, I was only twenty

myself when I married." He went to the table and picked up the decanter. "Will you have a glass of this excellent Madeira with me now?" he suggested, with his usual relapse into the impersonal.

"Yes, thank you," said Mrs. Temple automatically, and set down the tea-pot with a suddenly nerveless hand. Constance turned her head slowly, and their eyes met across the room. *Now I've done it*, thought Mrs. Temple contritely. And then—*Well, it's best to know.*

The room was now so still that the fire could be heard, and the simmer of the tea-urn, and the tiny guggle of the wine through the neck of the decanter into the glasses. Constance rose and squared her shoulders. Married? Of course he was married, she had known all along that he must be. His wife naturally would not be living at the farm while the house was let. She would go home to her people, probably. And yet—all these weeks and never a word from him to suggest—*my wife—my son*— But equally he had never said—*because I never married*—or —*before my wife died*—. His complete indifference to anything but the most commonplace kind of friendly intercourse was natural enough in a man whose ties were of such old and intimate establishment that he never felt the need to speak of them. Perhaps he was ashamed, too, that his household had to be broken up at the whim of any outsider who chose to rent Queen's Folly for a few months. Besides, there was no need for him to account for his wife to his temporary tenants. Or perhaps they

246

didn't get on together—he wouldn't care to talk about that either, to a stranger.

It was a death-blow so casual, so heedlessly given, so quick and clean, that she had not yet had time to realize its exquisite pain. Her first impulse now was merely to get away. Her first revulsion of feeling was not so much for Peregrine Brand as for the queer house which had brought her to him, and which now represented only a tragic fabric of dreams so fragile that it went into shreds at a touch. She wanted to leave Queen's Folly at once, and at a dead run. The incredible interlude was over. She would go back to London where she belonged, she would go to night clubs again and dance—theatres— parties—champagne—clothes—she must buy a lot of clothes—Paris, of course—absurd to think of skipping Paris—anything that was Queen's Folly must be instantly wiped out. She had so nearly made an eternal fool of herself. She had so nearly let him know. . . .

"We all need a drink," she said. "You see, I've had bad news. And that means we'll be returning to America at once."

He turned to her, a full glass in either hand. His face was very grave.

"I'm sorry," he said with deep concern. "I had no idea—you seemed so gay at luncheon I never dreamed—"

"It was waiting for me here," she said. "I guess I was expecting it, and now it's come. We'll have to go up to Town tomorrow."

"I'm sorry," he said again. "The house likes you. Had

you noticed?" He handed them the glasses, and turned back to the table for his own.

Constance glanced up at the portrait of Elizabeth with a somewhat twisted smile. *You might have told me*, her eyes said to it. *You needn't have led me on.* And Elizabeth gazed back at her enigmatically, doubtless a little contemptuously, for she herself had never run away from anything in her life.

"The house won't care," said Constance, "so long as it has you—and her."

"Oh, *I* don't matter," he said cheerfully. "She's never thought much of me. My father was the sort of man she liked. He made her expensive presents all the time. She dearly loves presents." He raised his glass. "The Queen," he said solemnly, and they drank.

## V

He saw them off in the blue roadster before noon the next day. Constance was white and silent, with shadows under her eyes, and even Mrs. Temple was subdued. He tried to imagine what sort of disaster could have so quenched their normal spirits—and because money loomed largest among his own worries, he assumed that they must have had some sort of financial reverse. Their silence on the subject, after weeks of confiding loquaciousness about everything under the sun, was puzzling, and added to the gravity of the mystery. Any ordinary mischance would have come out without a second thought from them, he was sure.

At last he could bear his own uncertainties no longer.

"Anne, were there any cables or telegrams yesterday?"

"No, sir," said Anne, making it harder, and added, for she knew well enough what was in his mind, "Not even an American mail, sir. Just a few letters from London."

He told himself that it was none of his business anyway. He had no right to pry into the girl's private affairs just because she had happened to live in his house for a summer.

Life went on at Queen's Folly much as it had done before they came, but the year had turned the corner into winter. The weather was cold and rainy and dreary, and the dahlias on the terrace were mud-spattered and forlorn. Peregrine moved back into his own bedroom above the Queen's parlour, and blamed his imagination for the delicate whiff of fragrance which remained in the wardrobe and the drawers of the bureau and commode where Constance's clothes had been.

One rainy morning in November he carried his account-books and papers into the parlour and spread them out on the big table there in order to manage with only the one fire. Anne was on her knees on the hearthrug polishing the brass fire-tools. He liked to have her there, and she had chosen her time to do it while he was in the room. They both sought each other's company these days, glad of another human presence in the great emptiness of the house. He and Anne had been through a lot together, beginning with his teething, and her attitude toward him was still likely to be more that of a nurse than a housekeeper.

The tale his figures told was a bad one, but he was strangely calm about it now, strangely resigned and unresentful, for the remedy was to his hand and he had decided to use it. He told himself bitterly that the only feeling he had left was of positive relief, the way a man felt who had decided to have a tooth out.

For months he had known this day would come, and for months his mind had refused it, like a nervous hunter at a gate. Now the winter was upon them, and the roof would not last another year; already the damp was coming in. And the roof was a job he dared not begin without the money actually in hand, because there was no possible way that he could ever get ahead enough to pay for it in even very easy instalments. The best barn too was leaking, and the stock must be made comfortable before the cold weather set in. Repairs at the farms were long overdue, chimneys must be cleaned, water-pipes seen to. Suddenly, in an accumulation of neglect and patchings up, the place demanded thousands, to save it from falling to pieces.

There was no more land or timber that would fetch a price—only sheep-walks and a bit of meadow, park, and orchard. An itemized list of the house's belongings and contents, including all the silver and furnishings at probable auction prices came to a total which, laid be-

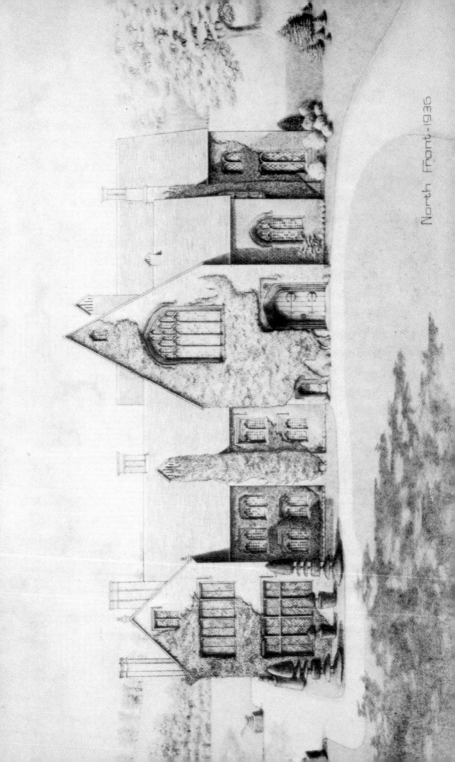

North Front - 1936

side the debts and the inevitable expenditure, was hardly
worth the sacrifice. If he stripped the rooms entirely
and closed off the east wing, he would still not be much
ahead for long.

But there was one thing in the house which would
do the business alone, and a bit over. No painter's name
could be found on the portrait of the Queen, and it was
painted much too early to be the work of the great
Gheeraerdts it resembled, but its incontestable pedigree
made up for that. It was worth almost any price he chose
to name. Its sale alone would save Queen's Folly, and
for some time to come—for the length of his lifetime,
perhaps.

"Anne," he said suddenly, "there's a Mr. Burford coming here today. We'd better give him lunch or tea, I
suppose, when he arrives."

Anne gave a startled glance up at him and then down
again as quickly.

"Isn't he that antique expert from London?"

"Yes. Been here before. Dried up chap with a mous-
tache."

"I remember," she said tonelessly. There was a long
silence, while he wrote busily in his ledger. Anne looked
up at him again, and away, making up her mind, her
strokes with the polishing cloth steady and strong.
"Seems quiet without them, doesn't it," she remarked
at last.

"Who?" he said, abstracted. "Oh, you mean Mrs.
Temple and her niece. Yes, doesn't it!"

"Must say I'd got kind of used to them," Anne went on, speaking as though half to herself. "They weren't like any of the other people we've had here. Seemed like Miss Ingleby loved the house for its own sake, like." He went on writing. "Maybe they'll come back next year," she suggested, very busy with her polishing.

"I doubt it," he said without looking up.

"Would have been nice to have them back."

"Yes." He paused to contemplate that radiant possibility, and then left off philosophically. "Well, you know how those rich girls are, Anne. They get enthusiasms—and then they cool off again."

"Is she rich?"

"Terribly, I believe."

"Funny," said Anne. "It didn't show."

"How do you mean, it didn't show?" He was always interested in Anne's views on people.

"She wasn't spoilt, I mean—or bored—nor she didn't give herself airs. I liked her," said Anne insistently.

"So did I," he agreed almost without thinking first. "There was something—you could talk to her about things that mattered. I mean to say she wasn't—" He came to himself abruptly. "What are you driving at, Anne? I'm too old a bird. Don't start getting ideas into your head, at my age!"

"I suppose we should be grateful for her having been here at all," admitted Anne with a sigh.

"Yes. We can always be grateful for a glimpse of

252

something beautiful. We mustn't be greedy and fret because we couldn't hold on to it forever."

"No, sir," Anne agreed humbly, her head down.

For a long minute he drifted among suddenly poignant memories.

"She was here, wasn't she," he said at last. "We didn't just—dream her?" He caught Anne's eyes upon him and returned hastily to his accounts. Constance's absence was a thing he refused to contemplate in relation to the inner desolation he had been enduring the past few weeks. He preferred to attribute his acute state of mind entirely to his decision to part with the Queen.

"She put quite a lot of money into the place in the course of her—enthusiasm," Anne was saying on the hearthrug.

"Put money into it?" he repeated stupidly.

"Things it needed. Little things—like in the kitchen and the bathrooms. Very practical-minded she was, sir. And she got Gregson a new garden hose—said maybe you wouldn't notice and make a fuss till after she'd gone, and you didn't! But I call it very thoughtful of her."

"Very. What else did she do?"

"Little gifts to people on the place, sir. She got a bed-table for old Mrs. Hickson—like in a hospital, with a shelf-thing that comes out across you so things don't have to rest on your stummick. Maybe you've noticed it, down at the cottage?" He shook his head vaguely. "And a bicycle for Tom's eldest boy—and a doll for our Sallie's birthday—and a complete outfit for the new baby down at the home farm, the loveliest things you ever saw, all sent down from that grand place in London—"

"Anne," he interrupted. "Why didn't you tell me all this? Why have you waited till now to tell me?"

"Well, it never seemed to come up, sir," she explained guiltily. "And besides—I was afraid you might put a stop to it."

"I should have tried. I mean—she was paying a good price for the lease—that was enough."

"I thought maybe you'd feel that way about it, sir," she agreed meekly.

"You did, did you!" He regarded her bent head for a moment, then gave the whole thing up and resumed his figuring.

There was a long silence, broken by an occasional small sound from the hearth where Anne was at work on the brass sides of the bellows. The house waited, listening, like the watchful Queen.

"Master Peregrine—what's going to become of the place when you go?"

"Go?" Her meaning reached him like a cold douche, and he gave a humorous shiver. "You're in a dismal frame of mind this morning! It must be the weather!"

"Well, sir, with no heir at all, as you might say—outside the Cheshire cousins—and no *prospect* of an heir here, so far as that goes—"

"Yes, I know, I know," he interposed hastily. "But don't let's talk about it, I'm good for a few years yet!" There was a pause. "Besides, I shan't need an heir when that time comes. My death duties will leave nothing to inherit. I'm the last." And after another minute—"If I had a son growing up he would have to see Queen's Folly pass out of his hands for lack of money to keep it. So perhaps it's just as well—" He shook it off with an effort. "For heaven's sake, Anne, how did this awful conversation get started? *You* began it! Now what about Mr. Burford's tea, don't you think you could make some of those nice rock cakes for him?"

"I dare say," she conceded, a mite ungraciously.

"We must be polite to him, Anne," he told her with a sympathetic grin. "He's written us a very polite letter and he controls a great deal of money."

"Is he coming to buy again?"

"That's his idea, yes."

Anne sat back on her heels to look up at him.

"What will it be this time—if you don't mind my asking?"

"Yes, but I do mind, I—haven't decided."

"What's he after?" she persisted fearfully. "Silver?"

"Pictures," he said, not looking at her.

"What pictures?" But she knew the answer. The family portraits were none of them by famous or fashionable artists, except the Lawrence of the second Nicholas's wife, which had gone five years ago. There was only one other picture. . . . *"The Queen?"* said Anne in a whisper of sheer horror, and he nodded. "Oh, Master Peregrine, you *can't!*" He sat drawing meaningless little scrawls on the paper before him, unable to meet her eyes. Anne stumbled up from her knees and went to lean on the edge of the table opposite him, pouring out her unpremeditated protest against the hard, cold facts written under his aimless hand. "I've worked in this house for nearly fifty years—I remember your father's wedding day, and the night you were born—I refused two good marriages myself when I was a girl because it would have meant leaving the place—I've given my life to it and to you—that gives me the right! You can't let *her* go— something dreadful will happen!"

"Something dreadful will happen if she doesn't go. I shall be sold up soon—turned out—lock, stock, and barrel, Anne. How would you like that?"

"But surely there's other things that can go first—"

"Oh, yes, I could stave it off a little longer, a few pounds at a time, by stripping the place—this table, the Restoration chairs, the silver, and so on. But that's no good. Because if she goes, everything else is safe for a long time. She's worth quite a lot of money, up in London. Mr. Burford will have a cheque in his pocket."

"Something dreadful always happens when that picture comes down off the wall," Anne repeated, her cheeks shining with unashamed tears.

"It's only come down once, that we know of," he reminded her.

"Wasn't that enough?" said Anne, and tried to catch his eyes, and failed.

"The first thing that will happen this time is a new roof for the house," he said firmly.

# 1936

"You don't *dare* do such a thing!" cried Anne in desperation. "The Lord only knows what will become of the place if she goes! She's always been there, since the house was built. The Brands will all rise up against you, Master Peregrine, if you sell the Queen!" She leaned toward him, and her voice dropped. "*Anthony* won't like it," she said, watching his face.

He showed only a moment's hesitation.

"It's that one picture against the whole house, Anne," he explained rationally then. "I can't go on. She gave us the house. Surely she'd be willing to save its life now."

"She won't be willing to leave it," Anne said darkly.

"Nor am I," was his brief answer to that. "But we can't both stay." He reached out a hand across the table to her. "Don't look like that, Nannie. I've tried everything else, honestly I have."

Anne took his fingers tight in hers, and tried to smile. For a moment they clung to each other.

"I must go run up those rock cakes for tea," said Anne, and left the room.

Mr. Burford arrived in a big black limousine through a mizzling rain about four o'clock, with twilight already coming on. He was a dry, genial man with a genuine love of old things. Anne showed him into the Queen's parlour where the fire was and where Peregrine still sat over his papers, and after an exchange of greetings and the usual English commiseration on the weather, Mr. Burford turned to make the portrait a little bow.

"Good evening, Madam," said Mr. Burford to the Queen.

"She doesn't like you, Burford, I can see it in her eye. As a matter of fact, we're neither of us one bit glad to see you, so it's no good being bright and cheerful like a doctor. To be perfectly frank, we hate the sight of you, Burford, have you got that cheque?"

"I have," said Mr. Burford, unoffended, and produced a strip of bluish paper from his wallet. "Look at that! Really handsome, you must admit."

"All in one bank!" said Peregrine wonderingly. "How does he do it?"

"Not many of those drifting round these days," commented Burford brightly. "I happen to know he's shifted quite a lot of other stuff on account of it. Got rid of some of his Italian things, he's so dead keen on her. He calls her his picture bride," said Mr. Burford, with a snigger.

"She won't take to him, Burford."

"Maybe she'll hoodoo him," Burford suggested with interest. "I've heard of such things." He eyed the portrait whimsically. "You know—I don't think I'd *like* living with her myself. She's got her eye on you, what?"

"You want a clear conscience—that's all." Peregrine sat down at the table again, like a man too weary to stand, and stared down at the cheque on the table before him, his chin in his hands.

"Got one, old boy," objected Burford, his gaze still riveted on the portrait. "Nothing to do with *me*. But you're right—she doesn't like me." There was a long silence, while he went on gazing at the Queen, and Peregrine stared at the cheque between his elbows. "I say, Brand—does she look at you like that?"

"Like what?"

"Well, I mean—" Burford moved to one side so that Peregrine's line of vision to the portrait was clear. They both contemplated it a long moment, while the Queen looked back at them, wrapped in her watchful dignity, and yet somehow cornered—trapped—at bay—but too proud to plead. And the guilt they both felt as they faced her was the ancient guilt of treason.

"She knows something's up, that's all," said Peregrine at last. "The whole house knows. Can't you hear it?" But all Mr. Burford really heard was the whisper of the fire and the hiss of fine, wind-whipped rain against the many window-panes. "A man will be here in a minute to take the picture down," Peregrine went on, matter-of-factly. "Have a cigarette?"

"It must be the weather," said Mr. Burford, shrugging off his sensations.

"You'll have a cup of tea before you go," suggested Peregrine politely. "The portrait will have to be carefully wrapped."

"Yes, of course," said Mr. Burford. "I mean—thanks very much."

He lighted a cigarette and sat down on the chesterfield by the fire. "This is a great coup for me, you know. By the way, I was to phone my client at the Ritz at once if the deal went through. Great coup for him too. He wants to have her photographed properly at once, to go with the story—be in all the papers."

"Yes—as though she had committed a murder!"

"As a matter of fact he—he asked me if I could get some photographs of the house as well, to show where she's been all these years."

"No," said Peregrine.

"Oh, I didn't bring a camera with me or anything like that," Burford reassured him hastily. "But I thought perhaps you wouldn't mind—"

"I said No," said Peregrine, his teeth on edge.

"Perhaps you're right," admitted Burford, and there was an uncomfortable pause. "I say," he blurted suddenly, "is this house haunted?"

"What? My dear Burford—"

"Yes, I know. Middle of the afternoon, and all that. Listen, Brand. I've been in this business for years. I've been in old houses all over England. But this is the damnedest place I've ever felt! There's something going on here!" He glanced about him with a small involuntary shudder. "I feel—well, I feel damned queer! Never noticed it before." Peregrine had risen and was standing beside the table looking at nothing in particular, his long body in its old, well-cut riding-clothes relaxed, one hand in his pocket, his face set. He seemed not to have heard. "I suppose you're used to it," said Mr. Burford, feeling his way. "Ever seen a ghost here?"

At that moment a very old man appeared at the doorway, peering in uncertainly, and lugging a ladder under one arm.

"Anne said you wanted a ladder, sir—?" he suggested with incredulity.

Mr. Burford, whose back was toward the door, leaped nervously off the chesterfield, and Peregrine smiled.

"Come in, Thomas. I want you to take down that picture."

Thomas stood staring at him, rooted to the threshold.

"The *Queen*, sir?"

"Get on with it, Thomas," said Peregrine gently.

Thomas came a few steps into the room, caught the portrait's eye, and stopped dead.

"I—I don't think I'd better, sir—"

"Hurry up, Thomas." The quiet words were inflexible.

Unwillingly Thomas came forward to place the ladder beneath the mantelpiece, and when he had done so he cast an appealing glance over his shoulder at the master, who showed no sign of letting him off. Gingerly, Thomas began to mount the ladder. . . .

"Oh, sorry—Anne said I was to come right in," said Constance from the doorway.

## V I

When she drove away from Queen's Folly in September she had decided to catch the first boat for New York. Paris wasn't far enough.

Mrs. Temple very wisely did not argue that day on

the drive up to Town. They could not get their favourite corner rooms at the Berkeley because they had not booked them ahead, so they went to bed in less attractive ones. When Constance woke in the morning she announced firmly that she would not stay in such a hole, and demanded the *Morning Telegraph* for the Shipping Intelligence.

"Look," said Mrs. Temple then persuasively, sitting down on the edge of the bed. "There isn't a decent boat for days, I happen to know that, and everything will be booked up anyhow. Let's not go home, they're having an election over there. Let's—"

"All right," said Constance agreeably, for she didn't really care where she went any more so long as it was away from wherever she was. She sat up in bed looking pale and heavy-eyed, with a long yellow plait over each shoulder. "Let's go to the Russells' in Scotland. I feel savage. I'd like to watch people shooting things."

So they got into the blue roadster that same morning and drove to Scotland. And by the time they got there Mrs. Temple had managed to point out that they might have been somewhat hasty about leaving Queen's Folly like that, without giving things a chance to clear up a little.

"After all," she reminded Constance philosophically, "not everybody stays married for twenty years. In fact, what with one thing and another, the average is pretty low."

# 1936

"Well, it's too late now," said Constance drearily, her eyes on the road.

"Too late for what?"

"To ask questions. Or shall I send him a telegram: *What have you done with your wife?*"

Slowly, however, the idea began to grow on her that she might have jumped at conclusions a bit. Nevertheless, no nice girl likes to discover that she has been throwing herself at the head of a man who is already married; especially if the man has given every indication of being satisfied with his private life exactly as it stands. She was the first to admit that Peregrine had never encouraged her. He had never, in fact, behaved as though he wasn't married. And so in a panic of pride and humiliation, she had fled.

A month in a gaunt Scottish seat whose bare stone interior walls were studded with old armour and ancient stags' heads, and hung with priceless threadbare tapestries which stirred ghostly in a perpetual draught, resulted chiefly in nostalgia for the sybaritic life they had led at Queen's Folly. From Scotland they went to a moorland hall in Yorkshire of the stupendous Vanbrugh vintage, with a Corinthian colonnaded portico, a yellow marble hall with pillars, cold white mantelpieces supported by naked busts, spindly ironwork stair-rails, and massive crystal chandeliers like exquisite ice. Classic sculpture in chilly semi-nude postured eternally in niches in the dining-room. The "boudoir" was full-blown rococo. In "the pink bedroom" with French *boiseries*, Constance went to sleep each night hugging a tepid hot water bottle. Aunt Dolly's room adjoining was an immense bride-cake effect in white and gold. There was no central heating at all, and the bath-water always gave out.

And here in the bosom of a large affectionate family whose eldest daughter had brought home her new baby for its first visit, while the youngest was drifting blissfully about the edges of things with a new fiancé, Constance took to holding long ruminations with herself on the question of what she was going to do with the rest of her life. Of course I could buy another house, she thought suddenly one morning in November—she wasn't sleeping well, either, and woke very early, and couldn't get back to sleep. I could put money in it, she told herself, staring up at the pink taffeta hangings of her preposterous bed. I could fix up some other house to be almost as lovely and even more comfortable than Queen's Folly. What have I got money *for*, if I don't use it to save my own life? When a woman loses a child, she argued, sometimes she adopts another to take its place. I've lost Queen's Folly. But I'll buy another house—a nice old red brick and timber house in Sussex. . . .

She got into a velvet house-gown and slippers and dodged downstairs to the vast Regency library to rummage out a copy of *Country Life* she had seen on the table there. It was six weeks old, but she took it back to her room, encountering nobody on the way, and crawled into bed with it again, her teeth chattering with cold. She opened to the advertisements in the front. *Centre of*

*Old Berkshire Hunt*—no—*Charming Elizabethan Cottage Residence*—where you cracked your head on every beam—*Perfectly Appointed House*—and very ugly too —*Beautiful Part of Southern Home Counties*—Kent was hard to get to—*Superb Position on South Cornish Coast* —too far from London, nobody would come to see you— *Charming Old House with Walled Garden*—and with one bathroom to twelve bedrooms—*Enchanting Old Sussex Farmhouse*—and not one word about plumbing of any description—*Unique XVIth Century House in Rural Hants*—she threw down the magazine with a sigh. None of them would do. None of them seemed to have gardens that were old and sunny, nor a Gothic door, nor a Jacobean drawing-room with two fireplaces. None of them was dedicated to Queen Elizabeth.

She got up and dressed warmly, with a tweed skirt and knitted jumper, put on her brown suède jacket and a tam, and backed the blue roadster out of the garage without saying anything to anybody. It was still early. Some of them were already at golf, some of them had not yet come down to breakfast. She wanted to think things out alone.

The car slid smoothly down the drive and a few miles beyond the park gates came to a main road leading south. *Sheffield*, said the sign-post. *Derby. Lichfield.* There was a sort of café attached to the garage and petrol pump in the village, where she had a cup of bitter coffee and an excellent bun, and then turned southward, the road good, the car running well on a full tank, her mind preoccupied. Sheffield would do as well as anywhere.

So this was how it was when one was crossed in love. This daily desolation, this odd, eternal emptiness at the pit of one's stomach, this lack of interest in things which had once been amusing and important. But surely it didn't go on like this, one must eventually get numb? I'd like to be a *nice* old maid, not a gloomy one, she thought. Why must everybody bore me so, she wondered. Why must the life they lead seem so footling? How small one's world can get, she marvelled, and how helpless one can be before one's own inescapable memory. There were things that she could never see again without a stab, she knew—a field of yellow mustard under a stormy grey sky hanging low over Cotswold—the smell of pink climbing roses in the sun—raspberries, warm from the stem—red poppies by the roadside—long afternoon shadows under yellow, slanting sunlight—the sturdy pound of a little car along a dark road. . . .

Round lunch time she ran into an old town, with statues in its market-place, and a cathedral. Lichfield. Already? She was hungry. A policeman directed her to the *George*, and she ate with more relish than she had done for days. A queer, subconscious excitement possessed her. Somehow the drive was doing her good.

She paid her bill and came out on to pavements dark with rain, and took the car to a garage to have the petrol tank filled up. She thought how nice the English garage boys always were, in their one-piece grubby mechanics' suits, and their air of pleased surprise over tips. Her mind went back to that new white garage and petrol pump at the crossroads outside Evesham, where the boys all knew Peregrine and humoured the sad little Rover. As she drove on, preoccupied, another sign-post caught her eye. *Birmingham. Alcester. Evesham.* Evesham. What a coincidence.

Automatically she swung the wheel and took the road southward again. I could get to Evesham for tea, she thought. That place by the river. I could get petrol there where we used to go. They might just happen to mention if he had been in today. . . . What a state I've got to, she mused, when it's something just to see a dirty-faced lad who has spoken to him since I have—when just to drive along the same roads he uses is worth going on for. If I keep this up I won't get home tonight, she thought. Wonder if I could buy a toothbrush and phone Aunt Dolly and stay over some place. No luggage. Oh, well. . . .

She drove on.

But as she left Lichfield behind, her heart began to beat more quickly, for it knew before her head knew what she meant to do. Straight to Evesham she would go, and on, toward the hills. Just as far as Folly village with its gay gardens spilling over the grey walls above the single steep street, its well-mannered dogs and friendly children, its air of permanence, and peace, and security—just as far as the foot of the lane that led up to the house—perhaps just to leave the car and walk into the park a little way to catch a glimpse of the north front behind its great yews, making sure, of course, that she could not be seen from the windows. . . .

Her heart beat faster, faster, as the car sped on. Why, if everything was very quiet and deserted she might even tap on the kitchen window and beg a cup of tea from Anne. Anne would be glad to see her. Anne would talk. From Anne she would learn soon enough if a mistress had come back to the house after she left it. And if, after those twenty years since his marriage during the war— (until Aunt Dolly pointed it out she had not realized it could be so long)—perhaps if the house hadn't got a mistress any more—why, then, perhaps she might even have tea in the Queen's parlour again, with—with . . .

Peregrine. Fantastic, haunting, unforgettable name. Maybe I wouldn't feel this way if his name was James, she thought, doing sixty along the road toward Alcester. At sight of that little old town something collapsed in her mind with a whimper of relief. Evesham next. Less than thirty miles now, to Peregrine. I don't care, I'm coming back, I'm coming back. . . . Her heart went on thumping uncomfortably fast. *Peregrine.* I'm coming back, I don't care, I don't care. . . .

On through Evesham and out by well-remembered turnings into the flat orchard land to eastward of it, toward the first steep rise of the hills beyond. It was raining hard now, in wind-blown gusts, and getting dark.

# 1936

It would be quite dark by the time she reached Queen's Folly. I don't care, I don't care. . . .

The car began to climb.

Would she know, as soon as she saw the house again, if another woman was living in it now? What had become of that other woman? One need not have been such a fool, one could have asked Anne, one could still ask Anne, unless—unless the woman was sitting there this minute, underneath the portrait of the Queen, pouring out tea. (Her hands were cold and damp inside her driving gloves.) What sort of woman would he have married, at twenty? How could one explain oneself to a woman who was his wife, who offered one tea, and—and whose no doubt polite and unquestioning hospitality one would have to accept for the night?

The lamps were lighted in Folly village, the children were all inside on account of the wet. It looked lonely and secretive and patient, withdrawn and fatalistic, in the sweep of her headlights along its one brief street. At the bottom of the lane real stage-fright set in. She would have to walk into a brightly lighted room, herself blind from the twilight, wind-blown, chilly, not looking her best, and shivering with nerves. She would have to face—what? Why had she come, how had she *dared* to come? But the car kept on, unfaltering, like a homing pigeon, hurrying upon her ordeal.

There were lights in the kitchen windows, and light lay in a golden panel on the ground outside the tall north window of the Queen's parlour. Someone was in there—and please God there would be a fire. There was a long black limousine drawn up before the Gothic door. It's those Garstin-Ponsonbys come to tea at last, she thought hysterically, as she brought the roadster to a stop behind the big car, whose chauffeur might, for all she knew, be in the kitchen having his tea with Anne and the maids.

For a moment she sat still behind the wheel, staring at the limousine in surprise, while rain beat against her windows and the steady whir of her windscreen-wiper became unbearable in the silence—making up her mind to drive away again without being seen. And even as she reached this decision, she was switching off the wiper and climbing stiffly out of the car into the rain, and ringing the bell. I don't know what's the matter with me, she thought vaguely as she did so. I can't go in if he's got guests. I'll just get that cup of tea from Anne and—and slip away again. . . . Her teeth were chattering now, but not with cold, and her knees felt queer. A frond of ivy hung loose below the clipped edge, its leaves dripping in the rain—she caught it between gloved finger and thumb as she stood waiting, and tucked it tidily back in place, as a mother smooths back a lock of hair from a child's eyes. . . .

"Anne, I've come back," she said absurdly, as the door opened.

"God bless you, miss. He's in the Queen's room."

"I can't go in there, there's somebody else with him.

He—he didn't know I was coming, will you give me a cup of tea in the kitchen?"

"Tea's just going in, miss. You go straight along to the fire. It's only a Mr. Burford from London."

"Never heard of him. Will he stay long? I only—"

Anne laid a strong hand on her shoulder and she found herself crossing the vaulted hall to the library door.

"You go along in and get warm," said Anne quietly. "You're just in time."

In time for what, she wondered, proceeding obediently in the direction of the Queen's room. Tea, of course. Who was this Burford? Anyway, one could hardly make a fool of oneself before him, so perhaps it was all for the best. She felt light-headed, outside herself looking on. It was as though the house itself, not Anne, had thrust her forward across the stone floor of the vaulted hall. The library, dimly lighted, seemed to preen itself under her dazed eyes, lovelier than ever before, and yet unchanged, unchanging—books she had read aloud, demanding again the touch of her hand—the portrait of Nicholas, who had never set foot off his own land except on occasional market-days, watching for her above the mantelpiece. . . . Oh, Peregrine, *darling*, I've come home. . . .

The Queen's parlour seemed to be full of people.

"Oh, sorry—" said Constance on the threshold. "Anne said I was to come right in."

## VII

Peregrine swung round and saw her standing there—the girl he had convinced himself that he would never see again—the girl whose slow voice had stayed in his ears as persistently as the scent of her belongings had clung about the room which had once been his entirely.

For the blank second before he pulled himself together enough to speak to her, she seemed to his startled eyes wholly an apparition. And even after that, his mind continued to fumble confusedly at what it seemed to consider some dim association between the Queen's extremity and Constance's return. *Something dreadful always happens*, Anne had said direfully. But Constance in the doorway, warm flesh and blood, with raindrops shining on the edge of her hat—Constance dropped from heaven—this was not dreadful.

And yet—out of the corner of his eye he was aware of Burford's pleased surprise at sight of such a pretty girl, and of Thomas petrified on the ladder, staring—pretty dreadful, after all. She had caught them.

It was only a second that he stood there, paralyzed with astonishment and a sort of racking joy. Then he started for her impulsively, and on reaching her, shook hands with great propriety.

"But we thought you'd sailed—!" he gasped. "I mean—do come in—"

"If I'm interrupting anything—" she began uncertainly.

"No, no, I—we—" He drew her on into the room, a hand at her elbow. "Only it is a little surprising, because we were talking about you only this morning, and now you—suddenly appear like this! This is Mr. Burford, he—"

"How do you do?" said Constance, disposing of Mr. Burford as she began to get the full significance of Thomas, halfway up the ladder, grinning a welcome. "Good evening, Thomas—how's the grandchild?"

Thomas scrabbled back down the ladder like a man released from an evil spell.

"Doing fine, thank you, miss," he said delightedly, with a glance at the master—a sort of what-did-I-tell-you glance, which indicated that he understood the whole ladder business had been a mistake all along.

"Say, what's going on here, anyhow?" she inquired, bewildered, and stood a moment taking it in—the ladder against the mantelpiece, Thomas's irradiating relief at escaping from his position on it, the strange man, the air of constraint. Then she wheeled on Peregrine. "What is this? What are you doing with the Queen?"

"That's all for the moment, thank you, Thomas," said Peregrine, and Thomas departed with such alacrity that he left the ladder where it was without another thought. Whatever was going on, Thomas was blissfully confident that Miss Ingleby, bless her kind heart, would put a stop to it, and bring the master to his senses. "Er—" said

Peregrine, somewhat at a loss, "—will you stay to tea—
I mean dinner," he continued, trying to pass the thing
over somehow.

"Yes," said Constance firmly, taking off her gloves.
"I will. It's going to be damned awkward, I should think.
This isn't any of my business, and I'm going to the bottom of it, aren't you glad?"

Mr. Burford was enjoying himself, but he felt superfluous.

"I say, mind if I use the telephone?" he began tactfully. "My client said I could reach him at the Ritz
round tea-time. He's a bit anxious to know if—if—" Mr.
Burford cleared his throat.

"If the deal goes through," Peregrine finished his sentence for him courteously. "Tell him it's all settled. The
telephone is in the little room off the hall—" He started
toward the door.

"I know, I know, in the office—used it before—please
don't trouble—" Mr. Burford took himself off.

They were alone now, except for the Queen.

Constance, after so much stage-fright, was feeling unbelievably calm and collected. Her back was to the wall.
She had no idea where they would go from here, her
whole life hung on the next few minutes, but at least
the worst had not happened—there was no other woman
seated before the fire, serenely at home in Peregrine's
house, dispensing tea in her own right. A bright conviction was growing and growing: except for the Queen
there was no other woman in Peregrine's life.

"What deal?" said Constance bluntly, and—

"You know, it's awfully good to see you again," he began simultaneously. "We thought—"

"Was that Christie's or somebody?" she demanded, refusing to be sidetracked.

"Something like that, yes," he admitted.

"But not—*Elizabeth!*" she cried incredulously.

"Would you mind very much if we didn't talk about it?" he suggested, with a diffident attempt at begging the question which was instantly unsuccessful.

She laid her bag and gloves on the table, pulled off her hat and put it on top, loosened the slide-fastening of the suède jacket and removed the soft woolen scarf from round her throat.

"Yes, we are going to talk about it," she said decisively, marvelling at her own self-possession. "I turn my back on the place for a couple of months and *this* is what I find!"

"I couldn't very well consult you," he said, trying to face it out. "I didn't know you were still in England."

"We've been in Scotland and Yorkshire. Yorkshire is all very Georgian and draughty, did you know?" she ran on, feeling her way along his defences. "I went out in the car early this morning just to have a look round before breakfast, and—and the first thing I knew there was Evesham! So I said, 'What a coincidence,' I said—"

"England's such a *little* place," he chimed in solemnly, finding refuge gratefully in her ready nonsense. "Lunch at Berwick-on-Tweed—Penzance at tea-time! You can't help yourself! Is your aunt well?"

"Oh, always!" said Constance, and dropped pretence. "Look here, am I too late? I mean—"

"No, no, just in time for tea with Mr. Burford!" he assured her obtusely. "I was just going to ring for it."

"Can't you get rid of him?"

"Well, you see—I didn't know you were coming, did I, and—"

"You've got to get rid of him," she said urgently. "I want to talk to you—seriously."

"Well, he's doing a trunk-call," he reminded her, and began to fill his pipe so as not to meet her eyes. "We're all clear for roughly half an hour! As a matter of fact, I want to talk to *you*. I've just found out you played fairy godmother to everybody on the place last summer."

"Who told you?"

"Never mind. I wish I'd known, that's all."

"It wasn't much. You can't give them much, they're too upstanding."

"You might have told me they needed things," he argued unreasonably. "I—"

"Oh, don't make a fuss, please! You're even worse than they are! I happened to admire that bedridden old lady, so I got her a gadget to make things easier. How is she?"

"Just the same. Live forever. They always do."

"And as for the new baby things, I suppose you think you could have done that better than I did!"

"No, but—"

"Did it arrive all right? The baby, I mean."

"Oh, yes, right on time, I believe."

"That's good. They're such grand people at the home farm, I wanted to help out a bit, that's all."

"But that's my job," he insisted, holding to his grievance. "I don't mean to be difficult, but it was rather rubbing it in, wasn't it!"

"Rubbing what in?"

"That I couldn't do enough for them myself."

"Oh, my dear, I never thought of such a thing!" she cried, stricken, shy, and full of a guilty pity for his pride. "You mend their roofs and try to keep their drains from whiffing—you can't be expected to keep track of all the little things as well—"

"Yes, I am, I can, I do!" he cried angrily, in sore revolt against his own helplessness. "I knew they would need help when the time came, but I hadn't got round to it yet. I'm all they've got to look to—and I've been so in debt for years my hands are tied. It's sickening. Forgive me for mentioning it. It's my own futility that gets on my nerves."

"You didn't think I was—meddling?"

"Oh, Lord, no, please don't take any notice of my tantrums, I—" He took one impulsive step toward her, halted, clamped his teeth on his pipestem and turned away, to strike a match and hold it to the bowl.

The dear, remembered fragrance of his tobacco drifted across her nostrils. For a moment she stood looking at him, her mind working clearly two moves ahead, like a chess-player's, striving to formulate this sentence and then that one, to drive him into a corner and get the truth from him—and at the same time to do it in such a way as to save both their faces in case the truth should be—embarrassing.

"Look," she said slowly, in her most persuasive tone. "You can't go on like this. You can't let *her* be taken away!"

"It's the roof," he explained simply. "It's got to be all done over. And that on top of everything else—I can't quite manage."

"Then let *me* do the roof—as a present to her."

Almost he seemed to hesitate, and her heart began to hurry again. She was out in the open now. There was no retreat any more into casual foolishness. *Check*, she had said, and it was his move.

"She's sorry," he said after a perceptible pause, "but she can't accept."

"But I thought something awful always happened if she was disturbed."

"It does," he admitted dispiritedly. "There are manifestations, death, and disaster. Perhaps the sky will fall on Worcestershire—and then perhaps it won't matter to me any more." He folded up suddenly in a chair by the table and put his head in his hands, hiding his face from her. "*Must* we go on talking about it?"

"What would the first Peregrine say to all this?" she insisted, hardening her heart.

"I've been wondering. But, you see, I can't, unfortunately, run a sword through poor old Burford. Anyway, it's not his fault."

Constance looked down at him where he sat with his face hidden from her. Just beyond him the bluish strip of paper which was the cheque lay exposed on the table, where he had laid it. Her scarf was under his elbow on the table, and his free hand had unconsciously gripped a fold of it. Her eyes rested on that hand, thoughtfully, as though she laid hers on it.

"Don't tell me that's the cheque already," she murmured.

"Yes, that's it," he answered without moving.

"Mind if I look at it?"

"No, do look, it's a beautiful sight."

She picked it up gingerly, between finger and thumb, and gave a gasp as she saw the signature.

"But you can't possibly sell the Queen to *him!*"

"What's the matter with him?" he inquired without interest.

"I know him," she said, holding the cheque as though it might sting her. "He's the sort of man my father wouldn't do business with. He's terrible. She won't like him."

"Well, if she doesn't, he'll probably be sorry," he said philosophically. "Maybe she'll leave him and come back home."

"If you could *see* his house—it's incredible! I know, because for my sins I have spent a week-end there. You see—at one time he wanted me to be his third wife. Two have already died on him."

He turned slowly to look up at her as she spoke. He had known, of course, that there must be any number of people who wanted to marry her, but to hear it like this was nevertheless a shock. The same fellow who wanted the Queen had already tried for Constance. Well, whatever else might be said of him, the blighter had good taste. And from the way she spoke, he wouldn't get them both. Peregrine, who had already in his heart said good-by to each of them in turn, was conscious only of commiseration.

"I don't think he can be so terrible—the man obviously has a deep appreciation of the beautiful."

"Aunt Dolly said it was because I went so well with his drawing-room curtains," she explained flippantly, because she did really dislike the man who wrote cheques. "It's a blond sort of room, like the inside of a jewel-casket."

"Well, you might accept now," he suggested, watching her, "and keep Elizabeth company there."

"No," said Constance, grave again, her eyes fixed on the cheque. "I'd leave him too and—come back home."

The quiet words lodged like a pain in his heart. She loved Queen's Folly as no woman in its whole history had done. And he—he faced it now, and deceived himself no longer—he loved her, as no Brand had ever loved a woman before. They belonged together, the three of them, and the Queen. But the Queen was not theirs any longer.

# 1936

The Queen was forfeit, like his own happiness, to a world that was out of joint. Constance had come too late for Queen's Folly. And so she would go away, as the Queen must go—to some man who had managed to be a success in these queer times the war had left behind it. And finally—unlike himself and, perhaps, the Queen—she would forget last summer, or remember it only as a pleasant interlude. . . . But a voice somewhere inside his head said that such thoughts were rubbish, old-fashioned poppycock, and that he was a fool to let her go. . . .

"Do you really feel that way about the place?" he asked quietly, and his fingers moved on her scarf with a sort of caress, unconsciously, while its familiar perfume set his senses tingling again.

"I lost my heart to it the first day, when we drove up. I'll never forget my first sight of it, with its green lawns, and the forget-me-nots and lupins blue against the grey stone, as though the house stood with its feet in flowers— I wanted to cry—I wanted to take it in my arms—" He was staring up at her, his hand still caressing her scarf, and their eyes met and clung, and something in his made her fine courage veer aside, and started her heart to hammering so that she fumbled for words, lost her place, began again on a lower note, but still drove forward desperately along the line she must follow. "Please don't think this is just an impulse. It's been nearly two months now since I left Queen's Folly. I wanted to be sure. And I *am* sure. Now—don't bite my head off, will you? But—

will you sell me Queen's Folly?" (*Check!* cried the referee who seemed to be watching over her shoulder.)

The fingers on her scarf were quite still. His pipe had gone out from neglect. His heart was a lump of lead within him. He might have known, he told himself. A fool, was he. Well, yes—but not the kind of a fool he had feared.

"I'm afraid not," he said, looking away from her.

"You were bound to say that, of course. You think I'm just an American girl with a gob of money, wanting to gratify a whim. It's not that. The *feel* of the house has got me. It owns me. It was glad to see me, just now when I drove up. I want to pet it—cosset it—give it presents. I think in my very abbreviated way I feel something the way you do about it. Of course its hold on you is infinitely greater and longer—ever since Anthony. There's one thing I've just got to know. Why does Anthony come to that door and look in? Why that particular door?"

"I suppose he wants to make sure the Queen is still here, where he left her."

"But after today she won't be."

"No."

"Pretty hard on Anthony."

"Isn't it?"

"Have you ever seen him—yourself?" she inquired levelly, deliberately.

There was a long silence. He sat motionless, not looking at her. Then he spoke quietly, his voice as casual as though her last question had never been asked.

"You know, you'd find Queen's Folly much less attractive in winter, I'm afraid. These cold rains, day after day, can be very trying." While she stood staring at him, fascinated, he rose, still without looking at her, and drifted to the window to stand gazing out blindly into the blue-black evening. "Even Burford's been imagining things today. I'm used to it, of course. I suppose one would have to be, to live here alone and like it."

*Alone.*

Exultantly, she squared herself to the last move.

"Peregrine Brand."

"What's the matter?" He turned to her, in spite of himself.

"I'm going to do an outrageous thing. Will you be nice about it?"

"I'll try to be," he smiled, mystified.

"That day we drank the toast," she proceeded with difficulty, for her breath was coming very unevenly as though she had been running uphill, "you said something about having married at twenty."

"Did I?" He was lost.

"Well, you don't seem—you don't seem to be married now," she pointed out.

"No," he said unemotionally. "My wife died in childbirth the next year—while I was in Flanders. The child," he added after a pause, "was born dead."

"I'm so sorry—" She was almost voiceless with embarrassment and constraint. "I—I had to know."

"Quite all right. It seems rather a long time ago."

"I don't know how to go on," she gasped. "You're not helping, you know."

"Helping?" He was surprised.

At that moment Mr. Burford arrived inoffensively in the doorway, having put through his call, and now entertaining hopes of tea.

"Well, I must say, I never heard a man so pleased," he was beginning cheerily, and Constance whirled on him in a sort of frenzy, with clenched fists and eyes bright with tears.

"Oh, go away!" she cried wildly at his astonished face. "*Please* go away, and give me a chance!"

"Oh—I see—sorry—" Mr. Burford backed out, full of incoherent apology, and took refuge in the dining-room.

Constance faced Peregrine in the middle of the room, while he drifted back to the table and leaned there, holding a dead pipe. Things had begun to swirl round him.

"She won't let me off this!" cried Constance with a gesture toward the watchful Queen. "She's dragged me back here today—oh, yes, she did, I never meant to come —that is—I thought it wasn't any good. She's dragged me half across England in a pouring rain in time to stop this, and she won't let me off! Peregrine—I haven't got quite as much money as he has—" She nodded toward the cheque. "—but I've got enough. And it all belongs to her—to this house—to *you*. I tried to stay away because you were blind and stupid and thick-headed and wouldn't look at me. I swore I didn't care, and I meant to let you go to blazes, and the house with you! I thought I had

284

some pride!" Her breath caught on a sob. "I haven't! *She* won't let me have any pride! Maybe she's sick of pride, you've got so much! But the house has got hold of me again, as though it had hands to cling! It won't let me go. And you, *you*, in those clothes, smelling of pipe-smoke—" She stamped her foot at his expression of idiotic astonishment, and her hands went up before her face. She was half laughing, half crying. "Go on, make me say it *all*, don't let me off anything! Peregrine, I'm in love with you, damn you, and I'm asking you to marry me!"

"In—l-love with me?" he repeated, stunned, after an endless silence. Then he started for her impetuously, wavered, and finished the few steps to her side uncertainly, uncertainly laid his arms round her. Her face was still in her hands. "But, my dear girl, I—you—there must be a catch in it somewhere, I—you're not *crying?*" he demanded anxiously.

She showed him a radiant face, pink with excitement, a bit blurry with tears.

"But you must have suspected *something*—when I went away like that?"

"Good Lord, no!" he said with great sincerity. "I—I didn't know what to think."

"Well, don't mind me." She withdrew from him a little, bracing herself, gallant, humorous, fighting down a panic of shyness. "What are you going to do now?" she asked.

His eyes were on her, probing, staring, as though he

had never really seen a woman before. His hands lingered gently on her sleeves.

"I don't know, I—somehow it makes me feel the most incredible swine—"

"Because I've got money—or because I'm in love with you? Surely other Brands have married heiresses before now?"

"Very often," he admitted ruefully. "But—"

"But *unwilling* heiresses, was that the difference?"

"Constance, I—" he began, still not believing. His arms tightened, and she lifted her face to him for a kiss. As he took it, both her arms slid round his neck to hold him there. When at last he let her go, she buried her face against his shoulder, but he searched out her chin with his hand and made her look at him. "But—you *do* love me—!" He stammered with delight.

"Yes, stupid, I keep telling you!" she cried between laughter and tears at his heartbreaking incredulity, and he kissed her again, eagerly, breathlessly, long and hard. He had suddenly come to life, a man whose demands were imperious and thrilling.

"It isn't just the house you want," he said then, assimilating the idea at last. "It's me too."

"Now don't you start being jealous of the house!" she warned him, and he caught her closer with a breath of triumphant laughter.

"You've no idea how funny that is!" he cried, his cheek against her hair. "Oh, thank God you came back! I wanted you back—I wanted to ask you to stay—but don't you see, my darling, I didn't know, I couldn't be sure—I had no right—I'd got so used to doing without things I wanted—I couldn't believe you meant—I didn't dare to think—I—"

He was still babbling his incoherent, light-headed happiness when Anne came to the door to make sure that no one had rung for tea. Anne exchanged a glance of mutual congratulation with the Queen, and went away to give Mr. Burford his tea in the dining-room.

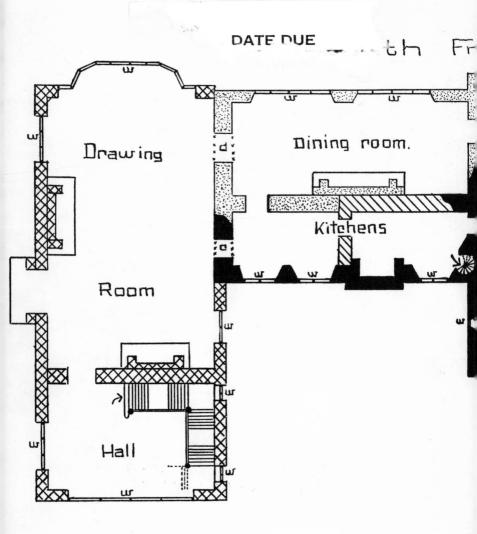

Drawing

Dining room.

Room

Kitchens

Hall